ULTIMATE DECADENCE

A collection of thirty erotic stories

Edited by Sarah Berry, Alyson Fixter and
Emily Dubberley

Published by Accent Press Ltd – 2009
ISBN 9781906373795

Printed and bound in the UK

Cover Design by
Sam Eddison

For Jean Dubberley, whose bravery and strength through her cancer was the inspiration behind this book; and to anyone who's been touched by cancer, and the charities that help them, particularly Macmillan.

Foreword

You recline, expertly: a pale aristocrat maypoled by slow ribbons of opium smoke. All around, thick curtains hang with such a weight of opulence that what's beyond them ceases to exist. Outside is not - not Vienna, not Prague, not Buenos Aires, Bangkok or Berlin; not day or night; not the nineteenth century, now or never. All that is, is pleasure; excess; dissipation; dissolution; delirium. You swan-neck a languid arm towards an attendant, to indicate you desire more of everything.

Here's the problem, though. You're probably not an aristocrat. Probably, you're a receptionist at Vision Express or part of a local government department 'tasked' with deciding what number each new building application form should have. Certainly, you need to know whether or not you're in Bangkok and what time it is because you have to be at work by 8.30am tomorrow to lie your way through this year's Personal Development Interview. What's more, opium is quite bad for you – and, man, *so* expensive, eh? Absinthe too. And a labyrinthine palace close to St Petersburg, every room tumbling with caviar and orchids and Remy Martin and ambergris and big gold hammers to idly smash big diamonds into bits you can throw at passing yacht salesmen to attract their attention. You can't afford that. Not even by putting it on your credit card – it's not 2008 anymore.

But wait! What's this? It's you, your smutty mind's eye, and some time to yourself. Unfettered sensual delight is, very literally, within your grasp. Cast aside the unattainably expensive and logistically awkward, their excess is excess to requirements. You have opposable thumbs, imagination, a closed door, a tin of chicken and vegetable soup and a length of tubing, right? What more could you possibly need? In fact, you could lose the soup and the tubing and, instead, get yourself an anthology of detonator cap short stories to set you off on a burst of hot, panting, frankly disturbing sexual intemperance. Sure, you'll have to improvise, but you're holding such an anthology *right now* – plus it avoids the need for Tesco's and Home Base and lots of unfortunate questions.

Best of all, this collection of throaty gasps and squelching obscenities is in aid of Macmillan Cancer Support. We're on this earth for only the briefest of blinks. If, during that time, we manage just two things – 1) to help those who need our help, and 2) to roar at the ceiling as our eyes roll up into our heads due to ecstatic syncope – then that's not bad, I reckon. That's not bad at all.

Mil Millington

Contents

Ultimate Decadence
by Poppy Winters

Davina loved money. She loved it so much she would do almost anything – jump out of a plane, eat a goat's testicle, sleep with Piers Morgan – if the price was right. But she drew the line at hard work, which was why after less than an hour as a cosmetics sales girl she'd thrown down her nail buffer and marched into the office of her new boss, Anthony Taylor, to tell him exactly what she thought of his job, and where he could stick it.

At nearly six feet tall in high heels, Davina made an intimidating spectacle as she slammed her hands on Anthony's desk – a real Amazonian goddess with long black hair and toned arms and legs. If she'd had a spear tucked under her arm, she'd have been positively terrifying. But Anthony, sitting at a teak-effect desk that bowed slightly in the middle, both hands resting casually on a nicotine-stained computer keyboard, didn't look terrified. He looked concerned, interested and ready to listen.

"I've had enough," Davina announced, sitting herself on the squeaky visitor's chair opposite Anthony and wondering, not for the first time, why a man who looked so expensive worked in such a rundown office. Today, for example, Anthony wore a sharp pinstripe suit and light pink shirt, with a platinum curb bracelet on one wrist and a 24-carat gold Swiss watch on the other. His thin, sandy blond hair was clipped and shaped in a longish designer style that swept across his forehead and, although he was nearly forty, he looked youthful and radiated good health. All in all, the man was totally out of place in this dowdy setting: Beluga caviar at a Butlin's holiday camp.

"I've spent the last hour watching women with prams make great big circles around me so I can't stop them and talk to them," Davina continued, "selling some bloody awful green chemical stuff that smells like toothpaste and barely making enough to cover my petrol. It's totally rubbish, Anthony. I quit."

She sat back, wondering if there was anything she could steal on her way out of the building that would boost a morning of rubbish pay, but there was nothing in this place worth anything. Even the computer on Anthony's desk was likely to fetch more from an antique dealer than a pawnbroker.

Anthony leaned back in his chair.

"You're interesting. Do you know that?" He rested a foot across his knee, revealing designer logos on his socks. "You've got … charisma. There's a spark to you. I like it." He tapped the desk lightly with his fingers. "What if I offered you another job here? Still promotions, but better pay and better … prospects."

Davina thought for a moment. "Would I still have to report back here? To these offices?" She stared pointedly at the corner of the desk, where the fake-teak covering was peeling away to reveal grubby chipboard underneath, one corner repaired with crumpled beige masking tape.

"The job's right here, in this building."

"No thanks." Davina stood up, knowing any job in these tumbledown surroundings wouldn't pay her what she wanted. The building was lovely from the outside, a beautiful – well she wasn't sure when it was built – but it was quite old; one of those flat, square-looking buildings with big windows and lots of pointy lines and details on it. What a shame the inside was so seventies and falling apart.

She'd made it as far as the ill-fitting plywood door when Anthony said:

"I know the offices aren't ideal, but there's plenty you haven't seen in this building, believe me."

Davina's hand lingered on the door handle. "Like what?"

"Upstairs. It's very different up there – a whole other business. Let me show you and you can decide for yourself."

"You'd have to promise me a lot more money."

"I promise you can make at least two hundred pounds a night."

Davina's hand dropped from the door handle.

"I don't believe you. There's no way anyone in this place earns anything like that."

"See it for yourself first, then decide."

In spite of herself, Davina was feeling more and more intrigued. "See what?"

As the old elevator winched its way to the top of the building, Davina began to feel a mixture of apprehension and excitement. She had no idea what Anthony was about to show her, but she was guessing it had something to do with money, and money always made her excited. But then again, there was something exciting about Anthony too. Maybe it was just because he was standing so close to her.

As the elevator doors rolled open, Davina's dark red nails flew to her mouth.

"Oh my God. Look at this." She stumbled out on to a thick, dark-red carpet and gazed at her surroundings. How could this space be here, in this building, with all the dilapidated furniture and worn-out carpets downstairs?

They were standing in a wide hallway. Three chandeliers hung from the ceiling, casting soft light and crystal shadows over the thick carpet. The walls were covered in thick plaster, carved with swirly scalloped patterns, and at the end of the hallway were two exits: one huge pair of white double-doors with blocky brass handles and one small door, white and carved with simple squares in that old-fashioned style that seemed to run throughout the building.

"Why's it so different up here?" said Davina, taking a step down the hallway and letting her fingers trail along the scalloped walls. "Is it a restaurant or something?"

"It's much better than a restaurant. Wait until you see it."

Anthony put a confident hand on her shoulder and led her down the hallway. He stopped outside the smaller door.

"This is the dressing room," he said, pulling down the

handle. "You can get changed in there."

"Why? What's through those other doors?"

"You'll see in a minute. This room leads through to the next room, anyway. The dressing room is the staff entrance."

Anthony pushed the door open to reveal a large, light dressing room, very square with three big windows that let in lots of afternoon sunshine. The light was amplified by the twenty or so art-deco style mirrors hanging all over the walls, all of different sizes and offering whoever stood in the centre of the room a view of themselves from every angle. Around the sides of the room were free-standing clothes rails hung with hundreds of vintage ball gowns, evening dresses, glittery stage costumes, underwear, sparkling diamond bracelets, chokers and diamond-set watches. Everything was immaculate: antiques undoubtedly and probably 80 or 90 years old, but in perfect condition.

"They're ... oh wow," Davina gasped, going right into the middle of the room and turning around and around, dazzled by the hundreds of outfits.

"Why don't you try something on?" said Anthony, closing the door behind them. "Pick anything you like – think of it as part of the interview. The girls dress up in here before they start work."

"Can I?"

It wasn't really a question, as Davina had already picked up a hanger strewn with diamante waist and neck chains: silver chains and strings of crystal dangling like little curtains to cover intimate areas – if moving strings of crystals could ever really be said to cover anything. Having decided this would be her lingerie, she cast her eye over the rest of the clothes rails for something to go over the top and decided on a halter-neck dress made entirely from pear-shaped crystals strung on slim white ribbons.

She put both items carefully on the floor and undressed: pink high heels off first, then unzipping her silk shift dress and letting it fall away, revealing what she knew to be a spectacularly firm body – devoid of underwear since she never bothered wearing any. Naked, she stepped carefully into the diamante chains, taking time to position them just right. As she fastened the chains, and then the crystal dress over the top, she grinned at Anthony and swung her hips left and right.

"What's this all for, anyway?" she asked. "All these clothes and everything."

"The costumes? I told you, they're for the girls who work here."

"Really? If I worked up here, I'd get to wear these clothes? I'd really love that, this feels amazing. OK, so tell more about the job."

"I pay £200 for the evening and you'll work 8.30 p.m. until midnight. You need to pass a few physical tests, but after that the job's yours."

Davina moved her long dark hair from one shoulder to the other.

"Physical tests?" she said. "What do I have to do?"

"Not in here." Anthony went to the side of the room and stood by an innocent-looking white door – a door Davina hadn't noticed until now. "Through here."

"OK. Oh, wait – I want to put one of these necklaces on." Davina picked one of the twenty or so diamond, ruby and blue-opal necklaces that sat in an open jewellery box at the bottom of a clothes rail: the biggest, brashest one of course, a pendant of silver swirls set with five diamonds. The diamonds were real, Davina knew just by looking, and each necklace was probably worth a few thousand pounds. Fastening the chain around her neck, she went to Anthony, who wordlessly opened the door and let Davina look into the room beyond.

Davina sucked in her breath and stared. Just stared.

It was some sort of bar or members' club: much bigger than the dressing room, probably big enough for fifty standing guests, and perfectly square. At first glance it looked like an upmarket cocktail lounge from years ago, with curved, cushioned red sofas, a glittering red-and-black floor and soft yellow light glowing from gold chandeliers, which hung from a high, domed ceiling.

But scattered over the glamorous antique furniture and floor were hundreds of old-fashioned pound notes. The notes lay

5

everywhere, brown and grey: over the curvy legged sofas, the round glass tables with their grooved silver stems and the chequered floor. Worthless now, of course, the faded print and stylised 'one' indicating a currency of years gone by, but it was amazing nonetheless to see all this money thrown about the place. The money wasn't just scattered over the floors and furniture, it also decorated the walls in an elaborate patchwork: lacquered bills with Bank of England written on them in swirling writing, stuck higgledy piggledy over one another to form a sort of wallpaper.

Of course, if it had just been a question of old bills scattered everywhere and stuck to the walls, Davina would have been impressed, yes, but not absolutely astounded. No, the old money alone wasn't enough to astound her. What astounded her was the giant green and gold Dom Perignon bottle, about 7ft tall, standing in the centre of the room on a glittering, concave base of black gems. The bottle stood like a triumphant statue under the domed ceiling, its glass sides glittering with warm yellow light from the chandeliers above.

"Why?" Davina said, when she eventually regained powers of speech. "What's all this doing here?"

"It's for … entertainment purposes," said Anthony, taking a seat on one of the sofas. "Believe it or not, this was a prestigious building years ago. Very prestigious. Film stars, princes, kings – all sorts of high-profile guests. It was world famous. Anyone who was anyone spent an evening here."

Davina nodded, only half listening. She went to the nearest wall and ran her fingers over the lacquer-covered notes, feeling paintbrush marks and hardened bubbles.

"So it's a nightclub, then? Like an old nightclub from years ago?"

"Not exactly. It's more than a nightclub. A lot more goes on, if you know what I mean."

"No, not really. What else goes on?"

"You don't get £200 a night just for making drinks. The girls have to work harder than that."

Davina got the picture, and thought: *if this place is what I think it is, I'll want a lot more than bloody two hundred quid a*

6

night.

Anthony went to the far wall, where there was a brass rectangle of black switches and buttons, like an old-fashioned stage-light control panel, and Davina followed him.

"Let me show you something," said Anthony.

"What?"

"Wait," he instructed, flicking three of the switches and pressing a button. After a second or two, there were gurgling, whooshing sounds like someone hosing down a car.

"Anthony, what's that noise?" said Davina, turning around. As she did so, she nearly fell over in shock.

The giant champagne bottle in the centre of the room had exploded with water, shooting frothing, fizzy liquid from its neck high into the air. Fizzy water rained down, splashing onto the glittering, concave base of black gems that made a wide circle around the bottom of the bottle.

"It's like a fountain," Davina gasped.

"Do you want to go under it?"

"What, you mean stand under it?"

Anthony nodded. "The water's heated."

Davina went to the fountain and held her fingers under the spray. The water was warm and fizzy. It made her skin tingle and with a whoop she jumped under the warm water, laughing and shrieking, throwing her long arms into the air, letting water froth all over her, on her hair and shoulders, dripping from the crystals and diamante hung about her body. She lifted her head up and opened her mouth, letting water fill it up and flow over her lips and chin, holding her fingers out and letting the liquid rain between them.

Anthony took a seat on a sofa next to the fountain and watched her twirl around and laugh and run her hands along her arms and through her hair, body soaked, hair lying in shiny waves around her tanned shoulders.

After a moment Davina noticed him sitting there and, all of a sudden, in his sharp suit and designer shoes, sitting on a sofa covered with money, he looked like the most attractive thing she'd ever seen. Her arms fell to her sides and she stood limp in the fountain, the raining water around her totally forgotten.

The next moment, Anthony was beside her, undoing the fastenings at her neck and back. The crystal dress fell on the hard floor, crashing like a chandelier, but Anthony left the diamante chains untouched. She felt firm hands stroke and squeeze – almost too firm.

He pulled her out of the fountain and threw her onto the sofa, where she fell willingly, front first, breasts pressing into scattered pound notes and swaying strings of crystal, exhilarated and eager for whatever was coming next.

Anthony was behind her then, taking a handful of notes and rubbing them over her buttocks and shoving them between her legs. Then he threw her on her back, taking a single note and rolling it into a loose tube. He pushed the bill inside her, watching her look pleasurably shocked as he did so.

"You've got the right body for this," Anthony whispered, feeling along the back of her strong thighs.

"The best girls here have some flesh on them – it suits the outfits better." While he pushed the note deeper inside her, his free hand undid his trousers and freed a very long, very hard cock, which he manoeuvred towards her mouth.

"Of course, you have to show me you can do the job." He pressed his cock against her lips.

Davina looked up at him for a moment, uncertain. Then she took his cock into her mouth and sucked it with vigour, until Anthony stumbled and had to catch himself on a glass table. He took her head then, and forced his cock further into her mouth, seeing how far he could push her before she recoiled.

But she didn't recoil, and he pushed his whole cock into her mouth. While she sucked it willingly, Anthony searched around in his trouser pocket and produced something resembling a shiny gold coin. He pushed Davina back so she fell against the sofa again, on her back this time, and held the coin a few inches from her face like a magician about to perform a trick. It was a condom, a gold one, and Davina watched with a sense of eager dread as he rolled gold rubber over his cock.

Anthony was pleased by her lack of resistance. If she was happy to let him fuck her within minutes of taking her clothes off, she'd more than likely let clients do it for £200 a night. Mentally, he began to calculate how much she could earn him over the next few weeks and months. £200 was nothing to what the club made of an evening, and he knew she could earn him ten times that figure.

He grabbed a handful of notes and rubbed them around her pussy, enjoying her moan as paper and strings of diamante moved between her legs. She was already wet, but after a few minutes of rubbing she was more than ready for him and had opened her legs wide.

He pinned her shoulder down with his free hand and rammed his hard cock inside her, fucking her harder and harder and harder until the whole sofa was shaking. Pounded into her again and again, he rubbed notes over her body and into her mouth. She had a firm pussy, just like the rest of her, and he could easily imagine her servicing six or seven clients per shift. The thought made him harder than ever, and he fucked her remorselessly, banging her into the antique upholstery.

Davina couldn't stop herself then, and reached down, rubbing and rubbing her clit until she came: a throbbing, fierce sensation that spread through her body and made every bit of her near-naked body feel electric and alive. She moaned and clenched her thighs together, barely able to breathe.

"Oh no, oh no," hissed Anthony, as she grabbed his buttocks and pulled him deep inside her. "No, NO." And he came. Even though he never did with the girls who worked for him: it was one of his rules. He fell on her, grasping the base of his pulsating cock.

"That wasn't supposed to happen," he said after a moment, his neck flushed and throbbing.

"What wasn't?"

He didn't answer. Instead he pushed his cock, sheathed in limp gold, back inside his trousers and pulled her up from the sofa. "Come on. We can't stay here, it's opening up soon. Get changed and you can start tomorrow. 8 p.m."

After Davina had dressed and re-hung the outfits, dropping the necklaces back into the jewellery box, Anthony showed her back into the lift and pressed the button for reception.

9

"So I'll see you here tomorrow," he said, a resounding authority in his tone. "8 p.m. Don't be late – you'll need time to get changed." The elevator doors rolled open and he gave Davina a slap on her backside as she stepped out into reception.

"OK." She nodded, then sashayed across the reception area and out through the creaky glass doors with their retro triangle patterning and on to the street.

The fresh air felt good. Liberating. As Davina walked towards the car park, her coy smile turned into a big grin. She couldn't resist taking a look inside her handbag at the five diamond necklaces she'd manage to stash while she'd been putting her clothes back on. They were worth, in Davina's estimation, at least £3,000 each – maybe more. Poor Anthony. He was so focused on making money, he hadn't noticed when another shark, someone just like him, had swum into his tank. She had no intention of working for a living, and Anthony, with his collection of vintage jewels, had just given her enough money to live very comfortably for a couple of months. Davina smiled to herself as she got into her bright-green Mazda and thought to herself: isn't money wonderful?

Beautiful Things
by Kitty Meadows

All she could see was blue; the perfect blue Mediterranean Sea which sparkled in the midday sun and seemed to stretch out for ever, her view framed by the white cotton drapes billowing gently in the breeze at the windows. All was still, with just the sighs and sounds of kisses and love in the afternoon. White cotton, blue sky, white-washed walls and blue, blue eyes smiling down on her.

"Shut your eyes, *querida*," Jan whispered. Decca smiled and lay back, eyes fluttering closed. She could feel Jan's breath, soft and sweet at her neck, then strong fingers trailing up and down her face, smoothing and soothing her brow. Kisses; first barely-there butterfly kisses gently planted around her eyes, across her cheeks, teasingly circling her mouth, then stronger, firmer ones, along her neck, nibbling at her ear lobe … slowly moving down to trace her collarbone, moving down to flick her already-hard nipples with a warm, wet tongue, licking, sucking and sending Decca straight to heaven. She moaned with pleasure and reached up to circle her tanned arms around Jan's neck, to push that dark head between her legs.

"Lick me there, baby," she breathed. "Let me feel your mouth on my pussy."

But Jan resisted.

"Patience, *querida*, wait …"

Decca wriggled with anticipation and bit her lip. Nothing could make Jan change pace … *Why rush something wonderful, mi amor?*

Why indeed? But what if fast was what was needed? Fast and hard … and now?

11

Decca's eyes snapped open. Time to take charge, she decided, and swiftly pushed up with her left arm, deftly rolling Jan over, laughing as she silenced the protests with a deep passionate kiss.

"You taste so good," Decca smiled as she snaked her hand down and slid her palm between Jan's legs. "Now I'm going to taste you there too."

She wriggled down the bed and pushed Jan's legs apart, burying her face deep inside her girlfriend's cunt. She loved to give head; to feel Jan's musky warmth get wet and slippery, to hear her moan with delight, begging to be fucked with Decca's fingers. She swirled her tongue around Jan's swelling clit and fastened her mouth upon it, sucking gently while slipping two, three fingers inside, curving them upwards to find that sweet spot and slowly rubbing tiny circles around it, just the way that Jan liked it.

Jan trembled as Decca's practised hands brought her to a shuddering orgasm and she wrapped her legs tighter around Decca's head, rocking her way to perfect pleasure. Jan took a beat to compose herself and then swung around to return the favour.

"Always, you're so damn greedy, always in a hurry," she chided. She reached across Decca and slid open the drawer in the ornate cabinet beside the bed and took out a scarlet lacquered casket. "I'm going to make you come so hard ..." she said, as she took out a pair of shiny silvery curved toys and gently hefted them in her hand. She swivelled the diamond and ruby-studded base. "See how prettily they sparkle?" she smiled as the jewels caught the light and twinkled. "Now open your legs, spread yourself for me."

Decca did as she was told and lay back on the bed, legs akimbo, and spread her pussy wide open.

"Open your mouth," said Jan, and Decca did so, licking and sucking the toy, making it warm, wet and ready to put inside her. Jan swivelled the base as she took it from Decca's mouth and it buzzed into life.

"Hold that in place," she said, and took Decca's hand and pushed the curved toy inside her so it pulsed against her G-spot.

Next Jan took the other toy, swivelled it into maximum speed and zipped it around Decca's clit. Decca moaned and her hips bucked as she felt an orgasm swiftly build inside her. She couldn't hold out against the toys, they were so strong, so perfectly tuned to the rhythm of the ultimate orgasm. She pushed herself towards it, desperately rubbing herself against the toy.

"Jan, yes, yes, now, oh God!" Decca's knees locked together as a wave of pleasure hit. She shrieked as she rocked against the storm inside, which then triggered another hit of pleasure from her clit. Flushed, she breathlessly flung the toys aside and ground herself down on her lover's cunt. Their juices mingled, tongues entwined as each lost herself in the pleasure of the other.

The phone rang, its bell cutting through the silence as the women lay tangled together. Decca groaned and rolled over to grab it. They had few calls at the villa and had neither cell phones nor internet access. Life was simple and that was how they wanted it.

"Hello?" Decca smiled across the bed at Jan, but what she heard next wiped the smile from her face.

"It's me."

"What?"

"We need to meet. I need your help. I'll give you all the photos. At the place with the cherries. Tomorrow night. Ten. Say yes."

Decca's face crumpled. "Yes," she whispered. And he hung up.

She stumbled over to the bed and sat down. Jan reached up. "Baby, what is it?" she said, but Decca brushed her away. Her head spun and the euphoria from the love making with Jan fell away, leaving her feeling cold and alone.

It was a life that she had left a long time ago. A world she'd tried to forget. A man she never thought she'd see again.

She stumbled into the bathroom, locked the door and splashed icy water on her face. Looking back at her reflection in the mirror her mind travelled back in time … ten years ago

...

She lay crouched on the floor, waiting for a signal. Waiting for Colt to show. She'd never stopped feeling scared about this part; waiting for him, waiting for it to start, her heart racing, trying to push down the fear ... but they'd done their research, knew everything there was to know and they'd get away with it ... they always did. The Carlisle Collection, the legendary Bundewein artefacts and even Prince Khamir's much-whispered about private collection.

Show time! The red laser dot flashed on and off twice; he was here ... It was always a blur from this point; time seemed to become liquid, to slow down, then spin fast, so intent were they on working perfectly as a team, working together to take what they wanted. And then, as they left, usually shimmying down a building, they were just a speck of darkness in the landscape of the night. Gone in the blink of an eye, leaving no traces, no trail to follow.

FLASH – a snap shot of them wrapped together on the bed, sweating, fucking intently as the adrenaline raced through their veins after a job ... His cock pumping hard inside her, her head thrown back, screaming, begging, pleading for more, more more. She was his, she'd do anything for him, anything at all.

She'd been just a petty thief when they'd met but he'd seen something in her and taken her under his wing, shown her that together they could do so much more ... take their wildest dreams and make them reality. They'd specialised in antiques, curios of a particular kind, decadent and outrageous. You've heard of Faberge Eggs? Well, the same skilled artisans also created an improbably decadent collection of sex toys and treats to delight emperors and queens, lords and their serving wenches ... For those who had the money and the entree to an upper class secret world of lust, sin and sex, the delights that could be enjoyed were many and varied.

The priceless Overmeyer white gold and rose diamond dildo, the golden and sapphire handcuffs of Princess Esme, the collection of rings and studs from a certain prince with certain piercings ... all these priceless gems were to be found in the homes of fabulously wealthy collectors, and Colt and Decca had stolen them all, living a life of criminal luxury, where nothing was too decadent, nothing forbidden. They played with everything they stole; he took hundreds of photos of her dripping with jewellery to match the toys. The emerald-studded nipple clamps, the flashing sapphire butt plug ... she loved how she looked in them all, wanton and wild, flushed with the audacity of their crimes. But then five years ago the fights had started. The coldness between them, then the churning sickness in her stomach as she realised it was over, she wasn't attracted to him any more, she didn't want to be a thief, she needed to move on.

Then the break up, the tears, fights and threats. He wouldn't let her go, wouldn't give her the pictures, but one night she'd decided to hell with it. She'd slipped a little something in his coffee and taken off in the night with more than enough to start again. All she'd taken of the spoils of her old life was the copy of a diamond and ruby toy that he'd had made for her with a modern vibrator inside. She'd kept moving for a year, always looking over her shoulder, always waiting for him to find her, but then she'd moved to the Island, fallen in love with Jan and tried to make the past a place she'd never have to return to again.

And now the past was in her present. Decca shook her head and took a breath. She needed to pack, to explain what she could to Jan and get a flight to Naples to get back to the cafe where they'd eaten nothing but cherries every day for a week as they'd planned that first robbery together ...

He was sitting stirring an espresso, and didn't look up as she sat down and signalled the waiter to bring another.

He passed over a bulky envelope and placed it on the table between them.

"That's for you. Thanks for coming."

She looked up and met his eyes. He looked tired. Far older somehow than the five years that had separated them.

"What's this about?" Decca asked and took the package,

tucking it away in her daypack, the one hold he'd had on her finally loosened. Her heart lifted. Whatever Colt wanted, she could deal with it now.

"It's about Wyatt. He's on to me – to us – I suppose. But I think he wants to cut a deal."

Decca's spirits plummeted again. Inspector Wyatt had chased them across Europe, just a few steps behind all the way. Tall, blond and absurdly handsome, in Decca's mind he'd always been the good guy yin to Colt's bad guy yang.

"What sort of deal?"

"It's the photographs," mutterered Colt. "I, I sent one to him when you left. I was angry, I wanted to frame you, I suppose. But he liked it. Liked it a lot. He sent it back and said that if I could find you, I was off the hook."

"I? Not we?" Decca's senses prickled. Something wasn't right. Something very bad was going to happen.

"Colt?" He wouldn't meet her eye. She looked over to the door and there he was. All six foot three inches of Inspector Zander Wyatt.

"You cowardly sack of shit, Colt." Decca stood up, leaned over and spat in his face. Wearily she turned to Inspector Wyatt.

"Do what you have to, but really – he's getting off?" She looked back briefly at Colt. His eyes were on the table and he looked a million miles away from the dashing hunk who'd turned her world upside down so many years ago.

"Your wrists please, Miss."

"Fuck," Decca swore and raised her hands up before him. Her eyes widened when she saw him snap on the golden and sapphire cuffs. "What the..?" Before she could say any more, he pulled a silk cloth from his coat and broke a fine glass ampoule within it, then held it to her face. "You lousy ..." Decca slipped into unconsciousness and knew no more.

She woke and found herself in a bed in an ornate room, with every wall covered from floor to ceiling in stunning erotic art. She gasped in amazement and sprang out of the bed. There, the lost Vermeer! There, could it be? An original Warhol! A naked

Monroe wrapped around a naked JFK, repeated over and over … Incredible. She looked around for the door and yet again met the steely blue eyes of Inspector Wyatt.

"What the hell is this, Wyatt?" For the first time she noticed that she was dressed in a simple silk shift dress. "And where are my clothes?"

Wyatt came over and sat on the bed.

"It's simple. I have a proposal. I'm very attracted to beautiful things, beautiful pictures. I want to recreate a photograph of you. If I can do that then I'll let you go. If that is not acceptable, then I'm afraid you'll have to come back with me to Zurich and explain to the department and the Lecruz Foundation exactly why I found these in your possession." He removed a slim silver box from his jacket pocket and Decca gulped. It was the Overmeyer set. A priceless, unique rose diamond and white gold dildo with matching nipple clamps. She remembered Colt taking photographs of her as she sat sprawled on a blue satin throw, hands cuffed over her head, legs parted, holding the toy deep inside. Could she do that again? Without Jan? Could she do that for Wyatt?

"What are my guarantees that you'll let me go if I do?"

Wyatt looked solemn. "I'm a man of my word. If I say it, then it's so. Don't be confused, I don't want to fuck you. Just see you use these beautiful toys. Do we have a deal?"

He held out his hand and, seeing no way out, Decca shook.

Wyatt let out a sigh of relief and smiled. "Good! I have wanted this, Decca, for years. Let's make it happen."

He led the way out of the room and down a corridor to a larger room with a huge bed with a curved hook over its head. Next to the bed was a cabinet and folded on the side was a sapphire blue satin throw. He picked it up and shook it out, watching the rich fabric smoothly flow across the bed. Then he reverentially placed the silvery case in the centre of the bed and gestured to Decca to remove her clothes. She breathed deeply, pulled the shift over her head, padded towards the bed and climbed on.

"Lie back, just relax. I don't believe in causing pain. I just want to see beauty," assured Wyatt as Decca involuntarily

17

trembled in anticipation. She lay there, listening to her breathing; shallow and fast. She tried to relax, to slow it down; she knew that if she was tense she couldn't take the Overmeyer set. What was easy when she was turned on would be impossible like this. She had to loosen up. She lay on her side, waiting for whatever would happen next.

It felt like a feather … a soft, light, almost tickling touch. She turned her head to see Wyatt beside her, a scarlet maribou fan in his hand.

"Please, relax," he said, and began to stroke her body from her toes to her head. He stroked her arms, her thighs, her belly and breasts, over and over again. It felt hypnotic, it felt … it felt sexy. She felt a stirring inside and her hips shifted slightly from side to side while Wyatt watched with a clinical detachment and saw a faint rosy glow spread over her cheeks and chest. Good, next step.

He reached across to the cabinet, where the oil that had been warming by candlelight was ready. He poured some into his hands and slicked it over Decca's breasts. Her nipples immediately sprang to life and he slowly rubbed the oil into each breast, circling the nipples with his thumb before taking first the left, then the right, between his thumb and finger, rolling and tweaking until Decca cried out a half-hearted protest. Next he re-anointed his hands and dipped his fingers to her pussy. With a flat hand he applied the oil in a circular motion,

"Hey," Decca said, confused. "What's in the oil? My breasts … they feel … tingly, strange. I feel woozy."

"It's a relaxant and also a sexual stimulant. I want you to enjoy this Decca. There's no beauty in real pain."

She lay back and closed her eyes. She could see stars. The world had reduced to Wyatt rubbing her cunt with his hand. The oil was working and she felt herself getting wetter and wider; she wanted to be filled, she felt so turned on. This wasn't what she'd been expecting at all.

"How do you feel?"

"I'm spinning … it's good, so, so good. I want this." She turned to look at Wyatt and smiled.

18

"OK, you're ready," he said, and scooped her into a sitting position. He took her wrists, snapped them in the golden jewelled cuffs, then looped them over a bar above the bed. "There, does that feel good?"

"Mmm ..." Decca smiled, enjoying the sensation of captivity. After all, if she was tied up, was whatever happened her fault? Of course not. She'd just have to go with the flow and take whatever was coming ...

Wyatt carefully picked up the glittering clamps and gently blew on Decca's rock hard nipples; they stiffened even more, so he opened the clamps to their widest setting and slowly applied them. Decca moaned with pleasure. It felt so good; her skin felt alive, each nerve end tingling, leaving her teetering on the edge of what promised to be a fierce orgasm. Wyatt ran his fingers deliberately along the connecting filigree chain that sparkled with hundreds of thousands of pounds worth of rare rose-coloured diamonds. The extra pressure caused Decca to let out a cry of pleasure-pain.

"Beautiful, just perfect," he said quietly, and slipped a hand between her legs and raised an eyebrow. "You really like this, don't you?"

"I do. I always did ... what's next?"

Wyatt smiled briefly and reached over to take the white gold and rosily shimmering toy. Decca parted her legs with a wicked smile. Experimentally, he rubbed it slowly across her clitoris. Unconsciously, her hips rose to take possession of it, to nudge it a little lower, to try to take it inside her. He didn't want to disappoint, so he slid it along and its tip easily disappeared in her body.

Decca caught her breath. It was so big, but so good.

"You're going to have to slide it in and out, very slowly, a little at a time," she stammered. "It's so big, but I know I can take it."

"I know you can. That picture's haunted me for years," confessed Wyatt as he began to fuck her, first gently, then deeper as she begged for more and rode the toy harder.

"Spread your legs wider Decca, let me see how beautiful you are."

She did.

And she was.

Her breasts were held high because of the glittering golden cuffs, her nipples covered in a cluster of jewels with a shimmering chain falling in a perfect U between her breasts. Her legs fell open to reveal the stunning jewel between her thighs. The base of the rose diamond Overmeyer Set was what made it special; a perfect hand-sized heart-shaped brilliant cut diamond, its fifty eight facets reflecting the light so clearly it looked like a living flame, dancing between her legs. It reflected off the blue satin and dazzled Inspector Wyatt.

Breathlessly he took in Decca's tanned, long legs and perfect small breasts. They were as wonderful as he'd dreamt they were. More wonderful. He'd seen only a still image of this; seeing it alive before him was more beautiful than he could ever have imagined. He needed to reward her, to thank her for giving him this amazing picture to keep and remember for ever.

"Decca, what can I do?"

"Let me come!" she groaned. "Rub my clit, please, let me come …"

Hastily, he tipped some oil onto his hand and as he thrust the Overmeyer in and out with one hand, he used the other to tease Decca into an orgasm that shook her from her head to her feet. Flushed with pleasure, dazzled with diamonds, she once again looked every inch the decadent hedonist that he'd been obsessed with for all these years.

It had been worth the wait …

"I still don't understand, *querida*, but I'm so glad you're home. And what a present!" Jan looked in amazement at the slim silver box that Decca had given her.

Decca smiled to herself. She hoped Wyatt would understand that some old habits never die. She'd left him with his beautiful memories; she just wanted to create some wonderful new ones with her love and, of course, the most decadent dildo in the world …

Blue, perfect blue sky, with the shimmering blue sea,

sparkling in the midday sun like a net of diamonds was cast across it … All was still again with just the sighs and sounds of kisses and love in the afternoon.

Blind Man's Buff
by Justine Elyot

In the room next door there is laughter and convivial chatter, the clinking of glasses. If I strain my ears I can catch unobtrusive jazz sounds from the loudspeakers, but I cannot make out individual voices or words. The door must be a solid one. I picture aged oak panels with looping grain and gold – or wrought iron? – handles.

"Are you ready for your close-up, Miss Trollop?" My lover's voice buzzes in my ear and his hands caress my shoulders, but I know those caresses. Their lightness deceives, and before I know it I am in a grip, in a bind, bound to do his will.

"Yes, I think so." Ready. If readiness means a constricted throat and a faintness in the head, I am certainly ready.

"You look …" A helpless intake of breath completes the sentence for him. I smile, and the uplift of my cheekbones causes the frilled edge of my blindfold to tickle my skin. "Thank you for this."

"I hope it will be a pleasure," I say with a rueful little laugh.

"It will."

Then the doors are opened – yes, concertina doors, I can now discern from the clacking and rolling noise they make, but that fades to insignificance against the human reaction to my entrance. Gil nudges me forward, across a threshold that is far more than physical, and I hear gasps, nervous laughter, a smattering of applause.

"Ladies and gentleman," says Gil in his courtroom voice. "May I present to you this evening's entertainment – Miss Venetia Valverde."

Now the applause is hearty and there are appreciative mutterings. How many are here? How many men? How many women?

"You've outdone yourself, Gil," says one older-gentlemanly voice. "She is enchanting."

"As you will see." Suddenly he takes his hands from my shoulders and snaps his fingers. The jazz sounds silence immediately. "Take a good look at her." His hand returns to me, a gentle but insistent pressure in the small of my back. "Up straight, Venetia. Chest out, shoulders back. I hope she is to your taste."

"So what's the entertainment?" asks a younger voice, female.

"I propose a favourite party game with a twist. Blind Man's Buff. Venetia here is our sight-impaired subject. She will try to get her hands on us as we move around the room. But each time she catches somebody, rather than swap blindfolds, she will have to lose an item of clothing."

There is chuckling, general approval. "She doesn't have that much to lose," objects a lady. It is true. I am wearing no more than a full slip in transparent lace, over a basque, thong and stockings. High-heeled mules restrict the speed of my movements. My quarries will elude me easily, if they want to.

Of course, they will not want to. Especially after Gil's next words.

"No, she doesn't, does she. So once she is naked, those she catches may use her body in any way they wish. Stopping short of penetrative sex. For now."

"That's inspired!"

"Any way we wish? Really?"

"Any way at all?"

The queries come thick and fast until Gil does something to stop them – hold up a hand, maybe? He is a master of the unambiguous gesture.

"Yes, any way you wish. With one exception. I do not want any of you to kiss her. Kissing rights are mine and mine alone."

I exhale a breath of gratitude. He understands my wishes on this score. He understands how the fantasies work, and what would make them fail. As if to underline his point, he cups my chin, tilts it upwards and kisses me, hard, tongue slipping through my glossy lips, for what seems like for ever.

Once I am marked and his possession sealed, he slaps me on the bottom and pushes me out into the room. "The game is afoot," he proclaims.

One of the mules almost tips me sideways, but I recover, placing a hand on the stinging site of his smack until the initial glow recedes. Where are the people? Their footfalls echo on the wooden floor, and the quality of the sound indicates that the room is of a large size. Is it sparsely furnished, or am I likely to bump into all kinds of occasional tables?

I swipe, sensing a nearby presence, and my nails snag in a necklace, pearls I think. A neigh of a female laugh, a hand on my wrist.

"Mind those, girl – they were my grandmother's." Her perfume is strong and rich, something like Opium, but not quite. "Well, then …" She begins to steer me towards something – a sofa – and sits me down on slippery cushions. "Let's lose these silly shoes, shall we? You'll wreck your bones, shoving them into those things."

The homily is unexpected, but rather reassuring. Once she has slipped the mule off my left foot, she cups it in her hand and begins to massage my instep.

"Oh! That's lovely!" I exclaim. "Bliss." The sensation creeps up my calf, tickles the back of my knee, tingles up my thigh to my crotch.

"I didn't ask for your opinion!" she says sharply, and I am humbled back into silence. By the time she has finished squeezing and stroking my right foot, I am puddling with desire, worrying about the expensive chintz. But then I am hauled back up and pushed onward with a laugh, to find my next victim.

He is male, wearing a rough tweedy jacket that smells of pipe smoke, and straight away he clamps hands beneath my armpits, then slides them slowly down the lacy sides, making a meal of each curve until he reaches the hem, which sits just on my stretchy stocking tops.

"We can lose this, can't we?" he says. His elder-statesman voice propels brandy breath into my nostrils. Obediently I raise my arms, while he shimmies the slip up over my hips and chest, up into the air and then away.

"Lovely arse," somebody comments, for now my oiled and powdered buttocks, bisected by a taut black string, are visible to the whole room.

"Yes." Gil's voice. "Would you like to touch it?"

Calloused skin makes frictive contact with my smooth globes, brushing them, then squeezing the underside. "There's a nice little patch of pink here where your hand made contact," observes the mystery man, talking to Gil. "I envy you, Markham – I suppose you get to spank this arse whenever the mood takes you."

"Indeed I do. And the mood takes me rather frequently, as Venetia would attest."

"I'm not surprised." There is a final pinch to my bottom and I am set off again, speedier on my stockinged feet, flitting around sofas, beginning to draw a mental picture of the room behind my blindfold.

I am aware of the bodies before I reach them; there is warmth and scent heralding their physical presence. If I do not like the smell, I try to elude them, but this one is peaches, lovely ripe delicate peaches. Or nectarines. When I catch her she laughs, low and mellifluous, and strokes my hair. She is about my height, and her touch as she unhooks my basque is exquisite.

"Oh, look, they are standing up for me!" Warm merriment in her voice, bathing me. Then she is pulling me back against her body – her dress is silk – and pinching at my nipples, demonstrating for the room. "Look at these pretty things, everyone." She reaches down to unsnap my stockings, then removes them. Her hair tickles my bottom and thighs and there is sweet breath on my skin. Once the hosiery is removed, she drops a gentle kiss on the inside of one thigh, then stands back up and repeats the action on the back of my neck. "Pretty things," she repeats, crooning it into my hair.

"Put her down, Saskia," says Gil indulgently and, to the

accompaniment of sighs, I am released once more, to pad about the room in no more than my thong. Their voices are giving away their location now, for they have broken into conversation, and their conversation is about me – or rather my breasts, and my bottom, and the curve of my hips and the tone of my skin.

"You're a lucky man, Gil."

"She is built for pleasure."

"Made for fucking."

"The perfect little slut."

I twist this way and that, in between the sound waves they produce, until eventually I trip over a shoe – a man's shoe, perhaps a brogue – and stumble into him.

"Oh, I have hit the jackpot!" he proclaims. "Let's get these knickers off then. Such as they are."

His thumbs settle inside the elastic, resting there for a while, snug against my hipbones, then he begins to ease them down, very slowly, very deliberately. He runs a finger down the string, releasing it from its captivity in my arse crack, then he chuckles – I knew he would – when my pubic hair is revealed.

"That's sweet," he says. "A heart shape. Look at this." He hurries to get the flimsy things off me so he can show my clipped, shaped mons to the world. There is a rumble of laughter and some clapping.

"There now, ladies and gentlemen," says Gil. "Your gift is unwrapped. It is now up to you to enjoy it. Catch her and you may use her in any way you wish – short, as we have established, of penetrative sex." His voice is getting closer, he is almost beside me. "Are you ready, Venetia?" His hand brushes my cheek. I nod. "Then let the real game begin."

Straight away there are hands on me, hands of all kinds, all sizes, all textures, but all of them are demanding, all of them want to take me and use me. They are in my hair, bunching it up and pulling at it; they are moulding themselves around my breasts; they are seeking and creeping into my crevices and holes. I am yanked backwards on to somebody's lap – male, wool trousers – and my thighs are parted to display the moist pink parts, the parts that are no longer private. From either side of me, hands and then tongues alight on my tits, while between my legs something eager perches itself and begins to fan hot breaths on to my clit.

I feel myself devoured and ravished; I lie back to rest my head on the lap-man's shoulder; his fingers knead at my pussy lips while another person's tongue begins to stroke the clit that swells within. My breasts are slick and chilly with the licking they are getting, my nipples beginning to sting from the constant attention. I can feel the lap-man's erection pressing itself urgently between my arse cheeks; he is jiggling a little, trying to ease it further in. The person who is at my clit sticks fingers inside me, spearing and thrusting.

"Can you hear that? She's so wet!'

"Make her come. I want to watch her come."

"Do it quickly, I want my turn."

I cannot count the mouths, the fingers, the tongues; they merge into one giant organism, working towards the common goal of bringing me to public climax. I begin to slip further into my darkness, a creature plugged and frigged and existing only for the purposes of sexual gratification, marked as property, yes, property, yes, that is what does it, and I come hard, on to an anonymous tongue and hand, my voice seeming enormous and alien as it leaves me.

I am soothed and petted and stroked and congratulated, but soon enough others want to take their place. Dimly, from behind the screen of pure sensation, I manage to count six people, seven if you include Gil, but I soon become confused as to who is having me and how, in the blizzard of cocksucking and pussy eating and arse licking and nipple nipping. I get spanked at some point, and at another my wrists are tied with curtain cord and I am made to crawl around the room and kiss feet. I come twice more, bucking and howling, and trying to push away the onslaught of more tongues and more hands and more cocks and more cunts, finally brought to the point of exhaustion.

"She is tired. Lay her down on the sofa," directs Gil.

My sore, well-used body, smeared with mingled sweat and semen, enjoys the respite, sinking gratefully into the velvet cushions.

The guests break into a low hum of conversation once more, discussing the food and drink, their last and next meetings. The chatter is lazy and enervated, their voices yawn.

I know that the hands lifting my head are Gil's, as is the lap in which it is placed. He is still fully-clothed, and I realise that I was right in my assumption that he had taken no part in the earlier proceedings. I know his touch exactly, and those frenetic encounters, rich as they were, had lacked it.

"Are you happy?" he asks me.

"Yes. Did I do well?"

"You did." Moistened fingertips run the length of my lips; I suck them into my mouth, using them as comforters. "And you had exactly the effect I anticipated."

He is right, for I can feel the iron ramrod of his erection crushing my ear against my head.

"Looking at you now," he continues. "Pawed and fondled by unknown hands and mouths, your belly tight with dried spunk, your orifices spread and stretched – it makes me want you more than ever."

His words stir me out of my torpor; the ache between my legs transforms to a pulse of need.

"Take me then." I form the words thickly, around his fingers.

He removes them. "What was that?"

"Take me then." My words ring into a suddenly quietened room.

"Is that what you want, Venetia? But it would be rude to leave our guests before the party has ended."

"Let them watch."

"Do they want to watch?" The question is addressed to the room. There is no need to answer; the sound of clearing throats accompanies a wave of air that I imagine to be them nodding as one.

Gil stands and helps me off the sofa, throwing the cushions to the floor for me to lie upon.

"Spread your legs," he says. "Show us what you have to offer." I can hear the sounds of disrobing, of unknotting ties, of zips and buttonholes. Obediently, I open up, as wide as I can, holding my thighs to keep them out of view.

"Lift your legs and hook your hands under your knees. Keep the thighs wide. That way we can see your anus too. Did anybody touch you there, Venetia?"

"Yes," I admit.

"Fingers?"

"Fingers, tongues."

"You liked it."

"I liked it."

"Well, perhaps next time you can take a cock up there. I'm not promising anything, though. Let's see how you get on. Who fingered her? Do you think she could take a cock up there?"

A man volunteers, "Yes, I think so. She liked having three fingers up there."

"Good. Right." I feel the swish of him, dropping down between my extended knees, then my shoulders are pinned down and swiftly, before I have fixed his position in my mind's eye, he swarms up to the hilt. Oh, the relief, the fullness, the rightness of it, as if I were born to sheathe his cock.

I feel the guests edge nearer and nearer while Gil sets to a brisk and efficient rhythm, keeping his moves tightly controlled.

"You're going to come one more time," he says jerkily. "One more time. While you're having your pussy fucked in public. One more time."

He repeats the 'one more time' mantra until it becomes a reality and I writhe under his pitiless thrusts, giving my throaty finale to the gathered crowd. He swoops down to my lips, kissing and kissing until I am bathed in his balm, locked down tight beneath his vibrating body, taking all the roaring heat from his pores and absorbing it into mine.

Later on, eyes unwrapped, I sit, leaking his juices on to a towel, drinking cocktails in the nude while I laugh and swap anecdotes with the guests.

Next time, I believe we will be playing sardines.

29

A Costume Drama
by Daphne Bing

"I can't say I wasn't … well, surprised …" Mary Highgate hesitated. "I really thought … Well, no matter what I thought. He does have a reputation, as I'm sure you know?"

Caroline smiled and smoothed out the silk on her gown. "Well of course he does Aunt, he's a Lord."

"A penniless Lord," Mary huffed. "A penniless lord who is no doubt attracted by your mother's inheritance. I can't believe my brother would countenance the match, let alone set it up! No doubt Bertie is dazzled by his title, but I really think he should have had more thought for you and the rest of the family." She covered her anger by patting her niece's hand. "You know, my dear, there is a reason why he's not been married before. His reputation makes him … undesirable with ladies of any sensitivity. But if you think you can handle him…?"

"I know he has a fearsome reputation with the people who work on his estates, but Papa always says that a man needs to rule firmly or people will take advantage."

Mary studied the chiming clock for a minute and considered her young niece again; she was the picture of perfect innocence. Large dark trusting eyes, full lips that were not afraid to speak out when crossed, and a figure that made many gentlemen stare at her in a most impertinent fashion. She suspected it was not just her niece's fortune that had attracted Lord Fleetwood. Mary went across to the bell and called the servants. When she'd ordered her nightcap she broached the subject again.

"Without being too indelicate, my dear, I think that Lord

Anthony Fleetwood will make a very demanding husband. Do you understand what I mean? Without your dear Mama to guide you I wonder if you understand what happens between a man and woman in the marriage bed?"

Caroline flushed slightly, nodded, and muttered, "Of course." She would need to sleep next to Lord Fleetwood and, somehow, in the night when they were asleep, their most private parts might touch and his seed might pass to her and she might bear him a child. She thought perhaps she would be able to limit this a little by wearing a very long nightgown that she would keep tight wrapped around her legs. "You must know, Aunt, that no one has ever been able to make me do anything I didn't want to do, and if Lord Fleetwood is ever impertinent to me he will soon find that to be the case."

Mary smiled. That much was true; Caroline had a very forceful personality, and it would be a strong man who could bring her to heel. Perhaps a man like Lord Fleetwood.

"I think you will find that his behaviour can be decadent. As his wife, the Church and the law demand that you submit to him as your master without complaint."

"I like Lord Fleetwood, Aunt; he always looks on me with very kindly eyes, and I'm sure Papa would not have arranged the betrothal unless he thought him a worthy man. Lord Fleetwood has done me many kindnesses and although I have seen a harsher, less gentle side with others, with me he is always most tender."

"So be it, but if you ever need me ..." She glanced up at the servant entering and knew to change the subject. "Well let us hope for good weather tomorrow."

It was a big wedding; it was only when Caroline walked down the aisle on her father's arm that she appreciated just how big. There must have been over three hundred guests. But the day passed without incident and at the wedding breakfast, as the toast was raised to Lord and Lady Fleetwood, she felt a pang of pleasure that she had secured a respectable place in society. She wished her mother could have been there to see her.

She glanced into the face of her new husband and fleetingly

caught a look she had not seen before in a man. His hand reached for hers under the table and he leant across to her and whispered in her ear, "Not long now," and Caroline wondered what he meant; they were married, so not long now until what?

His hand reached slowly up her leg, making circles with his fingers. She froze a little, and then her aunt, who was sitting the other side of him, said something that caught Lord Fleetwood's attention and his hand stopped its trail along her leg. She shifted to move it off and it fell between them. He turned back to her for a moment and gave her a strange look, partly angry, partly amused, and then was back talking to her aunt.

At around five the servants announced that their carriage was ready and waiting and, after many affectionate goodbyes, she found herself on her way to her new husband's estates, which were just outside Farnham. She smiled; he looked very handsome today, with everything in the latest fashion except a black cane with an ornate silver head that he carried. She'd not seen it before.

"Why do you have a cane, my Lord?" she asked, curious.

He smiled broadly. "I think we are now on intimate enough terms for you to call me Anthony, don't you think? And the cane, well, that's part of the intimacy I have planned for us." His eyes ran over her body and back to meet her eyes and she involuntarily shuddered and flushed.

He reached up to her face with his hands and held her so she had no choice but to meet his gaze, before he tilted his face, closed his eyes and kissed her on the mouth, where no lips had been before. His tongue probed and found its way into her mouth and she let her tongue meet his. She felt a surge of excitement which she didn't quite understand and the kiss became more passionate. She felt his hands bury themselves in the back of her hair and then tug at it so that her neck was exposed to his kisses. She let out a moan and he released her sharply. She sat back down, feeling hot and uncomfortable, and the man who had done this to her, her husband, merely resumed his seat as if nothing strange had just happened. She didn't know whether to insist he continue kissing her or slap him for starting it in the first place, but he was nonchalantly looking out of the window. She concentrated on trying to slow her breathing.

Eventually he turned back to her. "I heard you were strong-willed and outspoken, and your father said you were difficult to control. Is that true?"

"It has been said, I believe," she answered carefully.

He laughed. "Did you father or your governess never beat you into submission?"

She flushed and shook her head in reply.

"You poor thing, to miss out on that pleasure! I shall be correcting that."

She gasped, not sure if he was teasing her; his eyes were certainly smiling but there was something else in them that she couldn't understand.

"You intend to beat me?"

"It will be your choice. It will always be your choice; I will simply corrupt you into desiring it." His smile matched her scowl. "And now, if you'll excuse me, I will go back to studying the view outside. The one in the carriage is far too disturbing. We're nearly home and we probably don't want all the servants seeing quite how anxious I am to consummate the wedding, do we?"

So they sat in silence for the next ten minutes, with Caroline not sure whether her nerves, her anger or her excitement were going to win, while her husband used all his powers of control to think of anything but what he was at last going to be able to do to the woman who had disturbed his dreams more than any other.

Caroline looked around her new bedroom with interest. Her bags had been sent ahead so all her things were already set out for her. She had expected nothing less, but it gave her some comfort to see the familiar as she faced the unfamiliar. The bed dominated the room and seemed to be mocking her. How many hours before she would find out what was really expected of her? She had no doubt now that she had been naïve, and wished she had quizzed her Aunt to find out.

The light was already fading quickly and she started to panic, but in that state she recognised that strange excitement again. She put hand to her lips; she fancied she could still feel where his lips had been, the hand on the back of her head and the smell of him. To be closer to him had a certain appeal. She jumped as the door opened and the man himself appeared; he must have been in a dressing room next to the bedroom as he was now wearing only an open neck shirt and breeches.

He smiled at her. "Now, where were we before I had to control myself?" As he spoke he reached out and started to undress her.

Caroline stood frozen, watching his fingers expose her; she had counted on having another couple of hours at least.

"What about supper?"

"Later," he answered without pausing. His fingers knew exactly what they were doing and she flushed as her breasts were exposed to him. His hands cupped them and kissed her flesh before he took one nipple into his mouth and very gently in his teeth. She closed her eyes and gasped and he let her go again and went back to work on stripping her. She wriggled; fear and excitement were still muddled in her. She thought she might need to go to the closed stool, but there seemed no chance that her husband would release her. Her stays were falling to the floor and only her undergarments now remained. He pushed her onto the bed and stared down at her now half naked body. His own shirt came off over his head in one fluid movement and she stared in surprise at how appealing his body was; she had expected it to be offensive, but his toned, powerful torso made her think again that she needed to urinate. When he started to take off the rest of her clothes she wanted to help him; whatever this was building up to was far from unpleasant. Moments earlier she had thought she would be embarrassed when he finally saw her naked, but instead she felt quite wanton about it.

He got on top of her, kissing her everywhere, and she murmured in appreciation. She felt drunk with a strange cocktail of new feelings and she glanced down at him to see why he had stopped. He had been removing his breeches, and she let out a slight yelp when she saw him. There seemed to be part of him that was completely different to anything she'd seen before and she couldn't stop staring at it. The head was red and angry and was clearly leaking fluid.

But then he moved so that the thing was somewhere between her legs, probing her, and with alarm she suddenly realised what he was going to do.

"No," she said suddenly and pulled away. "It will hurt, it's too big, you can't, you can't …"

"Shhh …" he murmured in her ear. "You're ready, it will be a momentary pain …"

He pulled her legs right up and, with one of his arms, he pinned her right leg back up near her head so that she was totally exposed to him. She struggled again but she was no match for him. He kissed her gently on mouth. "Relax. It's better for you if you relax and don't fight me."

She tried to calm her mounting panic as his hardness started thrusting at her, she squealed loudly as it pierced its way into her. He pulled back a little and she thought that he had some compassion, but instead he thrust even harder and something inside her gave way and she felt herself entirely filled by him. Maybe that was it, she thought; it was over, he had her. She looked up to meet his eyes; all the time he had been staring into her face. She flushed at what they were doing. She couldn't believe the intimacy of it. Then he started moving rhythmically in and out of her. Her body started to respond; the sense of needing to urinate increased until she felt she would have to somehow get him off her or she would wet herself. His thrusts got harder and quicker and the old bed rocked and squealed in protest. Every nerve in her started to tingle and she gasped, trying to control herself. She found her body moving to meet him; she now needed him as much as he clearly needed her, and then she felt a sudden rush that was so pleasurable that she cried out and dug her hands into him. Moments later, she felt him juddering as she had and he collapsed on her, panting hard.

He fell off her and sighed in contentment. She moved to get her clothes and his arm came over her body. "I've told the servants to retire. We're not moving from this room until morning. That was just the aperitif; we have a whole night's pleasure before us."

"No! I have fulfilled my wifely duty by you and now need…"

He laughed, and leaned up on one arm to look at her. "Your wifely duty? I don't think it was such a hardship for you." He stroked her hair, "I knew it would be so …"

"I'm going …"

"Nowhere," he said firmly. "You promised to obey me in church not five hours ago. If you want to break that promise … well you'll find out what the cane is for then – perhaps I should demonstrate?"

She had moved off the bed as he spoke and he made a sudden grab for her and forced her to kneel at the foot of the bed, her face buried into the bed, her backside exposed. She heard him reach for the cane. Her insides tingled again.

"You can stop me," he said. "Any time, just scream out the word 'obedience' and I will stop whatever I'm doing. Understood? Carnal pleasures leave a bad taste in my mouth if the woman is not having fun too – even if she does need a little persuasion … And I do love the game of persuasion."

Before the last word was out of her mouth she felt the cane come down hard on her backside. She squealed in panic, "Obedience!" and, true to his word, he stopped and released her, but she stayed in position for a moment, realising that she was disappointed. She moved slowly back on to the bed to join him and his eyes glanced down appreciatively over her still-naked body.

"You're disappointed, aren't you? You would like to be properly beaten?"

"Of course not."

"Do you trust me?" he asked, and she nodded. "Well, let me beat you then. Maybe not today; perhaps next time you want to play at disobeying me."

"No," she said firmly.

He leaned over, kissed her gently and whispered in her ear, "Oh, you know you want me to really." She pretended to sleep.

Lord and Lady Fleetwood were hosting a big dinner party to celebrate the New Year. They had now been married two months. Lord Fleetwood had chosen the menu himself. It was not to his wife's taste, but she knew now when to obey her husband and when it was more fun to disobey him.

The first course was asparagus and Caroline found it difficult to eat. She attempted to be delicate but the butter dripped down her fingers, and if she tried to bite the heads off it just went stringy, so she sucked carefully in a way that did not go unnoticed by her husband. He watched her lips closing around the long vegetable and found himself hardening at the image. At one stage she even licked butter off her fingers, at which point he thought he would ejaculate on the spot. Never was a woman such an intoxicating mixture of passion and innocence.

Caroline glanced up and saw the heavily-lidded gaze of her husband, only now she knew what it meant. She sucked again on the asparagus tip and let the butter dribble a little more. She might not win arguments and he might subjugate her in the bedroom, but she had discovered a new power that was even more intoxicating. Most of the table had now spotted the lusting couple. They told themselves how appalling a display it was; the young woman must know what she was doing and it was not to be tolerated in public. Privately, they felt very differently and there were many children conceived that night.

It took a few hours to get rid of all their guests, or so it felt to Anthony, and then there was the night time ritual before finally they were alone and undressed.

He ran a finger along his wife's lips; "I want you to suck me in the way that you sucked that asparagus tonight, until I spill inside your mouth, and then I want you to drink it down like you would the most delicious drink."

His wife shook her head firmly. "That's outrageous! You don't mean it, I know you don't mean it. Such decadence – I've never heard of such decadence – I'm sure that's not part of my marital duties to you …"

He moved closer to her and undid the ribbons that fastened

her nightgown. In seconds the garment rippled to the floor, leaving her naked. He kissed her neck and down her shoulder, so tenderly she thought he had moved on, but then in one swift and violent movement he had her kneeled against the bed, her bottom exposed in a way that was now familiar to her. He pushed her back hard down on the bed with one hand and she knew what was coming next.

The cane was nearby and he beat her with it five times before he asked her again, "Will you obey me or do I continue?" She was about to come, just from the strokes he'd given her; they'd set up such a heavenly feeling in her loins. She wasn't going to let him stop now. "No! Never!" she cried, and the beating continued until her bottom was covered in a criss-cross of red lines and she was crying out in pleasure.

"Obedience!" she finally shouted when she had finished gasping and trying to cover the sounds of her enjoyment.

"Turn round and kneel before me." She did as she was told meekly and watched him strip off his nightshirt to reveal his manhood to her. She gently took him in her mouth and found the taste quite salty. He was leaking heavily already but it wasn't unpleasant. His hand came to rest on her head and he murmured words of instruction as she went to work on him. He started to thrust with his hips and he hit the back of her throat a couple of times, which made her gag. She knew he was close.

"Remember, drink it … drink it all, that's good …"

He started to judder and he held her to stop her moving on him. "Gently," he cried out, but the words were lost in a groan as he ejaculated into her mouth.

She swallowed most of it, just allowing some to dribble down out of the corners of her mouth, she smiled into his face and pushed it in with her finger, just as she had the butter earlier.. He smiled lewdly at her as he watched her get onto the bed naked; she knew better than to try to put her nightgown on when he was in this mood. Instead she wantonly let her legs fall open and mocked him with the sight of her body, fully exposed. His eyes were glued to her and he kissed his way up her legs until his tongue found her clitoris. She sighed and leaned back in pleasure with her husband's head between her legs. She loved their games; she loved going down on him and most of all she loved his childlike adoration of her body.

Endless Night
by Marcelle Perks

When Ella woke up, Joachim was still sleeping under a twisted coarse blanket. The old army coat he'd worn in Afghanistan when he'd gone there to make a documentary and ended up fighting with the Fundamentalists was somewhere in the tangle. Copious amounts of dope ash and the dead scrape of old sweat rolled under her skin. But the debris was mostly over him, because by now, with no proper sheets or covers to legitimise the thing they called bed, he'd stolen most of everything into a wreck around him.

In slumber his face was serene, the high cheekbones and arched eyebrows perfectly spaced. Once he was conscious, his diabolical temperament would manifest itself. He could be tetchy at the best of times. Smoked something constantly with a coffee in reach. On a bad day he might slash at himself crazily with a blunt knife, write her name on his body in his own blood. He was insane and unpredictable and never cleaned his flat, but every time he touched her, she simply melted. Just the merest brush of his finger tips over her skin was like sinking into a bath at body temperature. He had just the right touch. It wasn't sex, it was magic.

Joachim rolled over. He wouldn't be up for hours. Didn't do mornings – or even days, for that matter. The flat was draped in permanent night, with the shades down, candles burning and no clock anywhere to betray the real time. He didn't do normality. When she'd asked once, "Why them? Why the Fundamentalists, for Christ's sake?" his disdainful eyes had blinked and he'd given her one of his smiles. In between carefully crafted tokes on the joint he was nursing, he'd laughed into her face. "Because they were against smoking, and I thought it would be a good idea then to give up."

Ha ha. Just the kind of glib answer he liked to exude, easy as breathing. Joachim's face, however unwashed and underfed, remained a hearty pink, a fate he attested to his cursed Prussian breeding. Rather than washing it, he took to dressing his platinum hair with a variety of all-encompassing hats, letting it go unwashed for weeks till he ended up with things sweated into it, although underneath it remained pure gold. He had let himself go, smoked rather than ate and now that he had been kicked out of the film industry, dabbled with drugs the same way that he dabbled with his writing and caveman-like paintings. But with him, sex wasn't just a quick thing; he stretched it out so that an evening with him was like an entire weekend with anyone else.

It was like so. She'd arrive there on an ordinary night of the week. Say a Wednesday, a bit later leaving the office than she'd wanted to. It might even be after eight, but that didn't matter because they wouldn't waste time doing stuff like cooking or washing up. She'd get through the door and they would sit and smoke – joints or cigarettes, depending on how the mood took them. He might read her a bit of a script he'd done that day. And then it would start.

"Perhaps you should make yourself more comfortable?" he would say. No leer in his smile. He liked her to be naked in the flat as much as possible.

"You look better without these on," he'd say, throwing the knickers she'd left on to the side. She'd sit there wallowing in her naked consciousness and he'd look at her like he wanted to draw her, as if she was the only woman in the world. By now her skin would be tingling. She would have lost her self-consciousness, be on to her next cigarette. She'd observe how the leather sofa underneath warmed to her exposed flesh. Maybe sit with her legs slightly apart, so he could get a better look. All ever so casual, like nothing was really happening. Perhaps they'd look at the Chinese menu in between, although he always ordered the spare ribs, the only thing she'd ever seen him eat.

Under the pretence of ordering food, getting the next coffee in, he'd slowly begin to touch her. At first it would be non-sexual.

"I really like the nape of your neck," he'd say, stroking her with a warm touch. Hands always curiously soothing as if they exuded essential oils; the merest glance of a caress. She'd put her outstretched legs on his. Usually by now he'd be naked too, trying desperately not to let his penis go stiff. A former girlfriend had told him that to sport a hard-on whilst playing voyeur was plain rude. His tall, muscular body was ridiculously toned, and his penis always curled slightly to the right. He looked glorious in the buff with his tall, bulky physique. She didn't know whether to look at his sulky face or body. It was unfair, but her pussy could moisten without him knowing, although sometimes her face would burn with shame when she felt she could bear not to have him any longer.

When he kissed her, he traced the outline of her lips first. She allowed herself to be fondled and adored, and all the time a kind of energy was building that made her feel weightless. The trick was to slide slowly into her arousal until there was no turning back.

They'd be eyeing each other up, and she'd know the tremendous strain he was under to keep his erection at bay, to act normal. At times they could feel the work of each other's breathing, the slow bitty burn of the candles. Because they were both gasping for sexual contact, every little slip of skin that touched was a sensation. Even the hairs on his legs could drive her to distraction when they brushed against her skin. And with no clock, it made her feel as if she had stepped out of the rat race temporarily, that there was just this slow mounting pleasure, one endless night.

They took their time. In between they lit and rolled joints, although it was tricky being naked and not getting the crumbling ash onto their bare skin. Perhaps the dope clouded her perception of time, but their seduction ritual seemed to last for ever. At some point, the sofa would become too small for them. They would retire to the bedroom, fall onto the unmade bed.

By this time, Joachim would not be able to hide his erection. With the full length of his body he'd push her to the bed, press his cock against her so that he was non-penetrative but pushed firmly over her labia. Their bodies would knead together and all the time his cock would be pulsing on her pussy lips. In that position, genitals locked, they'd rock, grinding against each other like lesbians. It was the classic pre-sex position she had done at fifteen with guys in their jeans, except all her delicate parts were being directly exposed and the foreplay didn't stop. She felt like she was surrounded by skin, could even visualise the florid pink of his foreskin. It was not penetrative sex because Joachim felt weird about actually doing it, but it turned her on more than anything else he could have done.

They'd get hotter, louder and stickier. She'd look at his gorgeous face, kiss the sardonic lips. Her entire labia would be wet, running honey. He'd be humping her relentlessly, whispering in her ear, "Imagine a roomful of men just watching you, all of them playing with their dicks!"

She'd desperately want something inside her, a finger or a cock, anything! He'd look into her eyes. "Do you want more?" he'd say. But she'd not get it. Not there.

A few more grinds and she'd hit her first release of the evening, her clitoris fully creamed by the soft application of his cock; and usually her excitement triggered him to come promptly all over her thighs.

"Ohh, ohhh," he'd cry into her hair. And she could never tell whether it was seconds or minutes or even longer, but once in the bed they'd be after each other all night. The more he made her come without actually fucking her, the hornier she'd get.

"Help!" he'd say at some point, his skin golden with sweat. "I'm in hell because I can't stop myself from being turned on." He'd smile wickedly, turn his mouth down. "And it's just fucking exhausting. I am, as der Germans say, kaput."

They'd laugh, take a toke, although she was sure that the smell of the smoke did more for her than the actual inhalation. Even the cannabis worked differently than expected. And she didn't know if it was the drugs or the flat's gothic ambience that made everything different with him. But every night here seemed to stretch so that it was an eternity.

At some point, when the sun started falling into the sky, they'd drop into an exhausted stupor. Push each other away. She'd kid herself that if she could just get a few hours kip she'd be able to get through the coming work day which was approaching like a juggernaut. It wasn't like the perfect relationship, they both knew that, but in those few hours of gritty sleep, how beautifully she'd dream.

Freefall
by Emily Dubberley

It's Saturday night and I'm bored. This isn't an uncommon occurrence. It takes a lot to keep me entertained: I'm very much a 'live fast, die young' kind of person, I guess. Maybe that was what first attracted me to the music industry – known by everyone who works in it as The Industry, as if no other industry could possibly exist – which gives you an idea of the kind of arrogant twats I deal with every day.

I started working as a junior A&R (talent-spotter, which seemed exciting when I first landed the job and envisaged myself finding the next Beatles; now I think of it more as a shit-sifter, given the amount of hours I've spent watching clones of whoever's the latest hit churning out plagiarised pulp with excessive earnestness). Fast forward too many years to admit and I run my own label, sending junior A&Rs out to shit-sift for me. Sometimes I go to gigs, in the vain hope that I'll see a glimmer of saleable talent out there, but what sells nowadays depresses me, so I prefer to keep myself as removed from the process as possible and just count the money. Mostly, I spend my time sitting in my office, listening to the radio to see what shit's selling and flicking through photographs to see who's attractive enough to make it. It used to be that I listened to every CD but I've learned through bitter experience that if the face doesn't fit, the music won't get played so why put myself through the disappointment?

That's not to say the job doesn't come with perks. Everyone wants to be famous in this *Big-Brother*, *Heat*-magazine culture, and if you own a record label with a few hits behind it, there's never a shortage of parties to go to. Unless a weekend contains

45

sex, drugs and rock'n'roll, it feels like something's missing. Hell, unless a weekday contains sex, drugs and rock'n'roll, it feels like something's missing. Especially sex. Drugs got dull; once you've actually snorted coke off a hooker's arse there's only so much further you can go without fucking yourself up, so I only do it to stave off the boredom. Rock'n'roll just ain't what it used to be. So sex is the way that I remind myself I'm alive.

For years, I was satisfied with a quick shag with some pretty twenty-something – and that was easy enough for me to come by. Big tits, small tits, pert arses, killer legs, blondes, brunettes, redheads; whatever I wanted, it was there, and frequently more than one at a time; all fresh and dewy with the naivety of youth (even though it was generally a façade and they'd sucked three roadies' cocks to get an invitation to the after-show). Yes, there's always some hot chick desperately looking for a big break. And if she wants big, I'll give it to her.

Or at least, that was the way I used to think.

Then I met Louise.

She was a softly-spoken thirty-something – she never did tell me her exact age – who worked as an A&R. I spotted her the second I walked into an after-show party that would otherwise have faded from my memory as soon as I left it; all titian pre-Raphaelite hair, golden skin, green eyes and killer curves. Her tight jeans clung to a firm, round, high arse that just begged to be bitten. Her waist nipped in to nothing, which was hardly surprising if Dolly Parton was right and 'nothing grows in the shade'. Because, my God, those tits were to die for. Full, round and clearly natural from the way they bounced as she jigged from side to side in time to the music, I couldn't help but imagine how it would feel to slide my dick between them and watch her lick the tip while I fucked her tits. But I fought down that thought before I went over to introduce myself: no point looking over-keen, after all, and I didn't want my erection giving me away.

From the start, I knew she was different. Although she gave me every sign that she found me attractive, that was as far as it went. She made it very clear that unless I was prepared to put in some effort, I wasn't going to get anywhere. Usually, I'd just move on to an easier target, but her distance was teamed with a natural sexuality that made me think she'd be worth the chase.

And she was.

It took me six months to get her into bed. Six months. I'd got singles into the charts quicker than that! I'd tempted her back to my place with a promise of hearing the new, unreleased album from one of her favourite bands. She was still waiting on her copy from the PR – because I'd told my PR company not to send it to her. The bitch only made me play it to her, start to finish – including the bonus tracks – before giving into my charms. Every time I'd moved closer to her while it was playing, she'd just edged away and 'shushed' me.

But when the album finally finished and she deigned to let me kiss her, it was unlike any kiss I'd ever experienced before. We'd been drinking Jack Daniels and having a smoke while we listened to the music. When my tongue finally slipped between her lips, she tasted of rock'n'roll. And although it had taken me a long time to get to this point, once I'd finally made physical contact, she moved fast – and was insatiable. The kiss soon became clashing tongues, with plenty of biting and hungry grasping. She pulled one of my shirt buttons off in her rush to get me naked; and when I pushed my hand into her knickers, her clit was swollen and her slit was dripping wet. She ground up against the heel of my hand, thighs so tight around me I thought she'd break my wrist, chasing her own pleasure until I pushed her back onto the sofa and pulled my hand away, leaving her high and dry. She pulled my hand to her mouth and licked it clean, before passing me a condom and saying, "So are you going to fuck me then, or what?"

The first time I slipped my length into her sopping pussy. I fucked her hard doggy style over the sofa. Her pussy gripped me as tightly as a hand, muscles flexing my length in a sensual ripple, and she bucked back against me, mewing with pleasure. I was like 'the man', reducing her to nothing more than a lust-crazed body made for my pleasure. I plunged into her deeply, making her pay for making me wait so long. With every thrust I felt her juices spurting over my balls, her body trembling as she begged for 'more' and 'harder'. But just as I thought I finally had her, she turned her head and, smiling over her shoulder, said, 'Your cock makes me want to feel you in my arse'. The way she said it was so base, so animal, that I spunked inside her right there, right then. She immediately started grinding back against me, hand on clit, determined to get her orgasm before I stopped coming. And she did. Louise certainly knew her own body.

From there, we fell into a torrid relationship. There was no 'usual' escalation going on. Every time I thought things had got as hot as they could, she ramped things up a gear. The first time I saw her after that night – unplanned, at a gig – she was true to her word of wanting me in her arse. She wordlessly walked up to me, grabbed my hand, led me to the toilets and, with one hand on the cistern and her skirt raised, spat on her hand to lube up her tight hole.

"Get your cock out and fuck my arse," she said.

She was one horny girl.

After I'd shot inside her, she pulled up her knickers, rubbed them against her skin to trap our combined juices then slipped them off and into my hand before heading back into the venue. She didn't ask me to go home with her – didn't need to. She'd got what she wanted. I've since come into those knickers more times than I can remember.

There was no way I could ignore a woman that dirty so I called her the next day to arrange a proper date. I took her out for dinner – something I hadn't bothered doing for years – because I wanted to spend more time in her company. See, that was what was really fucking with my head: it wasn't just the sex, there was some spark about her that made me think about her in other ways too. Some joke would make me think of the way she laughed; a dress in a shop window would make me wonder what she'd look like wearing it. But I won't deny that every time I stroked my cock it was with her on my mind.

And she always had something new to bring to the party. It was after that first dinner that I first learned about BDSM. By the end of the night – or rather, 6 a.m. the following morning – she'd tied me face-down to an inflatable bondage device that she called a Cupid's Couch, spanked me, made me lick her pussy for hours and made me beg for my own release. And I'd fallen in love. She'd shown me real intimacy, looked into my eyes as she degraded me, and finally let me see her vulnerability, looking into my eyes as she used my cock to give herself an orgasm. At the point she came, there were tears in her eyes. Afterwards, she simply said, "I'm yours. And you're mine."

For some reason, I wasn't scared.

The next time we met, she cooked me dinner. And then she showed me her submissive side. Straddling her perfect body, pinning her hands down and wanking my cock over her face and tits until I shot my load over her is an image that will stay in my mind for ever. And when I released her hands, the first thing she did was move her fingers to her face, wipe up my cum and lick her fingers clean.

"Next time, you can take things further," she said. "I can take it."

So I did.

Sometimes I hate being me. It was all going so well with Louise. She was breaking through every boundary I thought I had, and a few I'd never even imagined existed. I was descending into true debauchery – my body was hers, and hers mine. But then, I was out one night and I saw Emma. Utterly different from Louise, she was a cute, innocent-looking 21-year-old. The type I'd always gone for before. I don't know whether it was the beer or my soul's attempt to save itself but I woke up the next morning with Emma in my bed. And the phone ringing. Louise. The music industry is small. I should have known better than to pull at a club. She said just two words. "It's over."

Of course, I didn't see Emma again. What was the point – she was a pretty but bland girl who barely knew how to suck cock, let alone do anything deviant. But Louise didn't care that it had been a meaningless night. I'd been hers, she'd been mine. And then I'd broken her trust.

So now, I'm stuck. There's no way that I'll ever meet a

woman who could do the things that Louise did to me. Part of me is scared to even search for it – when there are no limits, you're in freefall and you don't care about how hard you're going to crash.

And right now, it's the crash that I crave.

Blow the Candles, Baby
by Suzanne Portnoy and Simon Morgan

He was already awake when I opened my eyes, that morning of his birthday. He had his hands behind his head and was staring at the ceiling, contemplating his future. I took one look at him and could tell what he was thinking. He was in 'I'm forty and life sucks' turmoil. And he was right. He has a sucky life.

My boyfriend's the kind of guy who walks down the Finchley Road and is guaranteed to be attacked by nutters with that 'you're one of us' knowing wink. His last two books have been rejected. Pigeons the world over home in on London and the spokes of his pushbike to commit hara-kiri. A couple of months ago one flew into his back wheel right in front of al fresco diners outside a restaurant on Baker Street. That same evening we were walking out of Waitrose on his return from his shit job. Someone threw a sausage and mustard sandwich from a passing car. The sausage hit his head and the mustard dribbled down the inside of his Katherine Hamnett white linen shirt. He's one of life's natural targets. Even his much-prized Nokia 6310 decided on a 'Dear John' and propelled itself out of my car into a puddle where it was promptly run over by a John Lewis delivery truck. I'd said sometime ago, "Look on the bright side, it can't get much worse than this, right?" Wrong. His life is of tragic proportions.

"Happy birthday," I said while squeezing his crotch as some kind of conciliation. He looked at me without expression, no smile. His Spanish diesel hangover blankly said, "I want sex with lots of people tonight. I want the group thing. Organise it."

"Yeah, right, and I'm Heidi Fleiss," I said. He looked me up

51

and down and gave a derisory snort before turning his back. I remembered I had my hair in Swiss Heidi plaits.

I looked at him lying there with his back to the world. He just wanted the whole spinning thing to stop. He wanted the doors to open. He just wanted to get off.

I planted a kiss on his lips before saying, "Let me see what I can do".

Well, it's not your usual cake and candles affair, is it? But after all the shit of the past year, I felt a certain responsibility. Besides, it wouldn't be the first time we'd done this kind of thing .

I confess I hadn't planned any alternative. Actually, that's not quite true: I did get him a present – a soft brown suede jacket he'd been coveting for about six months. He'd put the deposit down for it and then, his finances being what they were, had never paid the balance. The shop owner had called earlier in the week and told him that if he didn't pay for it within the next five days, it was going back on the rails. Taking this as my cue, I paid for it myself, even though it was much more money than I intended to spend. It wasn't so much that he really wanted it as I couldn't stand seeing him wear his old suede coat any longer. Not only was the lining in shreds but it resonated with his sexual history. It said, "I'm a tramp and I know it."

I had about £50 in my wallet. Simon, as usual, had nothing in his. Even Tina at the local massage parlour charges more than that for filing her nails in front of you. I know this because I sent my boyfriend there late one evening after he shouted "Where's my blowjob?" in the kebab shop as we waited for a mixed doner special. I told him that wasn't really the kind of service I could perform in the Kebab Meister, so I suggested he walk across the road to the 'massage parlour' where I knew they did such things. He's never done the professional thing (and still hasn't) but he was through that green door, asking for a back rub. The madam asked him which girl he preferred. I was just in time to hear his perplexed response: "Well, which one prefers me?" The madam was thrown. She answered back that they both liked him (obviously) and so it was that he ended up with Tina and getting stung for £20 when his shoulder rub was unexpectedly cut short by the madam after I told her to let him know that his kebab was ready.

We later found out from some local guys who knew her that for £10 and a box of Quality Street, Tina would have done anything he wanted. Such is life. The thought did cross my mind to test out that hypothesis that night, but my boyfriend can be a little prudish at times. I knew when he said he wanted sex with lots of other people that he really meant he wanted to go out on the prowl without having to call in the professionals. Although, I've got to say, we are on the semi-pro circuit.

Racking my brains, I remembered a leaflet that I'd stuck behind a pile of free gym passes on my kitchen bulletin board. It was advertising a local 'naturist health spa' that had a Saturday Couples Night. Couples equals Swingers. There was something about the pictures showing groups of unattractive naked people 'lounging' in a Jacuzzi that seemed just the right side of might-want-to-check-this-out-sometime. I knew there was more than a 50 per cent chance it could turn out to be a complete waste of time but I was a little desperate to please my boyfriend. Thankfully, he has a sense of humour. If it was awful, at least we'd laugh about it the next day.

The place was already pretty full by the time we got there – about 200 people, all completely naked, save for towels wrapped around their waists. A little bar served free water, juice and tea, or you could bring a bottle which they'd put in the fridge for you. The barmaid wore a leopard print sarong and a pair of marigolds. £2.50 got you a toasted cheese sandwich. Nice touch, I thought. A toastie between mouthfuls, as it were.

There were Jacuzzis, steam rooms, saunas and a swimming pool. We wandered from one to another, getting hotter and hotter. You could tell by the eye-burning level of chlorine that the management were used to people fiddling with each other under all the bubbles in the Jacuzzi, but it certainly didn't seem to be the den of iniquity that we'd hoped for. Then we spotted couples being buzzed through a door which led upstairs. We asked one guy, who looked like a regular, what was going on, to which he replied in pure BBC yokel, "Ooooh! You need an open mind to go up there."

Our cue had arrived. My boyfriend grabbed my hand and led me up the stairs to the first floor. The place suddenly became quite dark, and we could see six or seven small rooms, most of them locked, although a few had been kept open just enough that you could see inside. They were not much bigger than a single bed and that's all there was in each one – just a small vinyl mattress on which you could see and hear all manner of things. This place, dear reader, was by no means the Ritz. On reflection, knocking on a door and saying 'room service' might have led to something interesting, but it all seemed very serious; no one was in the process of buying a pair of joke maracas, which I'd always thought was part of the joy of fucking, but there you go.

Next floor up there must have been about ten or fifteen couples writhing round in one big room. None of them were what I'd call beautiful but a few were attractive enough for a night's entertainment. That's the thing about swinging – it's great for the men who are just so grateful for all the attention and just about bearable for the women if they really, really concentrate on their fantasies. Any half-sensible woman would be wishing herself away from there. Some women were nearly three times my size. In fact I felt positively stunning and slim.

What the hell. We found a little space on a cheap sofa and surveyed the scene. It was time for an icebreaker.

"It's my birthday and I want presents!" my boyfriend shouted. The whole room erupted into laughter. That night we made a lot of new friends and my boyfriend's wish came true. He was actually very sweet and romantic. Some girl with the most fantastic tits I've ever seen challengingly asked him if he'd ever had his cock sucked by a Spanish girl before.

"No" he lied, "but it could never be better than from a New York Jew".

That's me, by the way.

New Blood
by Wersha Bharadwa

I'm thoroughly shattered as I step off the company's private jet. It feels like I haven't slept properly in years. Well, actually, I haven't. Not since 1999 anyway. Working as a lifestyle manager for the world's super rich does that to you.

Night in, night out, I busy myself with the orgy of excess billionaires require. Private doctors on demand as soon as they jet in from the Gulf, celebrity stylists for dinners with the in-laws, and Justin Timberlake et al for kids' birthdays. Not that the hours bother me. I'm not one to get up before dusk.

Last night it was a fashion show by Hussein Chalayan on board a client's £10m yacht in Ibiza. They never attend fashion week – ever – preferring to keep their elite club of squillionaires as private as can be. When you have £200m, mixing with normal people becomes a bit of a communication problem, you see.

Tonight I'm meeting with a new client: Ivan Cruz. Ivan's profile sounds distinctly oligarch-ish. Except he's not. He's from Romania – specifically a skewered little forest on the outskirts, which my boss, Ollie, has described exactly as such in his email but failed to lend a name to.

The rest of Ollie's email is filled with important client asset details. Ivan Cruz of Al Daurc Enterprises is a property baron, owns a La Liga football club, a smattering of global internet companies, a villa in Monaco, six polo ponies and a recently acquired exclusive SW3 postcode. One of those nouveau pads with a 2000 square foot underground basement extension boasting 10 bedrooms, a three storey garage for his vintage Aston Martins, a private cinema, a swimming pool, gym and subterranean tennis court to boot.

Ivan needs help getting his needs met. Normally I'd book myself in for a pedicure and manicure at the Mandarin Oriental in Knightsbridge to keep my talons in check (they grow at an absurd rate) on top of an essential spray tan session before a meeting of this nature. In my line of work a ghastly paleness puts people right off you. However, there isn't time tonight. I've only 40 minutes to drive down to Ivan's house before our 10 p.m. dinner booking at Le Gavroche.

My cab pulls up at a grand whitewashed house, but from experience I know it's a case of more than meets the eye. This part of my job excites me the most; seeing how my clients live. Ivan's only been living on this street a month and already has security systems and CCTV cameras to rival Fort Knox. Protection against kidnapping, I think to myself.

There's a clink at the door as it opens and I'm met by a man unlike any other I've ever seen. He's nothing remotely like a housekeeper, which startles me because, I promise you, these people seriously get off on having servants.

"Hi Alexandra. Nice to meet you," he says in a guttural drawl. "I'm Ivan." He has gone completely against protocol by greeting me himself.

"Erm, hi Ivan, it's great to meet you … It's great … I'm glad … uh … so good to have you on board," I say, my lips trembling. Hell knows why, but I've been reduced to a quivering, mumbling fool.

There's something … wicked about him. Not cheeky, wicked. Wicked, other worldly, wicked. He would've reminded me deceptively of one of those models from a black-and-white 80s Athena poster if it wasn't for his silver, foppish and foxy – no – wolfish, hair. Or the abnormally youthful face he has for a 50-year-old. There's not even a hint of experience on it. No laughter lines around his mouth from high times in Monaco or St Tropez and no eye crinkles from catering to the whims of high-maintenance supermodel girlfriends.

His face tells no story at all – other than never having been lived in – but, fuck me, it's gorgeous. He's gorgeous. Far too gorgeous for his own good.

Perhaps it's his misplaced accent. I love them. The drawn out Eastern European vowels have been Americanised, leaving me childishly hypnotised. He stands tall and defiant in his black suit and I wonder if he leaves every woman he meets as flushed as I am.

As I step into a hallway big enough to rival Claridge's, I'm greeted with insanely close-to-the-lips kisses on either cheek and cold elongated hands taking no time at all in clasping around mine. I pull away a little too quickly and defensively for a perceived professional embrace. This embarrasses me. He tucks his hair behind his ears and I lower my gaze, not wanting my eyes to let slip the crazy desire shooting through my veins.

In an attempt to regain composure, I clamp my sticky, glossed mouth together tightly and smile clumsily while nodding my head up and down like a woodpecker on ADHD medication.

"You look nervous," Ivan says, cracking an authoritative smile. He's obviously witnessed women crumble into tongue-tied heaps before.

Attempting to set myself apart from the swooning brigade, I defiantly brave eye contact again and pull out my notebook, ready to jot down all of his demands.

"So, how are we going to get you started?" I say, my hands trembling ever so slightly.

I wait for him to tell me he needs staff, or that he has staff lined up but they're still undergoing police background checks, or that he wants Gordon Ramsay to cater for his next birthday, or a private helicopter trip to the south of France or even a personal training session with an Olympic gymnast. Instead he lets out a huge sigh.

"Oh, I don't know." He shrugs. "I've never had a lifestyle concierge before and I'm not entirely clear why I've succumbed to having one now. I guess it's a good way to gain bedroom favour with someone as delicious as yourself, though, isn't it?"

Alarmed by his forwardness, I recoil from my polite

eagerness in shock. Inappropriate flirting is *de rigueur* with super wealthy males, but not at least until they've waited to get drunk or are four weeks into business with me. Even then, they have the decency to wait at least 10 minutes after I'm through the door. Just because Ivan happens to make my breathing patchy doesn't mean I'm going to let him gain any sort of favours with me. Especially the bedroom type.

Although, he does seem the sort who could give you something to sink your teeth into underneath the covers ... Oh would you look at me? I need to stop this train of thought NOW, I tell myself. As I refuse to acknowledge his blatant presumption, our eyes lock. The air is full of tension and there are fireworks going off in my La Perla panties. Like my insides are whooping with delight for a better acquaintance with Mr Cruz. But I never use my talents on clients. It's a thankless task. Ending with a P45.

There's another white-hot, seriously pleasant pang in my groin and I get fidgety and nervous. Especially because of the way Ivan is now looking at me. I don't like it. His charcoal black eyes have developed a sudden smouldering and alternating fixation with my face, décolletage – and then neck, specifically. He's giving me what I can only describe as a predatory stare. Horrible and dangerous, it's like he's trying to fool my silly biology into thinking I'm irresistible and he can't control his animal instincts so I might as well fall flat on my back, beg him to rip my clothes off with his teeth and impregnate me. Yuck. Looks like I've got another alpha male on my hands. One who's loaded and probably likes tying women up and beating them to a pulp too. Sadistic bastard.

"I hope you don't mind, but I've cancelled the restaurant tonight and have had my friends Jean and Caroline Sandrou deliver dinner round for us," Ivan pipes up, finally.

I have vivid images of being hacked up in his beyond lavish bachelor mansion with a chainsaw, *American Psycho*-style, before the name Sandrou brings my over-enthusiastic imagination back to earth. The Sandrous are Michelin chefs who charge roughly £500 a head for privately catered dinners.

He may not be a freakishly handsome but repugnant

psychopath after all.

"Come on through to the basement."

So maybe he is. Oh crap, I hate the way jetlag screws with your system. Besides, before I've had a chance to engage my brain to my mouth, I've let out a, "Sure, okay," and am following him down a terribly high, all-marble hallway anyway.

As we take the lift down to the dungeon these SW3 folk call underground dining rooms, I'm distracted from my psychoanalysing of Ivan's stare by the sight of a small bead of sweat running down his temple. Annoyingly, I tingle at the thought of licking it off him while wondering what he tastes like. He certainly smells divine. Like something you'd want to gobble up without even savouring for a second. This unnerves me big time. I've never smelt a man who's made me want to do that. Hermes, Guerlain, maybe? No, this scent is different. One which makes you feel out of your depth as soon as you inhale.

After mistakenly heading into a bathroom, a cigar and champagne lounge (yes, really) and a karaoke room (Ivan: "I'm still trying not to get lost around here …"), he seats himself at the table in a state-of-the-art, decadent dining room with Trompe L'oeil covered walls and pats the seat next to him while motioning me in.

"Come. Sit. I won't bite," Ivan says simply as he uncovers a plate of foie gras.

I shouldn't be climbing into the cast iron chair, but as he pops open a bottle of vintage Krug, I know my options are now thoroughly limited. He's staring at me wildly and I try to dampen his attentions by turning to the food.

"I'm really hungry," I say, peeking at his plate from behind a black calla lily arrangement.

"I'm hungry for you," he says devilishly, letting out an equally sexy grin.

Damn! Would you look at those teeth? There's a chiselled jawline and a cracked dimpled-smile framing a set of absurdly glossy white canines. I'd love to know who his dentist is. I've always hated my teeth for sharing a cross Chihuahua likeness to those Celine Dion sported before she got the full Hollywood blitzing.

"Do I make you uncomfortable, Alexandra?" Ivan asks.

"No ... No, not at all," I let out a disconcerted giggle.

Ivan's face darkens. "It's just your heart. It beats very fast," he says.

I'm quick to respond with: "I'm unfit, I haven't been to the gym in two days." Ivan finds it relatively easy to disarm me – something most men do not.

He tells me he's sorry but there's no garlic in the food as he's allergic. This proves to be our first good bonding point as I too reveal a heavy allergy to garlic. In an urgent bid to expand on this first slice of natural, 'normal people' conversation, I go on to explain how a teeny tiny sliver of it in my food makes me ill and any more than that could kill me by way of anaphylactic shock. He lets out a grunt. It's what, I assume, his kind call sympathy.

"You're not much of a talker are you, Ivan?" I say.

"What's there really to talk about? I'm just not the kind of pain in the neck who wants to bombard you with unnecessary bullshit to make up time before I sleep with you."

Huh? I push aside my champagne flute in outrage. And disgust. I mean, what's this arsehole's game? He's an old man. Probably with saggy balls and whites in his pubes. Stunned at Ivan's lewdness and atrocious manners, I swipe my handbag off the floor and get up to leave.

"I'm sorry, but I'm not paid to do this." I gesture wildly with flailing arms. "I've come here on business and you're clearly not interested ... so ... so, I'm going to have to leave. Speak to Ollie about a replacement for me. Sorry."

Apart from wanting to hit myself for apologising for his behaviour, I want to spontaneously combust with anger as I ambush the lift and hurry myself out of his house. I spend a few wasteful minutes looking for the exit button to release me from his front door and the inside of the security gates.

Tomorrow I will take him off our company books. I refuse to work with good-looking but perverted Romanian monsters who assume their money turns every woman into a prostitute.

I've worked way too hard to let a sleaze bag like him try and ruin my reputation by sleeping with him. I mean, couldn't he have just delayed being a tosser for a *week*?

There are three missed calls on my phone. All Ivan. I haven't calmed down an inch in the past hour.

I have eight missed calls and no voicemail messages. Again Ivan. It's 12 a.m. for fuck's sake.

The more I blank him, the more he calls. I wonder if he's as gruff-sounding on an answer machine? There is no way of hiding the strange sensation tormenting my body as I remember his voice. I lie on my sofa, body rigid, while my phone sits on my palm, and there's a heat coming off me that's almost liquefying. It's completely beyond me why someone I think is such a prick has begun to fill every one of my thoughts with his smell, his body, his flesh.

Too powerless to resist, I find myself insanely driving up to his house again. Ollie won't find out. Ivan will open the door to me and smile. He'll think he's won. And he'll think I'm easy. Who cares. I'm in for the mother of all shags.

There is no small talk when Ivan pulls me inside and slams his front door shut. It takes less than a nano-second before he's toying with the straps of my Herve Leger dress and steering me – quite forcefully – into the lift again. I take his hand and squeeze it tightly. It's a sure-fired signal for him to shag my brains out.

I feel a frisson of fright as he grazes his stubble into my shoulders and along my collar bone while his bottom lip drags along my skin. The rough of his beard and smooth wetness of his lips cause an aching chill to ripple across my back.

Instead of taking me on another accidental tour of basement floor one, the lift stops at minus level three. As the door slides open, Ivan leads me straight into the room opposite. It's his bedroom. It is opulent beyond my wildest dreams, with no mirrors and crisp white bedding layered over what looks like a sumptuous casket. While there are a dozen or so large Diptique candles burning on the floor, the room has an overbearing, earthy smell, betraying the fact that the candles are trying to mask it. It reminds me of foreign, wet soil.

I don't even have to entertain the idea of taking off my own clothes as Ivan is stripping me bare. We are standing at the edge of the bed and he is still fully clothed but I can make out the distinct outline of an erection pressing against his dark grey trousers. *Not an outline, more of a skyline,* I think to myself.

I am now completely naked.

Ivan leans over to the beside table where there is a single shot glass and an ice cold bottle of vodka. Good. This is all getting a tad intense. I watch him as he pours himself a careful measure. Oh, it's for me. He teases me by bringing the freezing cold glass up to my open mouth, but stops short of guiding me to sip.

I want him to drop to his knees and beg me to make love to him, but instead, dipping his index finger into the vodka, I feel Ivan rub the cool liquid across my moistened lips. I open my mouth against my better judgement and slowly suck his fingers as he rolls small wet circles around my softly swirling tongue. It's like that scene in *Cape Fear* where Juliette Lewis flirts with a murderer by sucking his fingers. Following her nymphet lead, I abandon myself to the sensation and it feels better than anything Hollywood could conjure up.

For the first time, Ivan leans in and kisses me succulently on the lips. I am intoxicated both by the sharp aftertaste of alcohol and the generosity of his full, meaty mouth. I gasp for air, pushing him off me, then reeling him back with my next breath.

I rub his ears a little and dig the tips of my forefingers into his temples. He likes that. There is an appreciative groan, a noise which sinks deep into my ear lobe and vibrates against my neck as he plants hundreds of gentle butterfly kisses along my collarbone. I like the way his hair tickles my chin a little and am thankful for his age and for how much of a neck man he is proving to be. I tell you, they really don't make them like they used to.

Ivan slowly licks my skin and he twirls me around. As he stands behind me, his nails dig into my curves urgently. I am filled with a bravado I've never seen in myself before and I push my hips back against his groin. He nibbles and gnaws and bites my nape so I hard I am startled to think he might pierce my skin.

He is so worked up I expect him to toss me on the bed any minute now but he doesn't. He takes his hands off me and for a second I feel like I'm alone in the room. Taken aback by his sudden withdrawal, I groan loudly. Where has he gone? Goddammit! I wanted him and I wanted him now. I turn around and instictively put my mouth to his neck. He has gone nowhere. My lips inhale his scent and my teeth tug at the buttons of his shirt before I slip my hand inside and feel a coarseness of chest hair. I run my tongue dramatically up to his earlobe. It's a wanton act of submissiveness; I want this powerful and stinking rich man to feel very much like he is in control.

And then I bite.

Deep, long and hard.

Deep into his neck and right into my favourite vein. And I suck. His blood tastes exquisite, like a juice I have never sampled on any of my many encounters.

I suck again.

And bite.

And suck some more.

He stops moaning – or is he laughing? Pleasure and pain do funny things to the body – and the room falls silent. I look down at his blurry but almost still body and for the first time in weeks am deliriously relaxed. I can't stop my eyes from closing.

I feel like I've had the best sex of my life and yet I can't remember any of it. My mind is deliciously … numb. Did we actually fuck? Surely I'd know. And I certainly don't feel satisfied. My hunger is back again but with a vengeance. Wait! Did the creep slip me Rohypnol? I pinch my legs to check for feeling.

I should be glowing with the injection of new fresh blood coursing through me, but my hands are still positively ashy. I feel sick. Did I not bite hard enough? I've been in the undead game for so long, could I have become sloppy?

I look down at the bed, expecting Ivan's handsome, perfectly preserved but bloodless corpse to be draped across the crisp white Egyptian cotton sheets, but he's not there.

He's not there.

And nor was his bed perfectly made up when I left it few minutes ago. On the bedside table there is a business card and a new bottle of vodka has replaced the old. The vodka has a tag with a handwritten message attached with ribbon to it. Frightened for my life for the first time since I stopped dining on rice crackers and instead on warm human arteries, I pick up the business card and the bottle and read the tag:

"You're really one of a kind. I'm throwing a bash at my Transylvanian castle in four weeks. Be sure to come and let me return last night's favour properly. D x"

Suddenly the air turns still behind me and I can feel his presence.

I raise my hand to my neck and feel the sting of two perfect and clean fang marks there.

I look down at the business card in my hand again.

Ivan Cruz, Managing Director, Al Daurc

A L D A U R C.

D R A CU L A.

Fuck. Shit. Fuck. Shit.

I've been fucked and bitten by Dracula.

But as soon as I realise what's happened, the blood that courses through my veins makes me feel more alive than I have done in years.

Roses
by Miranda Forbes

You arrive with roses. Deep red, long-stemmed roses, bound with a wide satin ribbon. Your eyes are dark, glinting, hard. "Kiss them," you say, "kiss each one."

I take the bunch, cup the first bloom in my fingers and take in the deep, musky perfume. The petals are velvety soft on my lips. I close my eyes, enjoying the fragrance, feeling my nipples harden, the folds of my cunt starting to swell.

"Take the roses upstairs. Strip, stand with your hands on your head. Wait for me."

I'm shivering as I wait but suspect it's more to do with anticipation than cold. I hear your tread on the stairs and feel a kick of wanting in my belly.

You're clutching a bottle of champagne and two glasses. You press the chilled bottle against my nipples. They are tight, hurting with the need to be teased.

"Please, please," I whisper, knowing you understand everything my body craves. You rub the hard, cold glass against my nipples and suck them into your mouth. I feel your sharp teeth hurting, loving and biting me.

You untie the ribbon from the roses and loop it behind my neck, pulling me close. Our eyes connect and you ask me if I want to be loved with the roses.

"Yes," I say, wanting them, wanting you, wanting release. You take the ends of the ribbon and circle my breasts, binding them tightly. They stand out, round and swollen, my nipples aching to be touched again.

Slowly you start to sweep the flowers across my breasts. The velvety petals are cool against my skin, the fragrance heavy, warm and musky. You build the rhythm and it becomes hard to stand there, my arms aching, my whole body wanting.

"Slut," you whisper as you feel between my legs and your fingers come back wet and glistening.

I watch as you rub the wetness into my nipples and think, "Yes, I'm a slut; your slut." My weak knees are grateful when you instruct me to lie on the bed.

I open my legs wide as you tell me and put my hands behind my head. My whole body is open, vulnerable, exposed and I shiver slightly as I wonder what you have planned. You trace patterns with the roses, caressing my body with wide, stroking, fragrant sweeps. Then the tempo picks up and I feel you start to slap them harder against my skin. Each breast gets twelve strokes before you tell me to spread my cunt lips. You swipe the roses up and down my exposed cunt and I smell my own hot muskiness mixing with that of the roses.

The blooms have shed some petals when you tell me to turn over. My bound breasts ache as they are pushed against the bed and I lie there wondering what is coming next.

Twelve, you say, twelve lashes for each rose. At first they feel quite gentle and I count out each stroke easily, but as the petals fall from the flowers the strikes get harder against my flesh. You work your way up and down my back, my buttocks and the backs of my thighs. Small thorns from the stems start to prick and pull at my skin. They bite and rip into my hot flesh. I feel I'm floating in a sea of petals, perfume and pain. The final strokes take me to the very edge of my endurance; I ride the waves to somewhere new.

And then I hear your voice next to my ear telling me how beautiful I look right now, and I turn and see the bed has become a sea of red rose petals. You lie beside me holding me close until my breathing has calmed and you gently unbind my breasts. You take each in your hands, rolling them, kneading them, and pulling on my nipples until I feel on the very edge of coming.

Carefully you wrap each nipple with a petal before attaching chained nipple clamps. You gather a couple of petals and place these on my eyelids, using the ribbon to secure them and blindfold me. I'm floating on waves in my dark perfumed seas as you spread my legs and I feel your breath on my thighs. The heady smell of the roses is heightened in my darkness and I feel I'm lost in an extraordinary erotic garden. Your tongue laps at my clit and I shiver with pleasure. I feel your finger exploring and entering my vagina and then you work to widen the entrance. Soft petals dance over my clit and then you push them inside me. Every touch is taking me closer to the release I crave.

"Please fuck me," I say. "Fuck me, let me come."

You turn me over onto all fours and plunge your cock deep into my petal-filled cunt. You take me very hard, making my clamped tits tug and pull against the chain as they bounce wildly with each thrust. I come almost immediately and feel your cock swelling and filling me, creating a delicious perfume of petals, cunt and come.

"Champagne?" you whisper in my ear.

I think about how you're going to use *that* and smile as I nod my acquiescence.

The Decline of Conversation
by MonMouth

It was a chilly morning, the commuters pausing after coming out of the ticket barriers, feeling the cold pour in off the street. The rush hour was almost over, and there was still heavy traffic at the coffee shop. I phoned Fifi while I stood in the queue.

"Just black coffee, please. No milk," she said, and I could hear her smiling over the phone. For myself, I bought something complicated with espresso and frothy milk to balance out the cosmic forces of minimalism and baroque swirling around the takeaway containers.

After parting with my money I joined the cluster of anxious caffeine addicts at the end of the counter. We stood around, waiting for our orders. The cafe was small and a tall man with a bulky laptop bag kept getting pushed closer to me. Our bags rubbed together, and I couldn't help thinking about how different their contents were this morning.

Fifi's flat was just off the high street, a few houses down from the coffee shop. Knocking on her door I found her standing just inside, a pile of mail in her hand.

"Mmm, hot coffee. And man. Delivered."

She shut the door by pushing me against it with a wet kiss. A bit of coffee spilled on top of the mail in her hand.

Upstairs, we took the coffee straight to the bedroom. Fifi, with a flourish of her arm, pointed out that she was an exceptionally considerate person, having just cleared the pile of paperbacks off the top of her nightstand, leaving room for the coffee cups. In the middle of the bed, like a present from the pervert elves, sat a big black file box marked with a white sticker and fat marker pen: Receipts.

"Doing the accounts this morning?" I joked when I spotted the label.

Fifi sat down on the bed, drumming the lid with her fingernails, smirking. "In a manner of speaking …" She reached inside and pulled out a small dildo and rested it mischievously against her lips. This was her toy box.

"So what's this toy you brought, then?" Fifi sipped her coffee, holding the dildo with the same hand like an obscene teaspoon.

I put my cup down. "Close your eyes and stick your hand out."

She waited obligingly while I rummaged in my bag. I pulled out the heavy steel buttplug, pausing for a moment to admire the heft of the thick, tapered head, and the elegance of the narrow tail, flaring out into a circle, designed for ease of grasping.

I dropped it into her outstretched palm, and she smiled at the pleasant shock of the cool mass of metal.

"Open your eyes."

Blinking, she weighed it in her palm. "It's beautiful."

I smiled to myself, thinking about the commuters, the coffee shop, and the pleasure of carrying a sex toy and not a laptop to a 9 a.m. appointment on a Wednesday.

We had our coffee lounging on the bed, up against a pile of pillows, chatting and removing our clothes one item at a time, very slowly. By the time we were down to underwear, the box had been displaced on to the floor and Fifi was lying on her back, legs spread, while I felt my way up the insides of her thighs, teasing the smooth curves of olive skin. Her dark hair spilled out over the cream-coloured pillows as she burrowed deeper into the softness with a smiling "mmhmmm" of encouragement.

Fifi doesn't talk much after she takes her clothes off. She doesn't bother stringing sentences together, relying on individual words or phrases to convey her urges. I peeled the lacy black knickers off her, and enjoyed the revelation of the pink of her labia peering out from in between the dark brown of her pubic hair, which is strangely straight and soft in contrast to the thick curls on her head.

Immediately when I touched her pussy with the tip of my tongue, Fifi took my head in her hands, pulled me up and with a great urgency said, "Uh-uh, fuck …" It was like a sudden realisation that the thing she wanted most in the world had to happen right away and could only be described by grunts and one-word requests.

I grabbed a condom and as soon as I had it on, she pushed me on my back and sank herself down on top of me with a great sigh from down below.

"Yes … mmm …" She fucked me with a focused need, "Cock … mmm … fuck."

She likes to come with a string of orgasms, one building right after the next. The first was a soft convulsion, her curls cascading around my face, my left hand cupping the large, brown aureole of her breast, pinching.

Short pause, then she started riding me again. Harder.

After a while I could feel the wetness between us, her pussy, our sweat, mingling on her thighs grinding together. Fifi lifted herself off me, the freshness of the cool air feeling good after the heat of our bodies.

"Behind … oh … mmmmfuck …" she purred, getting on her knees and wiggling the roundness of her bum in the air. Entering her from behind, I moved slowly, trying to tease her.

My own orgasm was building and I didn't want to come just yet. With one wet finger I began to caress the spread pucker of her ass in deliberate, meaningful circles.

Pushing back harder, urging me on, she opened up to the attentions of my finger, enjoying a small shivering orgasm while I fucked her slowly, my finger just pushing gently against the slick, round opening.

"Uh … dildo … mmm, fuck, yeah …"

Fifi pulled away and lunged for the toy box, pulling out a small, flexible vibrator and a lube dispenser. She put her hands around my neck and kissed me, still holding these things. Then, cocking her head in a faux coy manner she held up the vibe and smiled prettily, like she was inviting me to take a large bite out of a garishly yellow piece of candy.

"What? What do you want me to do with this?"

"Um, my arse?"

"You want me to put this in your ass?" I made a point of our different pronunciation.

"Mmhmm," she nodded, eyes wide, and got back on all fours, wiggling her bum at me in a most appealing manner.

I lubed the vibrator thoroughly, enjoying the view of her open like that, the glistening pink of her pussy waiting for my cock to return.

"Oh fuck … mmmm." Fifi was impatient. My cock slid easily into the wet tightness of her cunt. I began to fuck her slowly. Then, when she seemed to start getting a little frustrated, I twisted the knob on the vibe to the lowest setting and placed it against the pouting circle of her ass.

Pushing the toy in slowly, carefully, I enjoyed the vibrating sensation travelling down to the base of my cock. Fifi was quiet, concentrating on the spreading, tightening, pressing sensation filling her with throbbing, vibrating pleasure.

The soft vibe was bendy enough to fit up her bum without getting in my way while I fucked her. Once it was in as far as it went, the fat base resting against the stretched rim, I dialled up the intensity of the buzz. Fifi moaned deeply, burying her face in the cushions and pressing back against me, taking my cock in as far as possible. Her orgasm was building, and I couldn't hold back much longer with the twitching tightness of her cunt clutching my cock and the vibrations tickling me all along the top.

It was too intense to last.

Suddenly Fifi reached back with her hand and grasped the base of the vibrator. Firmly, rhythmically she began to fuck herself with it, in time with the thrusting of my hips.

"Harder … fuckfuck …" she growled, letting go of the buzzing toy to allow me to pound into her with the full force of my weight. Her orgasm seemed to last and last, rolling on with moans and whimpers, gripping my cock with an irresistible invitation to let go. Somehow I didn't want to come, wanting to hang on to the sensation for a little while longer.

I failed. Afterwards, I withdrew very slowly, removing both

my cock and the buzzing toy carefully.

A little while later, when recovering, Fifi sighed. "When you're turned on, it's incredible how difficult it is to just say the simplest things, don't you think?"

"Mmmm, uh, fuck, yeah …"

The Gilded Fountain
by Jeremy Edwards

A few days after Stephen and Jocelyn officially became engaged, Jocelyn revealed that she had a weekend treat in mind.

"I belong to a private club," she said casually, "and I'd love to bring you as my guest on Saturday."

"That sounds delightful," said Stephen.

"I think you'll like it there. I hope so, anyway."

Jocelyn's club was housed in an impressive eighteenth-century building in a quiet street. The moon came out from behind the clouds just as the couple arrived, and its glow gave the staid facade an exciting aura of promise.

They were elegantly attired. "There's no specific dress code," Jocelyn had explained. "Most people just find something dramatic or glamorous to wear – you'll see why. Everyone looks so interesting."

This was one of several hints Stephen had been given that there was more to this evening out at the club than met the eye. He was intrigued: what exotic world would his ever-fascinating Jocelyn be showing him here? She was hip to so many marvellous and unusual things. He'd resisted the impulse to ask a lot of questions, as he sensed that surprise was part of what Jocelyn intended him to experience. And he wanted to experience everything she had in store for him.

She was wearing a glittery, copper-coloured blouse that brought out the humour in her eyes and interacted felicitously with her tiny gold earrings. A short but classy black skirt, stockings and basic black heels completed her ensemble. Stephen was wearing his tux, at his fiancée's request. "You're so delicious in it," she'd opined. "It makes me want to do special things to you." After that provocative comment, he had required no further persuasion.

The building's interior had obviously been redone in the twentieth century. The foyer blended elements of Art Deco, postwar Italian design, Renaissance sculpture and contemporary-nightclub neon in a way that defied overall categorisation but nevertheless worked. The effect was that of highly aesthetic, cultured decadence.

"Very nice," said Stephen sincerely. Jocelyn beamed and took his hand.

The first thing Stephen saw, as they exited the foyer through an archway, was a strikingly attractive woman in a sleeveless silk top and a jewelled necklace. Stephen was surprised to note that she was naked from the waist down – and even further surprised to note that she was engaged in pissing voluminously, from a standing position, into an ornate marble basin. Woman and basin were both situated atop a pedestal.

"Oh! We seem to have wandered into the ladies' room," he spluttered to Jocelyn, groping for the best explanation he could find.

"Welcome, darling," Jocelyn responded with a smile. "This place is all ladies' room."

"What?" As perplexed as he was, he didn't take his eyes off the unanticipated spectacle before him. The woman and her stream were captivating, together comprising a dazzling, kinetic display of feminine beauty.

"This is my club's *raison d'être*, Stephen." Jocelyn was whispering now, as if to avoid intruding on the public privacy of the woman – though she, too, was staring at the performance. "It's a place for women like me to indulge a taste for erotic, exhibitionistic peeing." She took a deep breath. "Are you shocked?"

Frozen in place, Stephen had to think about this. "Not in a bad way," he replied at last. The phrase 'women like me' was reverberating in his mind.

He noticed that the pissing beauty's fingers were very active: she was not only manipulating her lips so as to guide and shape her stream; she was also masturbating. Just as Stephen made this observation, the woman shrieked. She threw her head back, eyes closed and pussy still flowing. She was having an orgasm.

"What did you say the club was called?"

"The Gilded Fountain."

Stephen finally tore his gaze from the orgasmic pisser so he could proceed further into the club with Jocelyn.

In a corner up ahead to their right, where two complementary floral wall hangings met, a pair of nude, curvaceous women with Botticellian blonde hair were titillating each other everywhere with peacock feathers – and peeing heartily. And to the left stood a glamorous, rock'n'roll-style woman in a red vinyl miniskirt, who was surrounded by a group of male and female admirers and who clearly needed to spring a leak soon. She was rocking in place with her legs crossed, and pressing herself through the front of her skirt in a completely uninhibited manner. Far from looking unhappy while she held back her water, her lipstick-vivid face instead showed intense enjoyment and her dark eyes sparkled lewdly at her fans. Stephen could see her erect nipples straining the thin cotton of her black T-shirt.

Focusing on this woman's face, Stephen remembered seeing a similar expression on Jocelyn's on one occasion, when the two of them were walking briskly home from the park because she needed the loo. Jocelyn had been on the brink of wetting her knickers, but she'd seemed to relish every minute of it – as if the cajoling tickle of holding it were foreplay for the orgasm of release.

Recalling that incident, he better understood why they were here. This organisation was a magnet for erotically sophisticated women who found refined sexual delight in the rarefied sensations of holding, then dramatically releasing, their pee, in a variety of imaginative and visually astounding scenarios. Within these walls, their fetish could flower into a wonderfully bizarre genre of decadent performance art.

Nor, in this context, was piss-holding a source of distress, or public peeing a misadventure. No, these women were totally, cheerfully in control of their own kinky indulgences, expressing their femininity through their pee games, engineering themselves into squirming excitement and free-flowing ecstasies.

And Jocelyn was one of them.

The appearance of a team of three efficient employees – dressed as Victorian chimney sweeps, but with mops, buckets, towels, hoses, and spray bottles instead of brooms – answered Stephen's next question before he had a chance to voice it. Where the peacock-feather ladies had just finished frolicking, the crew got to work, and soon the entire area was pristine and florally fragrant.

"They have everything arranged here to a T," commented Jocelyn. "That's why the cover charge is so high."

Stephen continued to take it all in.

"Ooh, look," said Jocelyn, pointing at a man whose lingerie-clad girlfriend had backed him against the wall, where she passionately embraced him, grinding her pelvis into him while peeing her panties. "Nice kiss-and-piss there."

There was evidently some lingo to be learned, Stephen reflected, as he studied the woman's pleasure-enlivened ass.

"Let's have a drink, shall we?" Jocelyn suggested.

As they moved towards the bar, Stephen caught the rock'n'roll girl in his peripheral vision, wetting the floor with her knees bent as her laughter echoed off the ceiling. Right before he and Jocelyn rounded a corner, the rockin' wetter turned her face his way and winked.

It was difficult for him to concentrate on the drinks menu, for several reasons. First, behind the bar flowed a large artificial brook, the centerpiece of an expansive 'outdoors'-themed adult playground. Various women, in various postures, were positioned along its banks, astride boulders projecting from the water, and even on a bridge. Some lifted their fashionable skirts to empty themselves; some had tailored slacks and silk panties halfway down their legs and derriere cheeks proudly exposed, so they could piss ambitious, male-style arcs into the water; and some simply dampened their designer bathing suits as they danced in ecstasy on the shore.

Nearby, women in crisp linen shorts played table tennis and croquet, all challenging themselves to make shot after shot while nursing their full bladders, each jiggling evocatively in place during her idle moments.

Nor did the bar's seating area represent a break in the entertainment. Almost every stool was occupied by a leg-crossing, crotch-clutching woman with a drink – all of them glowing with mischief as their bottoms wiggled and their feet twitched.

Immediately to Jocelyn's right, a redhead with a lager in hand was busily puddling her bar stool, her hips pumping in a high-quality business skirt, her tights glistening where trickles ran down them. She looked Jocelyn's way and grinned at her.

Stephen had never been so aroused in his life – and it was a revelation to him. If someone had asked him, the day before, if he appreciated the sight of a woman pissing, his response would have been a low-key assent like, "Sure, I guess." And if he'd been asked whether it was titillating to him to contemplate a woman feeling the need to pee, he would have said something along the lines of, "Yes, I suppose, as long as she's not uncomfortable." But no one had ever asked him these questions, and he'd never given these matters much thought: never given much thought to sensuous women who had to pee and deliberately hovered on the edge awhile … or horny women who intentionally wet their knickers … or remarkable women who had powerful climaxes from pissing in front of others. And now he'd been given all of this on a silver – no, a golden – platter, and he was incredibly turned on.

Jocelyn was glancing at his lap and smirking. "Sexy, isn't it?" she asked.

"Oh, God." He swallowed, and it took him a moment to say more. "You know, I couldn't have imagined London held so many women with these particular appetites."

"A few of them come in from the suburbs," Jocelyn allowed.

While Stephen had been absorbing the scene around him, she had ordered for them – Scotch for him, and a pint for her.

"Cheers," she said.

"Yes, cheers!" said Stephen, thinking of the effect an evening of beer drinking always had on her metabolism.

"Would you like to see more of the club?"

He indicated that he would indeed, and so they grabbed their drinks and left the bar.

The next room used a shifting landscape of fluorescent lighting and a soundtrack of chill-out music to create an otherworldly mood. And here the carnival of erogenous pissing continued, now familiar in its theme but ever stimulating in its variations. A kneeling man in 1960s paisley and beads held his lover's vintage minidress up at the rear, kissing her all over her bare bottom while she peed straight into the panties at her knees. Not far from them, a muscular woman squatted over mirrored floor tiles, gyrating her hips and fondling her own breasts through her lace teddy. As Stephen and Jocelyn walked by her, she reached between her legs, cleaving the split crotch of her matching panties, then cleaving her own fleshy lips. She poured like a spigot, managing all the while to churn her pelvis athletically in time to the music.

Jocelyn spoke wetly into Stephen's ear. "I have to go, too," she said. Her pint glass was nearly empty.

Stephen smiled. "I believe you've come to the right place."

She squeezed his hand. "I'm not going to do it yet. I'm going to wait, until the release will blow my mind. But I wanted you to know. I want you to be thinking about it. I want you to be watching me as the need becomes more pressing, waiting for me to do something about it – and wondering, with a club full of opportunities, how exactly I'll choose to do it when the time comes."

As she finished her monologue, they arrived outside a majestic set of inner doors.

"Let's go into the theatre," said Jocelyn. "It's almost time for the show." She gestured toward a poster.

"'Tonight at 9 p.m., Maggie performs her trademark piss-tease act,'" read Stephen aloud. "What in the world is a 'piss-tease' act?"

"You'll see."

The cabaret within the club was, like everything else,

lavishly and artistically decorated. Red velvet hung everywhere, and the tables and chairs evoked *fin de siècle* Paris or Vienna. Here and there sat and wriggled other patrons.

The lights dimmed, and for the next ten minutes they watched an act like no other. Maggie, a stunning, somewhat androgynous woman with short black hair, long legs and small round breasts, strutted out wearing only a pair of frilly, bikini-cut black panties and plenty of eye makeup. She stopped centre stage, acknowledged the applause, and then addressed the audience.

"Ladies and gentlemen, I have to pee," she announced importantly. She clutched her crotch suggestively and let an erotic shiver run through her.

A murmur of sex-charged approval greeted this proclamation. Then a curtain behind Maggie opened to reveal a sparkling, silver-plated commode, its seat ready to receive the quivering arse of a piss-rich woman.

"And perhaps," Maggie said softly, "some of you have to pee, as well." The audience tittered knowingly.

Maggie sat down on the toilet seat – still in her knickers – then instantly got back up. She laughed, and again squeezed herself.

Over the next few minutes, Maggie walked laps around the stage, parading her condition, stopping now and again to cross her legs or squat teasingly, often smiling or winking at the audience, and generally playing the situation like an acrobat on a tightrope. With knees rhythmically knocking together, she slapped her own buttocks and tweaked her own nipples. She took delicate, gingerly steps and great, bold strides. She pulled her knickers down, then up, then down – flirting now with pissing on the stage, now with doing it in the commode, and making a show of pretending she couldn't decide where, when, and how to let go.

"You never know if she's going to do it on the floor, in the loo, or in her knickers," Jocelyn told Stephen. "Sometimes she even lets the audience choose."

Tonight, after suitable deliberation and debate, it was the floor. And as Maggie's ostentatious waterfall shimmered in the spotlight and the cabaret star roared with the divine pleasure of giving in, Stephen heard the liquid hisses and heartfelt sighs of the several women pissing in tandem with Maggie.

He saw that Jocelyn was fidgeting next to him. "Are you going to do it?" he asked eagerly.

"Not here," she said. "Come on." She stood hurriedly, dancing in place and giggling while she waited for him to scramble up.

He followed her out of the theatre and along a space-age corridor, in a direction they hadn't explored yet. Just beyond a bench occupied by a platinum-haired leg-crossing enthusiast in a fine black raincoat and tense white panties, they stopped at a service window. Here Jocelyn addressed a club official, a handsome woman with penetrating eyes.

"I have a room reserved for an engagement ceremony," Jocelyn informed her.

Stephen felt a stirring in his heart – and, because of the possibilities promised by their location, another in his groin.

The official consulted her computer. "Ah, yes. Jocelyn. So you'll need four volunteers?"

"That's right." Jocelyn smiled, blushing slightly.

"You two can go on in," said the official. "I'm sure it will only take a minute to round up some friends. Everyone loves these ceremonies," she added to Stephen.

Jocelyn opened a door across the corridor, and escorted him inside. She closed the door behind them.

The room looked like a cross between a traditional private library and a postmodern sanctuary. There were oak bookcases along two walls, and heavy-framed paintings and mirrors on the others. There were deep couches and chairs around the perimeter; but the middle of the room was dominated by a sort of asymmetrical gazebo, lit theatrically by floodlights. Lounge music, incongruous yet appealing, was piped in through speakers.

Stephen sat on a couch, but Jocelyn did not join him. "I'd better not sit," she acknowledged. "At this point, if I don't keep moving I'll probably soak myself … and that would spoil what I've planned for you." She chuckled seductively, pacing back and forth, petting herself through her clinging skirt as she savoured her delicious restlessness. "Oh, fuck, I'm turned on, Stephen," she whispered.

Stephen had the insight, at that moment, that Jocelyn was not wearing any underwear, and his cock tingled as he imagined the sexy sensations his fiancée was experiencing as she touched her pussy through the thin skirt while enjoying the urgent thrill of teetering on the verge.

The door opened, and a procession of four women snaked in. One wore an iridescent evening gown, two were in bright little cocktail dresses, and the fourth was sleek as a cat in a turtleneck and slacks. Jocelyn, playing hostess, greeted them, introducing herself and Stephen. Then, without even waiting for them to give their names in return, she clapped her hands with enthusiasm: "Let's do it."

And they all knew what to do. The four smiling women converged on Stephen's couch. He relaxed, mesmerised, as each of them took one of his extremities in hand. Jocelyn, now digging her fingers deep into her crotch, waddled forward and leaned in to kiss him. "I love you," she said.

Then she scurried out of the way, allowing her four attendants to carry Stephen, face up, to the gazebo, each of them using both hands to support his weight.

"He's gorgeous," volunteered one woman.

"Mmm, yeah," agreed another.

"Wow, I really have to wee," giggled a third.

"Me, too."

"Me, too."

"Me, too."

Jocelyn moved into Stephen's field of vision, and the four women lowered him just enough so that she could step over him with one luscious, stocking-clad leg and then remain there, straddling him. And just as he focused his gaze on the magnificent image of his woman standing open-legged and knicker-free over his waist, he saw her face relax; and a dribble, then a cascade, of woman-warmed piss descended onto him.

"Baby," she cooed, looking into his eyes with a blissed-out expression of release and adoration. And, like a string quartet playing the first measure of a piece with synchronized precision, Jocelyn's volunteers all suddenly switched on their sprinklers.

Stephen found himself at the centre of an extraordinarily lewd tableau. The cocktail-dress woman holding his right foot was shuffling gracefully in place and wantonly splashing the floor, and the bearer of his left foot was pulsing around a darkening, slowly leaking trouser seam. Both women moaned – in harmony with Jocelyn, who appeared to be melting with pleasure. Behind him, he heard the burbling downpours of the other two goddesses, who were releasing their personal floods while still holding his arms.

"Ooh!" a pretty voice squealed at his shoulder – involuntarily, it seemed.

"This feels sooo fucking good," crooned the woman in slacks.

The whole room seemed to vibrate in a cosmic ecstasy built of abandon, sensuousness and between-the-thighs female luxuries that were too recherché for a man to fully understand.

In counterpoint to this grand effect, the immediate caress of Jocelyn's water on Stephen's tuxedo trousers was the most intimately sensual thing he had ever known. Inside his clothes, his erection throbbed gratefully while his lover rained on him. As Jocelyn and her lovely attendants, full of beer, pissed on and on, Stephen felt he was in paradise.

"Look at the lucky man," said the woman in slacks, breathlessly.

"We'd better finish soon, or he's going to come before she's ready for him," chirped the sweet-voiced woman holding Stephen's right arm.

Finally they all trickled to a halt, ending almost as precisely as they'd begun – like a string quartet gone slightly sloppy from imbibing.

"Let this outpouring be a symbol of my endlessly flowing love," chanted Jocelyn, her eyes tearing up.

Before Stephen could respond, she was unzipping his

trousers and springing his cock free. Now it was his turn to moan.

Jocelyn dipped her fingers into her sopping crotch, then grabbed his prick again. Then she steadied herself, standing solidly above Stephen, and nodded to the women behind him.

They took the cue, as did the women at his feet, and the four piss goddesses began to elevate him. Jocelyn guided his cock between her lips as it came up like an obelisk on a mechanic's lift, and Stephen trembled with the velvety satisfaction of being claimed by her.

When she'd taken him about halfway in, she nodded once more, and the attendants held him steady. Then Jocelyn began to bend her knees.

He'd never been fucked like this, so exotically and from such a physically passive attitude. Jocelyn brought herself up and down, milking his shaft with expert sensitivity. Stephen's gaze moved from her piss-streaked stockings to her bliss-streaked face ... then to the sympathetic figures holding his ankles, whose countenances were radiant with the damp raunchiness of what they'd done for him. He thought of their hard little clits in their warm, dripping-wet underwear, envisioning the orgasms that would crackle through them as soon as their hands were free.

Jocelyn had her pee-dabbed fingers on her own clit now; and though Stephen was close to exploding, she beat him to it. A bonus gift of piss poured out of her as she came, sobbing with joy, and Stephen howled as he shot into her, completely wallowing in the extravagant eroticism of it all.

The attendants put him down gently and left the two of them alone, exiting the room with pussy-gratifying hands already active in their wet junctures. With his trousers a pond of sacred water and his groin beginning to pulse with a pleasant, watery ache of its own, Stephen licked Jocelyn's pussy – tasting everything, and feeling so very, very engaged.

The Night at the Hotel
by Elizabeth K. Payne

I was late. Considerably late. Almost an hour. Everything seemed to be conspiring against me. Work took longer than usual, I cut myself while shaving my legs, and then, to top it all, the train I got on was delayed. I looked at my watch nervously, then my mobile phone – no messages from him. Had he received mine?

Even though in truth I was dressed quite modestly, in a black dress, a mac and a beret, I felt as though the passengers in the train knew exactly what I was on way to do, as if they could see the lacy underwear I was wearing underneath, or the contents of my suitcase – the paddle, the collar and the pair of heels I had purchased that day in my lunch break.

I got out of the train, and attempted to follow the directions he'd given me. I was tired, nervous and confused by the number of bus stops. I went round in circles, unable to find the right one. I texted him I was lost. He called and explained where I should go. His tone of voice was neutral. I apologised for being late.

"Yes, you are late," he said. No anger, but no effort to reassure me either.

Our common friend Hanna had introduced us, acting as a matchmaker, knowing we had complementary desires that neither of us had yet had a chance to fully explore. Not that I hadn't played before, but, having spent most of my twenties in long term relationships with relatively vanilla partners, I had only been 'in role' for brief periods. My ex-boyfriends had been more than willing to tie me up and tease me before sex, but I hadn't been able to persuade them to play for longer stretches of time – say whole evenings.

His story was similar. We spent an afternoon in the park, getting to know each other, walking and talking about what we wanted to experience. He had beautiful eyes with thick eyelashes, almost as if he was wearing mascara, and a pleasant voice, calm, friendly and intelligent. We sat on the grass, and I touched the side of his face lightly, inviting him to kiss me.

By mutual choice, wanting to get to know each other better first, we hadn't played that day and we hadn't played on the two quite traditional dates that followed, but the time for something kinkier had arrived – and I had finally got on the right bus, and found the hotel!

For the first time, we would meet in role and, as long we were both comfortable, I would be his pet for the evening. We agreed 'pet' had a nicer ring than 'slave'.

The hotel was luxurious. I expected him to be in the lobby, but he wasn't. I called him, and he told me which corridor to walk through, which room number to look for. In my sleep deprivation and nervousness, it all seemed so difficult, and I had to ask him to repeat his instructions a couple of times.

I sat on the bed, and he offered me a drink. I thought he would tell me off for being late, and generally being so ineffectual, but he said it was understandable that I was nervous, and kissed me. He was wearing grey trousers, a white shirt and a waistcoat. There were sex toys laid out on the bed. He asked to see what I had brought. He liked the heels I had chosen, but said I should iron the shirt I had packed. I was a little surprised.

"Is this a course in being a woman?" I said.

The iron was warm – he'd ironed his own shirt. Expertly, of course, whereas I was doing a poor job.

"Is this good enough?" I asked.

He pointed to a few creases. "What do you think?" he said. "You may want to make a good impression on your first day."

"Sorry," was my instinctive response. I smiled nervously as his probing gaze cut through me.

"You may not make eye contact with me, and you should not speak unless I ask you a question," he said, and ordered me

85

to walk into the bathroom and undress. I noticed a wooden bath brush was waiting for me there, a sight which filled me with excitement, and a little fear.

I took my clothes off, handing each item to him as I did so. He folded them neatly and put them aside. I stood naked for the first time in front of him, and he looked at me.

"Very nice," he said. "Step into the shower."

He ordered me to turn the water on. I panicked, again incapable of following the simplest instruction, finding even the shower taps too confusing. I felt foolish and cold, and started to shiver. Eventually, and with some assistance, I got the water running. Why was I so incompetent in the presence of this man? He applied shower gel, and started scrubbing me with the bath brush. He scrubbed forcefully – it was almost painful. He washed and scrubbed my face as well, then, with his hands, he soaped my breasts, stopping to squeeze each nipple. He ran his fingers lightly over my clit, but he did not linger as long as I wished. I made a face, as if asking him for more.

"Patience," he said, tapping me with the hair brush. "And remember, no eye contact."

He massaged shampoo, and then conditioner, on my hair. Once it was all rinsed off, he asked me to step out of the shower, and towelled me a lot more thoroughly than I would have. Then, with confident movements, he applied lotion on each part of my body. I savoured the sensation of his strong hands as they made their way from my feet to my neck. Even though I was still quite nervous, a part of me began to relax. He was in control – I didn't need to plan what to do next, and that was restful.

I was ordered to wear my heels, the pleated skirt I had packed and the shirt I'd ironed. Back into the bedroom, he asked me to walk in the heels to the door and back. This was not something that came easy to me, and he knew it – I had made it to my thirties without learning how to walk in high heels, a gap in my education he was keen to address. He stood close to me and observed.

"Again," he said. "With more feminine movements."

As I started to walk, I met his eyes, by mistake, and he slapped my face. He sat on the bed, slowly rolled up his sleeves, and put a pair of leather gloves on. He grabbed me by the arm, pushing me into his lap, and raised my skirt for a spanking.

"Time for some discipline," he said.

The smacks landed on my bottom with a satisfying noise. I liked the feel of the leather gloves – a first for me – and the fact that I was wearing heels seemed to add something to the punishment, making it more formal, more official, and me more elegant and vulnerable. The spanking lasted a couple of minutes, enough to warm me up, but not to cause considerable pain.

"Get up," he said.

He had a few more things for me to wear: a collar and wrist restraints. He attached the wrist restraints to the collar, so my hands were behind my back, then placed ankle restraints on my feet, and a chain between them. He unbuttoned my shirt, exposing my breasts, and turned me so I could admire myself in the mirror.

"Do you like what you see?" he asked.

"Yes, I look just like an S&M pet."

"That's right," he said. "You're my S&M pet. You have given yourself to me, and so I will require you to take care of yourself, do you understand?"

"Yes," I said. Of course it was a game, an act, and in the morning I would be off to work and back to my life. I wasn't really his, but it was delicious to pretend I was – and I hoped fervently that the game might last, in some form, and that even in between our meetings there might be moments when I would think of myself as his pet.

"You won't drink alcohol or smoke. You'll exercise. You'll always be groomed, well-dressed. You are lovely, and, for me, you will be the best you can be, all the time. If you are about to do something naughty, text me first. Ask for permission."

"I will," I said, feeling thankful, eager to please.

"Good pet."

He kissed the side of my face and blindfolded me.

"Walk," he ordered, ready to catch me.

I was unstable, of course. I had to trust him. I took a few hesitant steps and lost balance. He did catch me. I kept walking, enjoying the feeling that someone else was watching over me, protecting me, and I could just abandon myself to his will temporarily. I got to the door, and rested with my body against his. He fingered me with his gloved hand, and commented on how wet I was. But it wasn't time to fuck yet.

He ordered me to crouch, still blindfolded. It was easy enough, but I wasn't allowed to move and soon my feet started to hurt. I told him so.

"Does it, sweetie?" he said, in a kind tone.

"Yes," I said, my voice a little babyish, hoping he might take pity on me. "Can I move?"

"No, but perhaps these will take your mind off the discomfort," he said, and I could hear him reach for something.

Metal tugged at my nipples. It was my first experience of nipple clamps. The pain was sharp as he adjusted them, but it soon dulled down, until the sensation became pleasurable. My feet still hurt though. I whimpered a little. He kissed me gently, and rubbed my hair, but he did not let me move.

"I could just watch you all day," he said. Minutes passed, in silence.

"Get up," he said, finally, guiding me up and dragging me towards the table, making me bend down over it and lifting my skirt. He touched my clit, teasing me with his fingers. I was blindfolded and my hands were still behind my back, so it was difficult to control my upper body, and I knocked a plastic glass by mistake. Fizzy water poured onto the table and then down into the fluffy carpet of the hotel room.

"Look what you've done!" he said, removing my blindfold and freeing my hands. "Go and get a towel!" I did so, uncertain in the heels.

"Don't walk. Crawl," he ordered, and I obeyed.

On my return I handed him the towel, and he looked at me in mock shock. I giggled. Of course he wasn't going to be mopping the floor for me. What was I thinking? I pressed the towel on the wet patch on the floor, and dried his boots as well, as instructed.

"Crawl to the coffee table," he said, fishing in his bag for some rope. "This calls for punishment. I know you didn't mean to, but you have to learn to be less clumsy."

He ordered me to lie across the table, and proceeded to tie my arms and legs so I wouldn't be able to move. The nipple clamps were digging uncomfortably into my flesh. My ankles were tightly bound together.

"Point your toes," he said. "Now you are ready to be caned."

He lifted my skirt and reached for a little cane that was lying on the bed. He made it swish through the air, causing my body to tense in expectation of the pain. Twenty strokes followed, at a slow but regular pace, all handed out with the same strength. They were definitely not mild, but he was holding back, not hurting me as much as he could have. Even so, the pain was sharp, and I was soon attempting to move, as if to free myself and avoid to blows. But I could not – the bondage was tight, and even wiggling was out of the question. I could have used the agreed safe word, but too much of me was enjoying the experience, and, as the punishment neared its end, I stopped resisting the pain and started to feel oddly calm, almost as if I was floating, each blow bringing me to a higher state of pleasure.

"You are very wet," he commented when it was over, using the cane to stroke my cunt and raising it to inspect the evidence of my arousal. "And you look very pretty decorated with pink stripes."

He untied me and lifted me up in his arms to then deposit me on the bed. A nipple clamp lost its grip.

"We'll have to fix that," he said, readjusting it as I winced. It hurt, and, unlike the spanking and the caning, it didn't even hurt in a way which almost immediately turned into pleasure, and yet the thought that I was willing to let him inflict this kind of pain on me was both a turn-on and psychologically interesting – it made me feel as if I was truly submissive to this man, as if I could lose myself to the experience, letting him do as he wished with my body.

He undressed me until all I was wearing were the nipple clamps, the collar and the heels.

"You may look at me in the eyes when I fuck you," he said, reaching for a condom. "In fact, I want you to."

Facing me, and tugging the clamps lightly, he slid into me. I looked into his beautiful eyes as his cock finally filled me, but then I lowered my eyes slightly, forgetting his instructions, and he tugged at the clamps, than slapped my face, sending a sudden wave of pain and pleasure through my body. He lifted my legs so they were resting by my shoulders – stretched, the heels still on my feet – and started to fuck me hard. I kept my legs straight and my feet pointing (years of yoga were paying off!), wanting to be graceful for him, and finding that the position enhanced my pleasure further. Suddenly, I came, moaning loudly, almost surprised at the force and speed of it. He turned me round, and fucked me from behind, pressing his body against my skin, which was still in places warm and tingly from the punishment. Feeling a second orgasm building up, I reached for my clitoris. Soon I came, and a big smile spread on my face as I recovered from the explosion of pleasure. He didn't stop, but rode to his own orgasm, spurred on by mine, then let his body rest against mine and kissed me.

"Next time we will meet at the bar," he said later, spooning me. "Be early, and wait like a good girl. I want you to dress elegantly. Put your hair up, wear some make-up, your best jewellery …"

"And the heels?"

"Of course. And something else too. Under your evening dress, I want you to wear a little gift I have for you."

My eyes widened.

He reached for his bag and handed me a small parcel.

"Since you've been a good girl," he said. "Mostly."

I smiled, delighted, and unwrapped the parcel, revealing something I hadn't seen before, but had heard about. It was shaped like a butterfly and came with a remote control.

"Now, that's for me," he said, and showed me how the butterfly could be made to vibrate – quite silently, thankfully. He placed it against my clit, and gave me a little taste of what was to come.

"Bedtime," he said, with a pat. "Go brush your teeth."

On my return from the bathroom I saw he'd laid out some blankets and pillows on the floor, by the side of the bed. I looked at him in surprise.

"Pets sleep on the floor. Come here."

I sat on the 'bed' he'd made for me, and he lifted my right foot gently, and placed an ankle restraint back on, attached to some rope. He tied the rope to the coffee table nearby – there was quite a lot of rope, so I could actually move a fair bit.

"So you won't run away. Get in, then."

I did as told, and he tucked me in and kissed me goodnight. He got into the bed, the actual bed, and turned the lights off, while I wondered whether I dared disobey and climb into bed with him …

Swing Town
by Lauren Wissot

Odd that I would pass a bus ad for *Swingtown*, a new, retro TV show that follows the trials and tribulations of those wacky 70s wife-swappers, on my way to my latest gig. Having been happily ensconced in an 'adults-only' world off and on for over a decade, I thought I'd pretty much sampled every non-sex job the sex industry had to offer, from receptionist (at a body rub business and at a house of domination), to pro-dom, to stripper (albeit briefly as I lack the hustling gene). So when I saw the ad on Craigslist for a 'swing party hostess', I thought, "That's a job? I can really get paid just to watch folks screw?"

Well, yes and no. The standard swingers' party is for couples and single women only; no single men allowed, thus no need for hostesses. But because Erick – the fabulous black queen at the other end of the Craigslist ad – admits single guys to his debauched shindigs, he needs extra women to even things out. The hours are 7 to 11 on most weeknights, 10 to 2 on weekends, the pay twenty bucks an hour "plus tips". That salary arrangement could add up to pretty much nothing if you're mostly a voyeur like me, or pay your rent if you're an insatiable fuck-freak like Star, a towering Amazon of a black woman with huge tits and ass, which she parades around free of charge as she methodically attacks each and every man that enters Erick's candlelit and incense-drenched, three-floor midtown loft. In all fairness to this sexual Energizer bunny, I honestly don't know which men Star is charging for her services as she's like an indiscriminate tornado, sucking up every penis in her path, business dealings seeming a mere afterthought. Erick is forever asking her to slow down before she wears out all the customers.

I know she's not charging Wilson. Ahh, Wilson – one of the many former/current/aspiring porn stars that form Erick's vast entourage (did I happen to mention Erick is my new best friend?). The first time I saw Wilson enter the top floor lounge, my usual Pavlovian response to muscled Adonises kicked in and it took all my willpower not to drop to my knees, begging to body worship. Wilson is straight out of my 'Gaiety guys I must fuck' category. A pierced and tattooed Puerto Rican bodybuilder and personal trainer with a killer smile who eventually confided to me that he'd done gay porn in his 'younger days' (he's 26!) for Tony and Michael over at Lucas Entertainment, Wilson's only flaw is that he's, well, nice. Sweet and shy. A good guy supporting his girlfriend and four kids, not a bad boy bone in his body. Ick. Though I did manage to wrangle a taste of his big fat dick – after Jada, a sweet black stripper from the Bronx with enormous T&A had had her way with him, that is. While he was eating her out, she and Bianca, a young, innocent Latina hostess from the Bronx, gushed over how sexy Paris Hilton is. Wilson held up his pinky and waved it.

"Eew. You like her too?" I asked. He removed his face from Jada's vagina long enough to explain that he doesn't like thin girls. As my hard-on wilted, freestyle music filled the room, taking me back to those long-gone 80s.

"Oh, yeah, my mom used to play this when I was little," Wilson added. I felt like a skinny, creepy old queen. So I just contented myself with sitting temptingly near the Adonis, playing with his nipple piercings, inhaling the glorious testosterone – when he wasn't being greedily gangbanged by Star and her aggressive body parts. Technically Wilson's job is 'security plus' (wink, wink), but Erick's parties are so laid back that security doesn't seem to be an issue. It's not like the weird mix of cute couples, young, single and surprisingly decent-looking guys (everyone from white-shoe lawyers to blue-collar construction workers), porn stars and ghetto strippers all lounging around in towels are suddenly going to get up and riot. To wit, the only tense moment I ever saw occurred when the crap freebie 'NYC condoms' kept slipping off Wilson's dick the one time I was trying to blow him (I threatened to call 311 to complain, "The mayor keeps cock-blocking me!").

Of course, where there's a cock there's a way. Right off I'd suggested to Erick that he put an ad for 'Str8 Guys on the DL' on Craigslist so I could watch some live gay porn. The number of responses Erick received shocked him. Within a week I'd climbed the ladder from lowly hostess (dispensing towels and locks for the lockers when not cheering on the players, shuffling between the sparsely furnished, downstairs 'couples room' and the upstairs lounge with its giant couch, urban Brazilian porn on the TV and curtained-off boudoir area) to the chick who walks around flirtatiously whispering in every man's ear, "So. Do you suck cock?"

Such are the times when my gay male soul can shine through my biological female body without getting punched in the nose. Though for every, "Yeah, sometimes" there are always several, "No thanks", the effort can pay off. Like the night I got a cute black guy with an enormous cock to blow Erick's friend Anthony, a pretty Latin boy with dreamy eyes, as he was jerking him off. The black guy was a cock-sucking virgin, Anthony an eager young thing on the DL. Yum. Needless to say, I decided to hook enthusiastic Anthony up with my gay porn contact.

"Why are you trying to get all my friends to do gay porn?" Erick cried (uh, maybe because you have friends like the cute, straight Latin stripper who works the gay clubs – and even knows former Gaiety boy Tyler who now manages Club 20!).

"He sucks cock? But he's my friend! I never knew! How can you tell?" Erick endlessly wondered about this one and that, professing shock at my bi and gay-for-pay radar even as he was using me as an undercover DL spy ("Ask him!"). Simple, darling. I can pick up the scent of hustlers and rough trade from a mile away.

Not that these swing parties are all about the cock. No, there's erotic yoga as well. Jude, the fantastically fit, nearly fifty-year-old, pot-smoking 'cougar' hostess, a forensic psychologist who's married to her master and has been friends with famed BDSM filmmaker (and submissive) Blue for thirty years, has been known to perform a calisthenics regimen in front of the TV porn from time to time (so what makes this yoga erotic? The setting – duh!) And Jude isn't the only crossover from the S&M world to grace Erick's parties (not that Jude doesn't cross over from several scenes herself, having worked at the iconic punk rock Mudd Club – I was shocked when Thrill Kill Kult's *Sex On Wheels* blared from the speakers, courtesy of Jude – and more recently joined the political performance pranksters Billionaires for Bush). There's also Johnny, a nipple torture enthusiast who plays at Paddles and has known the legendary Lenny of *Hellfire Club* for decades. Plus Jude has some flexibility competition from Erick's friend Legend, a well over six-foot-tall black man with a to-die-for bod. I asked him if he played sports in addition to personal training. "Yeah, I used to be in the circus," he replied, detailing the years he spent with UniverSoul.

Then there's Liquid, a black bisexual hostess who won't do girls darker than she. "She's a white girl inside," Erick laughed, and indeed, Liquid sounds exactly like Elle from *Legally Blonde*. And there's also the sharp, twenty-something, Latin female/black male couple that arrive suited up in business attire, only to immediately strip, never to leave the boudoir area for the rest of the night! Turns out they've been together for three years and public sex is how they decompress after a long hard day. I have a feeling this relationship will last, with lots not to tell the grandchildren about someday.

And of course I can't forget to mention Erick's cousin George, a tall teddy bear of an ex-con with gold teeth, who bounces around the room like a kid in desperate need of Ritalin.

"It's my wife. Hi, baby!" he exclaimed, answering his cell during one of his rare moments of sitting still on the couch. "I'm sitting next to a dominatrix!" he added, handing me the phone. "Beat his ass for me!" the voice on the other end yelled. When the entire room suddenly disappeared to the second floor while I was in the bathroom I immediately went downstairs, looking for the orgy. What I found instead left me aghast.

Everyone was gathered around the speakers, shaking their towel-covered booties to salsa music like at some high school basement party. I was the resident pervert for sure.

When Star started devouring a little Puerto Rican guy half her height Erick coaxed me over to watch the show while he gave a play-by-play. "Oh, her wig is gonna fall off!" he whispered as Star's weave began to wave. "She's gonna crush him!" he exclaimed as Star flipped the small man onto his back with a move straight out of WWE. The guy turned out to be quite cool, though. After Star had had her fix he tried to pick me up but I demurred, letting him in on my 'secret'. Being a guy on the inside I fuck vicariously through man-on-man action.

"That's very interesting," he nodded, accepting and intrigued.

And I guess that's the best part of the swing 'gig' for me' the freedom to be my male self (swingers' parties are just gay bathhouses for straight-identified people after all!). I can wear undies and a T-shirt, no makeup, not like when I have to pretend to be a girl at Pandora's, posing as a corseted, high-heeled dom. When Erick shouts, "This is my favourite song!" he looks conspiratorially at me as the hip-hop lyrics sing, "Wave your dicks in the air!" It's me he sends over to freak out the straight black guy who does odd jobs for him, who he can't seem to get rid of ("You fool around with guys?" I bluntly asked the paint-covered dude. "Nah, I'm forty. I've got kids at home," he answered uncomfortably. "I won't tell them," I countered sweetly. "Nah, I'm good," he added, starting to panic).

I guess the only drawback is the low pay so I still troll Craigslist. Matter of fact, I just emailed a guy – a bi hustler in search of a girl to do joint sessions with his clients. According to Lorenzo's website he's an Italian-American, 6ft 3in, 210 pounds, bodybuilder …

More
by Donna George Storey

Who could ask for more?

Kendra settled back in the lounge chair and took another sip of her sparkling wine. The terrace of the bungalow had a stunning view of the Napa Valley, ringed with elegant, blue-green mountains. Neither the accommodations nor the aperitif came cheap, she knew, but it wasn't her credit card that would take the damage.

Jason's deep voice drifted through the French doors; he'd promised he'd turn off the Blackberry by six. *By six for sex*, he'd quipped. It was easy enough to laugh at his dumb jokes when he'd just suggested she pass the time with a massage at the hotel spa while he finished his business calls.

Of course, she was used to waiting for him. He was a busy man. She'd been waiting for this – a whole weekend away together – for quite some time. To make up for it, Jason promised he'd treat her like a queen, a class act all the way.

Kendra smiled with more than a touch of irony. Perhaps it wasn't exactly classy to shack up with a married guy, not to mention the chief investor in the start-up where she'd just been promoted to Controller. But it wasn't as tawdry as it seemed. Jason had assured her from the beginning that he had an open marriage. With wife number three, he'd made sure to spell everything out in the pre-nup. As for the risk of compromising their professional relationship, the truth was she was learning more about how to do her job well from him than from all of her business school finance classes combined. Jason had a way of getting inside things, figuring them out, making them his. Even as he did the same to her – or more precisely her body –

Kendra was watching, studying, building the skills she needed for her future.

She took another sip of the bubbly and ran her hand over the nap of the hotel's soft terry robe. The massage had been exceptional, her muscles kneaded to taffy by the capable hands of a young masseur named Narayana. Kendra always requested the services of a man when she wanted to be pampered. Though this relationship was strictly professional, there was something undeniably erotic about being in a low-lit room with a stranger who was rubbing his hands all over her. The heat of the man's gaze warmed her as much as his hands stroking her naked flesh. And she always listened for that catch in his breath when she let out a soft moan of pleasure. This Narayana – his real name was probably something like Mike, since he had blond ringlets and mentioned he came from Portland – was particularly attentive. *Your shoulders are really blocked with negative energy, I'd be happy to do another special session if you have time.*

He'd handed her his card with his private consultation number, a blatant breach of spa policy. Restraining a smile, she told him she'd think about it, charged his generous tip to the room, and floated back to Jason. Deliciously fuckable as her boy toy was, she had her limits. But she had no doubt she'd call on the brawny lad for a special fantasy session tonight.

These pleasantly titillating memories were now interrupted by the demands of her real lover, smiling down at her as he switched off his Blackberry with a flourish. Jason had already changed from his businessman outfit, his muscular calves bare beneath the hotel's robe.

Six for sex.

Kendra felt a twinge of lust between her legs. She was more than ready, but she knew Jason liked to play, so she pursed her lips in a pout.

"It's 6.20. You lied again."

"I'll make it up to you. I always do."

He sauntered back to the room and sank into the generous armchair, eyebrows raised expectantly.

She drained her glass and joined him.

"How was your massage?" he said, as she settled onto his lap.

"Great. It got all the stiffness out."

"I'm a bit stiff myself."

She laughed and petted his hard-on through the robe.

"That's nice," said Jason, "but right now I'm more interested in sampling your 'internal' technique. Be a good girl and get us a condom. They're in the outside pocket of my overnight bag."

Jason always started off their trysts by ordering her around, as if it took him a few minutes to peel off his 'captain of industry' persona like a suit and tie. But Kendra knew that before long she'd have him naked and on his knees, in more ways than one.

When she returned with the condom, he was ready for her, his robe open to reveal his muscular chest and thick cock, which poked up imperiously from the dark curls of his pubic hair.

"Put it on me." He was smiling, but his eyes had a steely glint.

She tore open the package and rolled the sheath over him.

"Now take off your robe and climb on."

Not a moment of foreplay? It was a good thing that hippie masseur had juiced her up well with his magic hands. As Kendra stripped, she couldn't resist throwing Jason a mutinous look.

He grinned. He liked it when she showed her spirit.

Squaring her shoulders, she straddled him on the chair and took him inside, one inch at a time.

His head lolled back against the chair and he groaned; a rich, sweet sound.

"God, you have the perfect cunt."

She couldn't help smiling. Sometimes her promotion from eager apprentice to boss was all too easy, as easy as sitting on his cock. Within seconds, he'd be babbling about how gorgeous she was, how brilliant and ambitious, how she'd leave him in the dust someday, once she'd sucked him dry of the meagre offerings he could give to a goddess like her.

She liked those words, but she needed more. So she'd pull off and taunt him. *You're lying, Jason. You're lying to me again. No more pussy until you tell me truth.* And he'd swear he meant every word and beg her, near tears, to let him back into paradise. There were even times, after she finally let him come inside her, that he would actually weep and declare his love. She'd say she loved him, too, although what she really loved was the way he made her feel in bed: proud, powerful, perfect. Feelings that almost made up for the vague humiliation of creeping off to meet him in hotels, or sneaking quickies in the empty office by the storage room, or keeping as quiet as a phantom when his wife called.

But other days he made her work for it, relinquishing his power only when she'd proven herself worthy. Like today when he held her hips fast so she couldn't move and said, his voice soft but stern, "Squeeze me, baby. Give me a massage with your hot cunt."

Kendra moaned assent and tightened her secret muscles, milking him as if her pussy really was a warm, fleshy mitten, smoothing away the stiffness from an aching limb. She remembered the melting pleasure of Narayana's hands. He was serving her, yes, but had her in his power, too. That's what she'd do to Jason.

"How do you like your massage?" she drawled, giving him an extra squeeze.

This was his cue to start spurting the praise, but to her surprise, Jason only frowned. "Can you work it harder? Too be honest, I don't feel much."

Kendra felt her cheeks flush. He didn't even feel it? She clenched her cunt muscles again as hard as she could, gritting her teeth with the effort.

"Nope, just the barest flutter. I know you're trying, but it's not enough. Have you been exercising like I told you?"

Her jaw dropped. What could she say? Of course she remembered the 'gift' he'd given her the evening they'd fucked in a suite at the Mandarin Oriental, a weighted, penis-shaped device that was supposed to make pelvic exercises more effective. But he'd only said, slyly, that it was a way to keep her happy when he wasn't around to do the job. At the time she'd thought it was a racy gag gift, nothing more.

Finally, she gathered up enough 'spirit' to reply. "Come on, Jason, with keeping up with my job and this insatiable older man I'm fucking, it's difficult enough to fit in Pilates. How do you expect me to find time to work out with a dildo?"

"I think you should make time," he shot back, his expression strangely serious, as if he were admonishing an employee. "There's room for improvement in your performance."

"But you said I had a perfect cunt." The words slipped out, her voice quivering, her eyes filling with tears. Apparently he *had* been lying to her all along.

His eyes softened. "No, now don't be sad. Your pussy's beautiful, baby, like you, but we all have to strive for more. In business and pleasure."

"Does it really make a difference?" Curiosity trumped the sting of his insult.

"You bet. I've known women with pussies like vacuum cleaners. It's incredible. And they say it feels better for the woman, too. I know you're a busy lady, but you want to be strong, inside and out, don't you Kendra?"

"Yes," she admitted meekly, unable to look him in the eye.

"Then promise me you'll practice with your little friend every day and when we get together I'll test you to see how much progress you've made. I think we have a win-win situation here. That's what you always aim for in any deal, right?"

She nodded, unable to speak. It was humiliating to be found so lacking. Yet, down below, her secret muscles tingled as if they wanted to be worked over, tested, proven worthy.

"The female body is capable of so much more than a man's," he continued, his hands gliding from her hair to her shoulders then on to her breasts. "If you always reach for more, Kendra, a smart, sexy woman like you will have the world at her feet."

She nodded again, the perfect student. She did want the world at her feet, but when she pictured 'the world', what she really saw was Jason, so wealthy, so powerful, a king in his little corner of the universe, crouched before her.

Jason hooked his finger under her chin and tilted her head up to meet his gaze. "I know what you want. You're like me; you always need a challenge, and I have another one for you tonight. Remember that bed and breakfast where they let us take a room for a few hours?"

She did remember, hazily. Yet another rented room with a wide, fancy bed. The grand view of the bay sparkling before her eyes as Jason lashed her clit with his tongue, swearing he was so thirsty for her, he'd suck down the nectar of a dozen sweet climaxes.

"How many times did I make you come?"

Her blush deepened. "Four."

"Four times in an hour and a half. I was proud of you, babe. Is that the most you've ever come with a man?"

"Yes," she admitted, suddenly wishing it were a lie.

"Let's try to top that tonight. Let's try for a new personal best."

"How about you? You're forty-five, how do you expect to keep up with me?"

"Don't worry about me. My goal is to hold off as long as I can. This is about your pleasure. You're in charge all the way. You tell me what you need and I'll do it."

Kendra had to smile. This was more like what she'd been expecting from a whole weekend alone with Jason.

"All right, I'm game. Double digits or die."

"That's my girl. Let's start right now. You can ride me on the chair while I play with your ass. That always sets you off like a rocket."

Already his finger was sliding down the valley of her buttocks, sending shivers of pleasure straight to her clit. She whimpered, half in shame, half in surrender. They both knew that when he touched her back there she'd do anything for him, a slave to the delirious sensations. He'd said she'd be in charge all the way, but of course he was lying again. Just as he'd lied about her perfect cunt, the open marriage, not fucking any other women on the side. If she had any pride, she'd pull off and refuse to play, until he did tell the truth, until the rules were fair.

His lips drew close to her ear.

"You want it, don't you, Kendra? You're so horny you have to climb on my lap while we're waiting for the board meeting to start. You know they'll be coming in any minute. Larry and Aaron and that horse-faced Marissa with a butt as wide as a barn. They'll walk in with their boring presentations and the dollar signs in their eyes and then they'll see you, naked, riding my cock while I stroke your pretty pink asshole. They'll see how much you love it, you dirty, horny girl."

"Oh, fuck. Oh, yes." Kendra starting grinding herself into him now, lost in his dream. Or was it hers? He always seemed to know how to touch her in just the right way.

"But I've got the perfect plan. If you come in a minute, you can wiggle back into your business suit and no one will be the wiser. And Larry will sit in the chair where we fucked and he'll wonder why it's damp, but he won't have the nerve to say anything in case I stop writing the cheques. We'll laugh at him all afternoon. Can you beat him? Can you come right now?"

"Yes. I'll try," she gasped. He was pinching her nipple rhythmically, sending double-pronged lightning bolts sizzling from her breast to her ass and cunt.

"I'll count the seconds, Kendra. When I get to sixty they'll see you. Do you hear the footsteps? They're coming closer. One … two … three …"

Kendra jerked her hips in a frantic lap dance – one, two, three times – and then she was doing it, she was coming, her orgasm tearing through her body, bursting through her throat in a shriek.

Jason hugged her tight, rocking her like a child. "You did it, angel, you did just what I said. Good job. Well done."

She collapsed against him, savouring the spicy male smell of him. Why this made her so happy she wasn't sure. She only knew she wanted to make this moment last, make their first night together be the longest, sweetest night of her life.

Of course, Jason was a busy man. He had other plans.

He gave her nipple a playful, almost painful, tug. "No rest

for the wicked now, we've got to get to work on number two."

Her body tensed in his embrace. She might indeed get her wish.

This could be the longest night of her life after all.

Kendra switched on the Jacuzzi, sighing as her body sank into the churning water. She was sore, inside and out, as might be expected of a woman who'd climaxed ten times in five hours.

She had to admit Jason had given her an evening to remember. Before she was fully recovered from her first orgasm, he guided her over to the bed and arranged her body, arms at her sides, legs spread wide. Then he pleasured her with his mouth, flicking and teasing her clit until her pussy drooled all over the sheets like a teething baby. The second time took longer, but, determined to meet his challenge, she managed to come again before too long. After that he pulled her on top again and diddled her while he fucked her. When he came, bellowing and shaking, it drove her over the edge, too, and she slammed down onto him like a jackhammer, announcing her own release with a bestial howl.

He allowed her a dinner break, and kept a solicitous arm around her as she limped down to the hotel's renowned dining room. But the meal was a test of another sort. He forbade her to wear panties and alternately ordered her to cross her legs and squeeze her thighs tight, then open herself wide enough that she could feel the air caress her bare lips. To Kendra's disappointment, he never tried to touch her under the table, but he did excuse himself once for a rather long time.

"Are you up for more?" he asked her, smiling devilishly.

This time 'more' meant resting against him on the lounge chair on the terrace, legs spread, her pussy exposed to the stars, while he rubbed her to number four.

A few minutes later dessert was delivered to the room – an aptly named 'chocolate orgasm cake' with whipped cream. Jason ate his portion from her breasts and ass and she scored number five to the sticky, sloppy slurping of his tongue.

For number six he made her kneel on the bed and masturbate while he spanked and scolded her for being so insatiable. Oddly, right in the middle of the scene a man from room service knocked once again and Jason sent her off to the bathroom with the assignment to finish herself off while he dealt with the interruption. Kendra considered defying him, but then she actually did find it a turn on to stretch out on the bathmat and finger herself to the mysterious murmuring of male voices from the bedroom. She was almost done when Jason pushed open the door and insisted on watching the finale. He promised a nice surprise if she completed the project to his satisfaction.

Kendra's heart skipped a beat when she eventually saw that surprise. An array of sex toys was laid out on the bed like platters on a smorgasbord: fur handcuffs, a butt plug, a curved G-spot stimulator in dainty lavender, and a silver egg that vibrated loudly when he flipped the switch on.

He'd had to give the man a special tip to drive down to Napa City, Jason explained with a grin, but it was worth it, even if the whole staff knew the lady in the Sunset Bungalow was in for stimulating evening.

Kendra stared at the display, her horror mingled with an undeniable pang of pure lust. She wondered if she could flog even one more climax from her swollen genitals, but she hadn't counted on battery power. With her hands cuffed, a buzzing toy inserted in her asshole and cunt, and Jason massaging her clit with the egg, she managed an electrified seventh climax, followed by an eighth, then a ninth, until at last she was in tears, begging him to release her.

Number ten was sweet and slow. Jason fucked her, in every position they knew, gently, sometimes holding himself perfectly still so that she controlled the movement. She was exquisitely sensitive and it took an hour, but she did it. She came one last time, a weary fluttering of her muscles, but it counted just the same.

Jason came again, too, then presented her with her long-awaited, final reward.

You're the best, Kendra. The fuck of my dreams. The goddamn sexiest woman in the whole fucking world. And I've known my share.

She floated there in his embrace, insults forgotten, wounds healed, that coveted 'sexiest woman in the world' crown resting lightly on her brow. She smiled and kissed him, with queenly indulgence, when he confessed that she'd worn him out, but he was up for pushing on to number twenty tomorrow. In moments he was asleep. Kendra relished the soft, even sound of his breath. He was like a child now, so trusting and defenceless in her arms. She had been to bed with Jason dozens of times, but she had never actually slept with him.

Then he began to snore.

After a restless half hour, Kendra slipped out of bed and ran herself a bath.

Now, grimacing at the sting of the heat on her well-used holes, she had to admit she was glad she was finally alone. Not that she was sorry for what she'd done, for him, and for herself. She just wasn't sure she could do it all over again tomorrow.

Maybe it would help if she got another massage?

Kendra laughed, softly, although she doubted there was any danger of waking Jason from his wheezing slumber. She'd been so busy watching her numbers, she'd forgotten to fantasize about that hunky masseur. The memory of those sweet strong hands, the tight young ass and thighs, would have been good for at least one more orgasm, if not two. Not to mention the thrill of cheating on Jason, if only in her dreams.

Her belly contracted, a sharp clenching of desire.

Why not go for number eleven right now? She'd proven she was a woman who could make dreams come true.

She stepped out of the tub, towelled off and fetched her cell phone and the card from her purse. It was past midnight, but chances were good a young buck like Narayana would be up on Friday, meditating or levitating or whatever he did to have fun.

He answered his phone on the first ring.

"This is Kendra, your four o'clock appointment this afternoon. I hope I'm not bothering you, but I have a bit of an emergency."

"Kendra! Don't ask me how, but I had a feeling you'd call." The pleasure in his voice was genuine.

"I think my *chakras* need adjusting," she said, grinning at her nude reflection in the bathroom mirror. Her flesh did have a lovely glow – maybe Jason wasn't lying when he called her the sexiest woman in the world.

"I noticed there was an imbalance, but I think I know just how to fix it. Can you meet me tonight?"

"Tell me where. I can be there right away."

In truth, it didn't take long to dress, snag the car keys from Jason's trousers and a few condoms from his bag.

She did pause a moment to gaze at Jason's sleeping body. "We both need recharging. It's a win-win situation, right?" she murmured before she eased the door closed.

Kendra's steps were light as she crossed the terrace in the moonlight. Her instinct told her it was worth the risk. If Jason did find out, he probably wouldn't like it, but he couldn't argue with the fundamentals of her plan.

After all, he was the one who'd taught her to ask for more.

Tube Journey
by Paris Orsini

Springtime on the tube is always a cocktail of heat and lust for me. All those people in skimpy clothes pushed up together, flesh touching flesh. As the weather gets hotter, I do too. The intimacy is overwhelming. Fuck thinking about work, shopping and security scares. I just want to think of this tube turning into a giant orgy: the ultimate decadence of everyone giving in to their own desires on a mundane Monday morning.

Sometimes I stand there just dying to be touched up. Yesterday morning was worse than most. I'd woken too late to enjoy my usual morning Rabbit session so was already feeling frustrated. The bus to the tube station had gone down some particularly bumpy road – a diversion that sent vibrations through me, making my knickers damp – which really didn't help matters. And I had a long journey ahead of me, right across London in the heat and the crush.

I stepped onto the tube and started eyeing people up, casually imagining what they had been doing at the weekend. The prim secretary with her neat hair, neat clothes and neat make-up: I bet she'd been thrashing around for all her worth, screaming and cursing as she received a magnificent fuck from someone who adored her. The spotty teenage boy with a skateboard in his hand had probably wanked himself into a frenzy after his Sunday lunch, locked lonely in his room. I moved my gaze on to more 'inspirational' targets.

What caught my eye this morning was an older city type, well dressed with a kind face but a naughty twinkle. He sat looking bored, casually looking around, presumably thinking about nothing in particular. I stood in front of him, thrusting my pert bottom in his direction, giving him something more interesting to ponder. I heard him shift in his seat and cough. He tried to move his feet further away from mine, an act of politeness. I made sure that he couldn't; I rested the outside of my foot next to his. He smelt freshly showered and clean. My mind started racing and I began to get damp.

In front of me was a much younger guy, probably about 18, undoubtedly thinking about sex. I smiled my sweetest smile at him but he looked away embarrassed. Undeterred I put my hand on the rail overhead, stretching my body upwards, accentuating my tits and making sure he noticed that my braless breasts were pert, with their very prominent, hard nipples showing that I was not a shy girl. He kept glancing but looking away quickly, wanting to look, wanting to touch, wanting me but not wanting to be caught.

By now I was really turning myself on. I wanted both these men to want me, to want to be in me, to feel how hot I was.

The next stop loomed and I was hoping that these guys wouldn't be moving. I wanted them there wanting me, I was horny as hell and they were going to be a part of the show.

The train emptied a bit more, people came and went but, to a certain extent, I was oblivious, I was vaguely aware of a guy standing next to me but my face was concentrated on the boy in front. I stared at his crotch, not caring if he saw me. I leant forward with the movement of the train and touched my stomach; lifting my flimsy T-shirt up slightly so he could see my taut, tanned flesh. I got the response I desired; a significant bulge was beginning to form in his pants.

He shifted in his seat, but couldn't help but look at me. I stared into his eyes and licked my lips. I wanted to know what his cock looked like, felt like, what it would be like to suck it. My heart was beginning to beat faster and I was aware that my breathing was getting louder. I was desperate to be touched, fingered, pawed, anything.

The businessman behind me must have been getting a good view up my skirt. I wasn't wearing anything underneath and the movement of the train would have been giving him glimpses of my tight ass.

I couldn't stand it any longer. I turned and caught him staring up at my legs and ass. He looked shocked and tried to move his legs together to hide his rising cock in his trousers but my foot was in the way. I leant down and whispered in his ear, "Please just touch me". He seemed even more stunned and looked around the carriage to see if anyone else had heard.

I was getting desperate, I was wet and desperate to be filled, and I ached at the thought of what I wanted. My cunt ached, my tits ached; I wanted to be touched and groped. I leant down again, my tits almost touching his face.

"Please touch me, I am wet and just need to be fucked. Please help me."

He broke into a smile but still looked nervous. I gave him a reassuring look and – result – he leaned towards me. The train was rocking from side to side as he slowly started to draw his middle finger from my calf, up the back of my knee, and caress the smooth skin on my thigh. He turned his arm and his whole hand gently grabbed my leg. I caught my breath and the man opposite couldn't help but move. He placed his bag on his lap, moving his hand underneath it. I was soaking now. I was grinning so much to see the control I had over him. He wanted me and, even better, I was exciting him enough that he couldn't resist touching his cock. Some people nearby started staring but didn't say anything. Conversations faltered and I felt eyes burning into me. This just increased my excitement. I wanted more people to see me. I was determined they were going to see me come, that they would want to be the ones fucking me, filling my soaking hole.

I just desperately needed to feel something inside me. Slowly but surely a smooth finger reached the top of my legs and gently stroked my wet lips. I was aching and aching and gripping the pole above my head. This was driving me crazy, he was teasing me and loving it. He knew what I wanted but was making me wait: this stranger was controlling me. I was breathing heavily, not caring what attention I got. I looked directly in front of me and opened my mouth. Talking was difficult but I managed to breathe, "Do you want to suck my tits?"

The 18-year-old looked as if he would explode, and wasted no time in jumping to his feet. His bag dropped on the floor and his hands went straight up my shirt, no discretion, no hesitation – he just grabbed as if it was the first time he had felt tits in his life. Maybe it was … The force of him pushed me backwards and a finger slid hard into my soaking hole. With shock, surprise and sheer lust I couldn't help but scream, not too loudly but enough to gain attention. Now there were lots of eyes on us.

I looked around at some shocked and some excited faces. We came into a station and some people got quickly off the train. Others just stayed rooted and mesmerised at their unexpected show. My hips began to move backwards and forwards. I needed to be filled. I was fucking his fingers and covering them in my thick juice. My T-shirt was half on my head and my tits were getting sucked furiously. I couldn't hold back much longer but needed filling more. I wanted to come with him inside me. As if he read my mind I heard his zipper open, and I reached behind and groaned as I felt his hard cock. Christ, I had to have that right now. He was tall, so getting him in me would be difficult. I was hanging off the rail with both hands. I angled my arse up towards him and put my feet on the edge of the seat. Nothing was going to stop me now. I needed to feel that inside me, thrusting, pulsating. He rolled a condom onto his dick and leant forward and nuzzled my ear. "You are one horny little bitch. I'm going to really enjoy fucking you."

He slipped just the tip inside me and I groaned. "Oh Jesus please just fuck me, fuck me hard," I begged.

He teased me by quickly pushing in and out with the tip. I needed it all. I strained backwards but he was still setting the pace. The whole train carriage was watching us now. I was ecstatic to see people massaging bulges in their trousers, rubbing between their thighs. All those eyes on me, wishing they were the ones who could fuck me like he was doing, pounding into me, bring me to the edge and back again, teasing me.

I pushed my hand down to the guy now sucking my hard nipples as his hand aimed towards my clit. My hand went down

111

his loose trousers and grabbed him. He was sticky and hard; his balls were tight and ready to explode. I tightened my palm around his cock and his hand reached in front to my clit. I was getting closer and closer.

Now the guy fucking me could not just tease me any more. I pushed backwards and his cock rammed up inside me. I was swearing and cursing and desperate for release now. I pleaded to be fucked harder. My hand squeezed the cock in front of me as sensation started to shoot from my clit to my tits. I felt tight and stretched. All around me I could see people straining to see my hole being filled by this muscular cock, sliding in and out, covered in my wet juice. I was starting to scream and cry with frustration. He rammed faster and faster and pinched my hard, hard clit. I felt on fire, my skirt around my waist, my ass thrusting backwards and forwards. The cock in my hand got even harder and I heard a groan as come shot all over my hand. This was more than I could take. My cunt tightened and I began clawing at the guy in front as he screamed his release, then collapsed against the rail, spent, and my orgasm took over my whole body. I screamed as my muscles trembled and flexed with bliss, looking around to see several pricks were shooting their loads into hands and laps around the train. A girl down the carriage was frigging her clit hard and fast and as I looked at her she sighed and came, gripping her seat.

I was being rammed hard and fast now and my legs began to buckle from the strain of standing on the edge of the seat. I reached between my legs and firmly squeezed the businessman's tight balls. Instantly, he cried out and filled me with hot come. Neither of us could move. I was dripping wet and sweaty and his hand was covered in my thick juice. I put my shaking legs on the floor. People around me were rapidly rearranging themselves and looking flushed. The guy opposite was slumped in his seat, sweating.

I turned around, looked at the businessman and saw his now limp prick hanging out of his suit trousers. I hugged him hard and kissed him gently on the cheek just as we pulled into a station. I hitched my shirt back down and rearranged my T-shirt and turned to the door.

I smiled at the carriage, which now contained stunned, wrecked-looking people, wrapped in the scent of sweat and sex.

"Have a nice day at work," I said, and skipped off the train feeling exhausted but supremely satisfied.

Maybe Mondays aren't that bad after all.

Wedding Day
by Jennifer Dark

It was 5 p.m. on his wedding day: a day blistering with heat. He looked around the sloping gardens at his guests, some standing in clusters, a few stretched out on the grass, bottles of champagne beside them, the shimmering afternoon creating a hazy stillness as well as an air of expectation.

The band was setting up at the far end of the marquee, intensity of action and purpose contrasting with the state of his guests – tired from too much excitement, drunk from too much champagne, bloated from too much food. Too much, weddings were too much. He didn't like weddings, and wasn't enjoying today, his own wedding.

He looked over to where his wife was sitting talking with her girlfriends.

"I'll be able to ban his phone now," she was saying, laughing and glancing towards him.

What had he done? She had been determined, her family determined too – pressure from her father, her brother. When was he going to make an honest woman of her? He had never felt so dishonest as when she had announced her pregnancy and his immediate feeling of abject terror had been quickly overcome by a vision of the house his parents-in-law's money would buy; the status being part of her family would provide him with socially and professionally. No, he'd never been more dishonest than when he'd pledged eternal love to his bride, a stranger at the party, knowing no one. Even his own friends knew nothing of his inner thoughts. Once he had promised his wife, he was alone – he had sold his soul and his body.

He looked across to the gazebo, a small building right in the far corner of the gardens, roses climbing up around the door frame. One or two guests were drifting in and out, collecting another glass of Pimms, passing by the chocolate fondue, absent-mindedly picking out a bit of fruit on their way back up the slope from bowls proffered by staff who looked stiff and cool in their black shifts and white pinnies. Cool and unavailable – but strangely fuckable. His cock hardened a little at the thought of fucking a black-shifted be-pinnied waitress, pushing her over behind the gazebo, pulling up her black shift, pushing her panties aside and fucking her from behind.

He daydreamed a little, before downing his glass of champagne, and walking over to the gazebo, feeling himself drawn to a woman there, a woman in a pink dress, standing alone.

By the time he reached the gazebo, she'd taken off her high heeled cream satin shoes and they lay carelessly beside her. She stood calmly, barefoot, slim brown legs shown off by her short pink dress. She was eating strawberries, picking them out, only the strawberries, dipping them in the chocolate and sucking it off with intent. He watched her sucking it off, as much chocolate as she could get on the strawberry, bending over the fondue, licking the strawberry and putting it back in the chocolate: the same strawberry – she didn't know anyone was watching her.

Her dress hugged her figure, scooping under her breasts and around her waist then tied at the back, but to the side a little. It looked like he could pull at the tie: undo it and swirl her out of her pink dress, he wasn't sure.

He leaned against a tree and watched her methodically dip and lick her strawberry. Her dress clung a little below her right breast, there was a hint of sweat perhaps, and her bending showed the line of her bottom, clinging a little to the inside of her left thigh while a waft of breeze moved the material and the tendrils of her hair which had escaped the pile she had scooped lazily up in a tumble of thick blondness on top of her head.

She stood up and smiled as a couple of guests joined her for some fruit dipping. They exchanged a few words, and she laughed with them then picked up her champagne glass, gulping down the remaining dregs, turning as a waitress instantly drifted over to top up her glass.

The woman in pink smiled at the waitress, then glanced around her, and saw him standing against the tree. She smiled at him and looked away. When she turned back and he was there still looking at her, she smiled again.

As he didn't move, she walked towards him, after bending to pick up her shoes. As she walked her dress clung a little to her thighs and he could see the slight mound of her pubic bone with each step because her stomach was so flat.

Her breasts moved just a little and the dress clung more to the left one where her dress was a little damp from sweat. She stopped in front of him and took a mouthful of champagne, then boldly reached up and took his tie in her hand, pulling his face to hers. When he opened his mouth on to hers, she still had champagne in her mouth. It trickled down her chin and onto her neck.

The woman pulled away from his embrace and lifted her face to the sun, thrusting her breasts towards him. She opened her mouth and closed her eyes. He slowly poured his champagne into her open mouth, watching it trickle out of the corners, down her neck and into her cleavage, wetting the material of her dress, making her nipples darken and harden under the coolness of the liquid.

He kept pouring and her dress got wetter, making him stiffen with urgent desire. Moving closer to her, he pressed himself against her and kissed her mouth, slowly, intimately. He explored the inside of her mouth with his tongue, gasping at her responsiveness. She wrapped her tongue around his and sucked on it gently at first, then harder; held it, bit it lightly, sucked again. She pulled away, then returned to kiss him first passionately, then gently, before stopping moving and just holding her lips on his, breathing his breath as the sun beat down on them. He could feel the sweat wet on his back and when he put his hand on the nape of her neck, the hair there was wet too.

They were in full view of the gardens. He moved away from her and she started to walk towards the gazebo again.

116

Following her a little distance away, he watched as she stopped by the table and picked out a piece of fruit – a strawberry again. She pulled off the stalk, dipped it in the chocolate and beckoned to him.

Holding the strawberry dripping with chocolate between her teeth and leaning towards him, it was clear what she wanted. His body gave him no option but to respond by biting on the other side of the fruit, their kiss a mixture of chocolate and strawberry and burning desire. She moaned as she kissed him – a very little moan, but he felt out of control, like he would just fuck her here, on the grass by the gazebo in full view of his wife and his guests, and as he kissed her, it fleetingly occurred to him that if he did that, if he fucked her here that he would be free.

As they kissed, he slid his hand up her thigh, under her pink dress. When he slipped his fingers over her clitoris, sliding his finger under the satin strip of her pants, the fabric was sodden.

She pushed his hand away and turned and walked down the sloping bank that led to the hedge at the edge of the gardens. She clicked the gate open that led into the woods and as soon as they reached the damp dark mossy earth beneath the trees, they almost fell as one to the ground, in a sweaty, champagne-and-desire-sodden tangle of limbs and animal abandon.

They still hadn't exchanged a single word.

He pulled off his trousers, socks and shoes, tore off his shirt, and was naked before her. His hand gripped her thigh, kneading the flesh. His fingers gripped her bottom, exploring, feeling the folds where her thigh slid away into the cheeks of her soft bottom and the wetness of her vagina. His fingers pushed up into her bottom from behind. He pulled at the tie that held her dress together and it loosened, revealing her right breast, naked for him to suck as he thrust into her. He groaned as he slid inside her tight hole; her sodden pants pushed to one side, two of his fingers pushing up into her bottom, a rhythm building in time to her shouts of delight, his muffled moans. Again and again he thrust and fucked, out of control, fleeing his life. She put her hands out and he saw she gripped at the moss, holding herself still as he banged deeper and deeper into

117

her, and her hair tumbled free.

"Stop," she said.

He didn't respond.

"Stop for a minute," she said again.

He heard her this time – and as he had followed her this far, he stopped and they lay together like this. Him on top, breathing hard until a calm came over them and they relaxed together. They remained like this under the dappled light, still feeling the sexual arousal moving all around their bodies and then as the energy started to fade they started again to move together, make love together, fuck hard again, breathing and sweating and moaning and fucking. And then they stopped again and lay together , connected – joined.

Several times they moved and stopped, fucked and lay, her dress wet against her stomach, his hand slipping over her thighs – and after repeating this ritual several times suddenly time suspended – there was no need for anything any more, they seemed to be floating in space – warmth and wetness, mingled with unbounded timelessness and no need for anything other than this moment.

The heat suffused their bodies and her moans grew louder as suddenly her thighs pressed hard against his and she arched her back into him, crying out as her pussy clenched and unclenched, bringing him to the edge of ecstasy and the biggest outpouring of cum he had ever experienced. She moaned and shouted and thrust as he let himself go in a way he never had before, surrendering, releasing himself as he spurted deep inside this woman's body – the woman still in her pink dress whom he'd never met in his life before. The woman whose name he didn't know. The woman who he now knew he could never turn away from.

Dark Horse
by Karen Krizanovich

She was tied naked to the horse, splayed on its bare back, her pussy spread over its wide back, her labia gently crushed open from her weight against it. Wrists tied in front of the horse's neck, she couldn't move or she would slide right off. The horse was too tall for her to dismount to the ground. Besides, she was drowsy, unable to focus. Her head pounded, then cleared.

Nervously, the horse spun around in its stall. It was dark inside the stable and the animal pawed the floor. Large, wide, black and strong, his coat was silky slippery, and the small woman had to use all of her strength to stop from falling down his enormous shoulder.

Clutching her knees on the horse's back, she twisted to move herself away from the animal's withers, which supported all her weight. The position was too close to her clitoris, sending electric sensations through her legs and back. She was in a precarious state, needing to stay on top of the horse lest she end up dragged by it, and having her womanhood ineluctably massaged by the horse's muscular back.

She tried to remain quiet, to stay still. Every move she made, even the smallest, made the horse start and turn, pushing her against her warm, pummelled vulva and sending shivers of near delight up her spine. She couldn't reach the rope that bound her to untie it. If she calmed herself, the horse seemed to lose interest in pacing around the stall, almost clanging her legs against the walls. There was nothing she could grasp, not with hands or feet, which would save her.

Finally, the horse settled and stood, breathing quietly.

Arousal was the last thing she needed. If she came, she was

119

afraid she'd lose her balance. She would slip off, still embracing the horse's neck, and be seriously injured. She was growing wearier and wearier. Her legs, spread wide over the horse's barrel, shook from fatigue.

A noise came from the barn door, making the horse jump slightly. She was caught off guard and as she clung on, unbidden pleasure swept over her. If she'd been in bed, it would have been exquisite, but, as it was her legs gave away their power and she was pressed helplessly against the horse's back. She came and lost control completely, her body convulsing in orgasm. A trickle of drool ran out of her mouth onto the horse's silky mane as she fought her body's betraying spasms. Going limp in overwhelming pleasure, her arms flopped to their tether around the horse's neck. The animal didn't care what was on his back, only that he didn't like it.

A man, fully dressed in evening clothes, came to the barred stall door. He didn't say a word, but watched the horse swing away from him. The man stood and gazed. He smiled. She knew him, from somewhere. The night before. This night.

Not recovering from the shattering, unwelcome orgasm, she could only let gravity hold her onto the horse's back. She could feel her own wetness flooding the horse's back, dampening her seat. She didn't like the man looking at her vulnerable, naked body, but she was helpless.

"Delia," the man said, "it is lovely to see you. You know we were delighted when you came to us last night. You have many fans. But I must warn you that horse is very valuable. He's young and unbroken to ride, which is why he is milling around so. He dislikes being in a stall, which is a bit remiss of me. It's not good for him."

"Why am I here?" she asked, her face muffled in the horse's neck and mane. "What are you doing? How did I end up here?"

"Delia, you don't remember? You don't remember the bet?"

"Bet?"

The horse started – apparently at nothing – and surged towards the man's face at the barred door. He arched his neck and almost threw the woman to the ground, but, haplessly, she gripped her legs at the wrong moment, and rammed her clitoris again against the horse's strong back. She murmured loudly in orgasm, yet again, ashamed of her lack of control, and that she was tied to this living orgasm machine, not knowing when or if she would be freed.

"Delia, you delight me. See? You are enjoying this. I can see how your body changes when you climax. Your back arches, and small tremors go through your legs and arms. It is very nice to watch. In fact, I find it very arousing."

She groaned and tried to stop the waves of pleasure sweeping over her. It wasn't that the horse's back hurt – it didn't – but she was afraid of falling, afraid of its slippery back and afraid of being too tired to hang on. Being in such a position where orgasm was almost inevitable, she was comfortable but also alarmed. Her tiny body was at the mercy of the shape of this animal which cared nothing for her being, only that it was something he did not understand and from which he wanted to flee.

The man watched her. From her face in the horse's mane, she could see him reaching into his trousers, perhaps touching himself as he watched, but his actions were blocked from her view by the stall door.

He smiled and closed his eyes, leaning back somewhat as if to stretch himself.

"Delia, you made a bet at the roulette wheel, my love. You bet everything on black 15. You ran out of money. Don't you remember? Or … did those champagne cocktails perhaps have something else in them?" He smiled, wickedly. He knew what he was saying, and had no seeming concern for her safety.

"Delia, you did promise me anything if I covered your bet … you promised me."

"So you drugged me and strapped me naked to a wild horse?" she howled, sending the horse spinning, milling and stamping in the stall. Gingerly, she balanced on the horse's back, try to keep herself away from giving the man more pleasure at her climax. But, try as she could, she felt the tingling of an oncoming orgasm as her vulva brushed against the silky coat, so smooth it was almost painful. She shifted and the arousal thankfully stopped.

"It was a very large bet, my dear. And I have been wanting you for a long time." The man unlatched the stall door, sending the horse rushing to the back of the stall. "No woman comes to the pleasure garden without knowing what is in store here."

He reached the halter and held the horse's head. The animal calmed and stood as the man ran his hand up the woman's leg, to her thigh, sliding his hands to the moistness between her legs.

"You are ready now – and dawn is breaking," he said, grabbing a rope from the outside of the stall door. "The payment of the rest of your bet awaits you outside. The light is almost with us."

"What do you mean? What? Please stop this …"

"I can't. You made a promise and you owe us what you promised."

He reached up and touched the knot that held her wrists together. "If only you were mine to enjoy, I would untie you now and have you myself. But … there are others who have bet and won – some very large sums – to see you like this."

He clipped the rope onto the stallion's halter and led him carefully through the door.

"Delia, watch your legs," he said, as the horse swerved somewhat. "I promise you nothing will happen, nothing that you didn't agree to. So you must choose – either I turn the horse loose or …"

He went silent, continuing to lead the naked woman, now almost too exhausted from struggling and climax to speak, and the prancing black animal to a large door at the end of the stable.

The dawn chorus had begun. Innocent birds singing in the trees. The smell of dewy grass. The door slid open, pulled on cue, and the crowd of men in evening attire, stepped aside to let the expected trio through.

Pink Champagne
by Laura Godman

When Hannah opened her eyes the first thing they focused on was the bottle of pink champagne on her bedside cabinet. It wasn't just any pink champagne though.

"Oh Chris, this is Krug Rose champagne!" she exclaimed to her husband, who was curled around her in spoons position, one arm propping his head on the pillow, the other slung lazily around her waist. He laughed.

"I know what it is – I bought the bloody thing." Hannah twisted round under the duvet so that she was looking up at him. His overgrown hair was tousled, a few locks sticking out ridiculously, but the sparkle in his eyes betrayed he'd been awake a while.

"But … it's expensive. Christ, have you got money to burn?"

"Yes, to celebrate five years married to most amazing woman alive, I have."

Hannah's heart fluttered as he reached out and stroked her hair, his thumb softly trailing down her cheek as he kissed her on the lips, his tongue slipping just between their plumpness. She responded in kind, sliding her hand across his hips beneath the duvet, but he pulled away.

"So aren't you going to open the bloody thing?"

He leant over to her and grabbed the bottle.

"What, now?" Hannah spluttered. She wasn't a drinks whizz but her granddad had been a bit of a fanatic and she knew a bottle of Krug Rose didn't come cheap – probably somewhere in the region of a hundred quid. She also knew that 9 a.m. on a Saturday, lying in bed in a pokey semi-detached house, was not the usual set of circumstances for cracking open a bottle of the stuff. There was meant to be a snobby waiter and a chandelier involved somewhere, at least!

"Yes Han, now. It's a champagne breakfast." Pulling himself into a sitting position against the headboard, Chris stood the bottle in his duvet-covered lap. It was green with a silver foil-wrapped neck and a pastel pink label framed with silver. "Now pass me those flutes."

Hannah passed him the two crystal-cut flutes that were standing on her bedside table and he caught her eye, smiling wickedly. She couldn't believe Chris – this was mad. Since when did they have the money to splash out on Krug? She watched him as he juggled the flute stems between his fingers and it occurred to her that the most expensive drink she'd ever poured in them had been £5.99 Cava from Tesco.

"Now, are you going to do the honours or are you too wimp to crack open a bottle of £215 Krug?"

"Two-hundred and fifteen?!" Hannah exclaimed wild-eyed as she twisted round to kneel in front of him, the duvet slipping from her body and revealing her creamy-skinned, rosy-peaked breasts. "Chris, you're fucking nuts!"

He chuckled and began unpeeling the silver foil from the bottle's head. Hannah lurched forward. God, if he didn't tear it too much they could sell it on eBay. But Chris wrestled it away from her and finished peeling off the foil, tossing it aside like it was so much tissue paper. Hannah watched helplessly as he set to work on the wire caging. Soon, she realised, with a sense of delicious curiosity, the only thing stopping the cork from its ascent was his thumb pressing down on the top.

"Come here, honey."

Chris motioned to her with his head and Hannah leaned forward.

"Put your hands around the bottle."

She did so and its coldness chilled her fingers. She was close enough to the bottle that her nipples were almost touching the glass body, and they stiffened in anticipation of possible contact and the forthcoming explosion.

"This is for five years together, having great fun, great sex and a great relationship all round," Chris announced. Pointing the bottle to the side, he pulled his thumb away, gently encouraging the cork to launch with an upward push. The cork shot off to God knew where and Hannah couldn't help yelping delightedly at it rocketed into oblivion.

"Quick, Han," Chris laughed as champagne starting frothing out the top of the bottle, fizzing its way back down the outside of the neck. Hannah eagerly lifted the bottle out of his grasp and tipped some of the champagne into each of the flutes. The liquid was a sweet salmon pink and Hannah felt awed as she admired the most expensive drink she'd ever poured.

"Well, don't just stare at it," Chris said and passed her a flute which she accepted with a helpless smile. God, he was gorgeous but, lying in bed, all ruffled, with his bare chest out and clasping a glass of pricey champers, he looked even more devastating.

"To us," said Hannah, chinking her glass against his and watching as tiny sunlit bubbles floated from the bottom to the surface, fizzing out into the air once they reached the top. Instinctively, Hannah and Chris linked arms and took their first sip, eyes holding one another's. Hannah's mouth flooded with fruity flavour and her tongue tingled as bubbles skittered across it. "Oh God, this is lush," she said, gulping some down. Chris mumbled his approval from behind his glass and Hannah took another sip. She spotted Chris watching her with a curious expression that quickly turned blatantly devilish. Then he purposefully took the bottle from her hand and placed it on the bedside table again before sitting back to consider her while stroking the stem of his glass thoughtfully.

"You know, this is really some fine bubbly, but I think it could taste better," he said.

"Christ, it's Krug, Chris. You don't get much better than that. In fact, if my granddad heard you say that he'd have a heart attack." Chris chuckled.

"No, what I mean is, it would taste *that* much sweeter if I were licking it off of your body. Say those delectable breasts of yours." Hannah's head felt light. She wasn't sure if it was the champagne or the excitement of his suggestion, but her pussy tingled in gratifying acknowledgement that she liked Chris's idea too.

"You know, I think you might be right," she replied thoughtfully. Leaning back on one hand she raised her flute above her chest and, after a momentary pause to consider what she was about to do, she dripped some of the pink fluid on herself. A thin stream of pink splashed onto her left breast, quickly rolling a cool path down over her straining nipple. Chris leant forward and intercepted the drip with his tongue, licking all the way upward till it was gone.

"Mm," he murmured, looking up at her, and Hannah lazily dripped some more out, splashing between her breasts this time. Again, Chris was quick to tongue the champagne trail away but afterwards he raised his own glass and poured a considerable amount over the top of Hannah's chest before furiously lapping her skin with his tongue; over her breasts, under her breasts and across her nipples. He sucked first one, then the other nipple and Hannah found herself lazily sipping her champagne as he continued his ministrations, till it was all but gone. When Chris next looked up it was with sheer lust – the kind of expression over the years she'd come to know meant he was absolutely desperate for her.

"God, you look sexy drinking that," he growled. "You look so powerful; so elegant. Like a goddess."

Hannah drained the last of the liquid away and found her pussy throbbing as thoughts of fucking Chris flooded her mind. Fucking him and drinking the Krug at the same time; screwing him slowly from on top; splashing expensive champagne all over his mouth and chest, then licking it off.

"Chris, pour me another glass," she instructed with a new, crisp tone.

Chris obliged, observing her face with excited interest as she watched the glittering fluid crash into the flute base. Then he downed his own measure and poured himself a fresh one before replacing the bottle on the side.

"Lie back," Hannah instructed him and he did so. Hannah pulled the duvet away from the bed, fully exposing them both. Her eyes feasted on his body. Even after all their years

126

together, she still got turned on seeing him naked. His olive skin stretched over moderate muscles – he worked out once or twice a week – and his chest was lightly dusted with hair that tapered down to his bellybutton. Beneath there, a thatch of trimmed dark pubes cushioned his hardened cock, the red crown straining out from under the sheath of his foreskin. Hannah was delighted to see a pearly drop of his come form on the silky surface. Straddling his knees, she bent down and lapped the droplet away with her tongue, before washing its salt flavour down with the sweet champagne – the two tastes blending in an oddly delicious combination. She held Chris' eyes with a determined glint as she finished drinking and he smiled with delight. He knew she was going to go on top. Hannah knew she had a way about her when she was going to dominate – she was more controlled than when he was on top. She became sure of her movements and oddly calm.

Hannah shuffled further up his body, so that his cock rested against her pubic mound.

"This champagne is making me feel light-headed, Chris," she said, trailing a finger down his chest. "It's making me feel a bit … careless."

Suddenly she splashed half her glass of champagne across his chest.

"Oops!" she mock cried and then slowly leant forward so her breasts stroked his chest and his cock was trapped between them. She rubbed her body against his and Chris grabbed her bum with his free hand, pushing her down harder onto his hot member. He grunted as her pussy lips unfolded around his balls, their inner wetness lubricating his sack. Hannah sat back up and reached for the bottle of Krug. She topped her glass up and put the bottle back.

"I'm gonna fuck you, Chris," she announced, lazily drinking from her glass, eyeballing him salaciously. From shoulder height, she poured her champagne onto his cock, then leaned down and took it into her mouth, sucking it heartily. The Krug's delicate flavour was diluted on his thick-veined shaft but still as delicious.

Chris grunted and spread his legs apart so he could feel her hair tickling his balls and inner thighs while she tended to him. Hannah squeezed the base of his cock, his pubes damp beneath her fingers and Chris began jerking his cock upwards, aching to be taken as far into Hannah's mouth as possible. But her body was bubbling for him to be inside of her. She pulled away and quickly straddled him, pressing down on his chest with her hand as she sank onto his hardness. His cock filled her unapologetically, intruding on her softness, and Hannah let her head hang back, her body brazenly arching as she took those first few raw, plummeting motions. Raising her head again she hazily saw Chris's expression was blissful.

"I can't believe I'm drinking fucking Krug for breakfast," she said huskily and Chris's lips curved into a satisfied smile as she began pumping him hard at the thought. She continued drinking her Krug, all the while fucking him, her free hand threaded through his chest hair, tugging it. Chris gripped one of her hips to help guide her up and down his shaft and Hannah poured the last half glass of Krug down the front of her chest. It dripped fast over her right breast and down her stomach, pooling around his cock and her pussy. "Lick me, Chris," she commanded, dropping the glass on the bed so she could pin his arms down beside his head. She dangled her right nipple in front of his lips and he lurched up to suck it, the tug of his lips on her sensitive peak sending fizzing sensations through her breast, down to her pulsing clit.

When Hannah pulled back, Chris's jaw was glistening with Krug. With a smirk, Hannah grabbed his glass from his hand and began drinking it, all the while sinking and rising on his cock. She sloshed some of the champagne on his chest and ran her hands through it. God, she was rubbing £215 champagne into his skin, Hannah realised and giggled before sloshing more over him, leaving the glass dry. She dropped the glass onto the carpeted bedroom floor and reached for the bottle of Krug. Chris, in his growing pleasure, still managed to laugh when he saw her tip it up to her mouth. Hannah found herself giggling woozily too, champagne escaping out of the corner of her mouth. She continued to fuck Chris, slightly losing her rhythm as she guzzled the remainder of the bottle and her head swam.

She briefly stopped to cry out, "I'm drinking fucking £215 Krug!" before she returned to her pumping even more enthusiastically, the taste of the pink champagne thick on her tongue.

Chris used both his hands to guide her hips in their rhythm as she tipped the bottle right up and champagne cascaded down her chin and body, splattering onto her stomach. Dropping the empty bottle onto the bed, she rolled forward so she was pressed up against Chris's chest. Then, her focus was purely on coming. She pumped him furiously with her pussy, their skin sliding together. The fruity scent of champagne seemed to clog Hannah's head and she felt like she was floating on air. Her pussy surged with lust as her clit rubbed against his abdomen. Chris was grunting now, telling Hannah she was a goddess. A beautiful fucking goddess who was going to make him explode.

"Keep fucking me, goddess!" he groaned and she upped her pace until she felt him buck and jerk beneath her, calling out her name. Her swollen clit was hot and heavy as she continued rubbing against him and then her orgasm, thick and rich, cascaded through her in one huge, intoxicating crescendo. She fell against Chris's sticky chest with a sigh, unable to move. Beneath her Chris's chest was still rising and falling in recovery from his climax.

"Oh God, Chris." Hannah murmured. Her breathing was heavy. "I love Krug. We really must … we really must save up for some more." Chris laughed faintly.

"Well, we've got till next year," he replied. "Until then, there's a bottle of Tesco Cava in the kitchen …"

Double Take
by Madeline Moore

Patricia Sheldon was the eldest – by eleven minutes, but that was enough to make her Jeannie's older sister. Just as well, for Patricia went first in everything. She walked first, said "Dada" first and was the first to read. Physically they were identical in every way. Nothing but their personalities distinguished one blonde, blue-eyed twin from the other.

Mrs Sheldon dressed them alike from top to toe. They both wore their wavy hair long, tied with identical ribbons. When they were very little they switched beds and giggled when their hoodwinked father kissed Patricia on the head and said, "Goodnight Jeannie," and then kissed Jean on the head and said, "Goodnight Patty."

Patty loved volleyball but hated maths, so she went to gym class for her sister, who hated volleyball but loved maths, and Jeannie went to maths class for Patty. This way they maintained high marks in everything and were never absent from a class often enough to raise eyebrows.

Mr and Mrs Sheldon took the twins to the Twin Convention in Twinsburg, Ohio every August. The girls loved the event because just being twins didn't invite attention, so they could vie for it like normal people, and be gratified when they got it. They sang duets in the Twin Talent Show and ate up the applause. The whole family looked forward to it.

They rode the float in the Year 2000 parade. A beautiful blond boy sat down beside Patty on the crowded, slow-moving float. "Hi."

"Hi," said a mirror image of the first boy as he sat beside Jeannie.

"Hi," the girls said, and gulped. Where had these two come from? Heaven?

"We're new," said the first, as if reading their thoughts. "We moved to Oregon this year, from Australia. But *you've* been coming to this Convention for years.'

"Uh huh," said Patty. His eyes were green. Green! If there is anything gorgeouser than green eyes and blond hair on a boy, she didn't know what it might be, except green eyes and blond hair on two boys.

"How'd'y'know?" Jeannie asked.

"We looked at the Convention pics online," he said, "and we thought you were the prettiest girls ever."

"Shut up," said his brother, blushing. "We picked you because – you'll never guess–"

"Try and guess our names," interrupted his double.

"I dunno," said Jeannie. She was as tongue-tied as the boy beside her. "Robert and Richard?"

The boys shook their heads. Jeannie twisted her necklace in her hands and shrugged.

"Peter and Paul?" Patty giggled.

The boys kept shaking their heads.

"Thing One and Thing Two?" Jeannie tried.

Gorgeous boy number one stood up. "I'm Gene," he announced. Gorgeous boy number two stood as well. "I'm Pat," he said. Together, they jumped from the float and disappeared into the crowd.

Jeannie sat, blinking, in the sunlight.

Patty grabbed her hand and croaked, "Oh. My. God."

Pat and Gene's carefully planned introduction was a complete success.

What fun the four children had after that! What innocent, sun-dappled, group fun they had that year, no twin giving much thought to which twin she or he was talking, swimming, wrestling or laughing with.

On the very night they met the boys, Patty whispered to Jeannie, "We're going to marry them."

Jeannie wholeheartedly agreed. Every night they'd whisper

into their pillows, "Oh Gene," and "Oh Pat," and then "Oh Pat," and "Oh Gene."

No promises were made that year, but all four understood that they'd see each other again the following August, and the August after that, and so on.

Eventually, gangly preteen boys greeted awkward preteen girls. The next year, tall teenage twin boys greeted girls with curves. And so on. They were fifteen the summer they paired off for the first time, alternating. The first kiss from Gene, for Patty, was fantastic, but so was the second kiss, from Pat, and the same went for Jeannie. One might think the two gregarious twins, Patty and Pat, would naturally be more attracted to each other, and the same with the shy Jeannie and Gene, but then, opposites attract too. So, while Patty loved swimming and playing baseball with Pat and Jeannie loved gaming and tech talking with Gene, Jeannie also loved dancing with light-footed Pat, and Patty loved conversing with knowledgeable Gene. All four of them loved singing in the talent show and the duet times two was a big hit. They got tons of applause and attention and they all loved that, together.

A year is a long time for anyone to wait for a lover, but especially for a teenager. It was easier for Jeannie as she was the more patient of the two girls. Patty was *itching* to have sex. Happily, they agreed on one thing – the more experience they brought to their first time with the twin of choice (whoever that might be) the better.

Patty was particularly impatient to be seventeen, because, as anyone knew, a girl who 'did it' before seventeen was a ho, whereas a girl who was seventeen or older was not.

Of course they'd been dating for a couple of years by the time they achieved non-ho status, but they'd held back, which had not been terribly difficult for Jeannie and not totally impossible for Patty. For at night, along with their muffled moans of "Oh Gene" and "Oh Pat" each was busy beneath her bedclothes. They weren't shy about trading information or technique, but when it came down to actual self-pleasuring, they made sure one of their iPods was docked and playing, to drown out any ecstatic sounds that might escape their mouths in the heat of the moment.

They saw each other naked all the time and certainly they'd compared hair growth and breast growth and, after that, labia and clits and nipples, but they didn't take it any further. They weren't interested in girls in that way, especially not in each other. So their exchange of information was mostly verbal, and usually travelled one way, from Patty to Jeannie.

"God, his French kissing was gross," Patty'd say as she and her sister huddled on one of their beds for their customary postdate chats. "Look at these hickeys!" She'd show Jeannie the ring of dark bruises at her neck. "I'll be wearing a turtleneck for a week."

The next week, Jeannie would make a point of frenching her current boy, just so she could report back to her sister, "He's pretty talented with his tongue." She'd show off her hickey (never more than one) with shy pride.

They were seventeen in August, after, sadly, the convention. In short order, little sister Jeannie was most definitely left behind once more.

"I did it," said Patty, triumphantly. Her face was flushed.

"Tell me," was all Jeannie said.

"We went to Jason's place. His parents were going to be out really late and his bratty little brother was staying at their aunt's. We ate pizza in the rec room, like we always do, only he had a bottle of sparkling wine so we had a glass each, and started watching the horror channel."

"Oh Christ!" muttered Jeannie. She couldn't stand scary movies.

"So I was screaming and hiding my face in his shoulder, like always, and we started necking, like always, and he put his hand under my shirt –"

"Like always," said Jeannie.

"Like *sometimes*," corrected Patty. "I pulled away, which surprised him. He was going to say something but I started unbuttoning my blouse. He shut up and watched. I unbuttoned it completely and took it off. Like so." She unbuttoned her blouse slowly, batting her lashes at her sister, and let it slide off her shoulders, revealing a skimpy satin bra.

"My bra!" Jeannie pretended to be scandalized but Patty wasn't fooled.

"I slid one strap down my arm," she said, demonstrating, "and then the other and I reached behind and unsnapped it and took it off."

"God, you're so brave."

"I have great tits. It's a fact."

"Me too."

"Of course." Patty continued. "Jason put his hands on my breasts and gently pushed me back until I was lying on the couch, and then he leaned over me and licked my nipples. It was terrific!"

"For how long?"

"I don't know. He went back and forth, and when he was licking one he'd twirl the other one between his fingers. My nipples were hard and pinker than usual."

"They still are," said Jeannie.

"God, you're right," said Patty, glancing down at her chest. "Show me yours."

Jeannie tugged down the neck of her nightie. The sisters appraised each other's chests. Jeannie's nipples were soft and pink, while Patty's were taut, swollen and scarlet.

"Neat," said Jeannie. She released the elastic neckline of her nightie. It sprang back into place. "Go on."

"He took off his shirt and lay on top of me. His skin was hot. He adjusted himself, inside his pants, and then popped the button of my jeans and slid his hand down, under my thong. I was so wet, Twinnie! As soon as his fingers touched my cunt I felt a twinge, almost like a shock, in my clit. I knew right then we were going all the way. I had to have it."

"Wow," said Jeannie. She was so taken by the tale she didn't bother to admonish her sister for her crude vernacular (Jeannie found the word "pussy" more pleasing).

"Yeah. I let him take my jeans off and he got between my legs, still in his pants, and started dry humping me. I swear I could've come but I didn't want to, and I told him so. Of course he thought I was protesting but I said, 'Take me to your room,' and he did. What a kick, moving through the living room, naked, with him in only his unbuttoned pants, the tip of his cock poking out the top. It was like being on a movie set or something. It felt dangerous and exciting, like those moments right before the serial killer leaps out and murders the teenage lovers."

Patty stood up and took off her jeans and panties, then tip-toed around their bedroom, her eyes wide with wonder. "I kept looking, from left to right, even as we went up the stairs. Then we were in his room. Jason dropped his pants. His hard-on was huge."

"How big?"

Patty measured out a span with her hands. "Six and a half, maybe seven. Big enough. I probably went pale at the sight of it. But he was cool, he really was. He put a towel down on the bed, in case I bled, and took a condom from his bedside table, and put it on."

"God, that is *so* cool.'

"Oh he'd done it before, that's for sure. I was sitting on the bed, watching, and he came and pushed me back. He bent his knees a bit. I knew he was going to do me, just like that, and I was keen. It was like all the heavy petting we'd done for the last few weeks had just that minute happened and I was totally psyched. I spread my legs a little wider and he slid into me, half-way, then jerked his hips so hard I felt his balls slap against me, just below my cunt."

"Did it hurt?"

"Not much. I liked it."

"Did you bleed?"

"No, but I'm not surprised. I think we both lost our hymens at that Wild West Riding Camp, don't you?"

"Probably." Jeannie nodded gravely. Whatever jealousy she felt about her sister vaulting ahead, experience-wise, was more than equalled by the relief that washed over her with the outpouring of her sister's story. Jeannie liked to go into things informed and once again Patty was a fount of information.

"He went slowly, at first, pushing all the way inside me, then pulling back even slower. He was grinning like I'd never seen him do before, a huge grin, and his eyes were half-closed.

He looked the handsomest I've ever seen him, and you know what that means …"

"Gene and Pat will be totally to die for."

"Right. Because they are, like, so gorgeous already. But Jason was terrific. We got a rhythm going and he sucked his thumb to make it wet and then diddled my clit until I was crazy, totally crazy! I was trying not to make much noise but he said, 'Go ahead, scream all you want. No one can hear you.'"

Jeannie shivered. "That sounds sort of threatening."

"I know! But he said in a really soothing way. So it was reassuring and threatening at the same time. I loved it!" Patty's eyes shone. "He kissed my mouth, and my nipples, and he put his thumb in my mouth and I sucked it wet and he put it back on my clit and I started coming. It was fantastic, having something inside me to come against, or, I guess, around. With each contraction it was like I was clamping onto a big hot hard…"

"Prick?" Jeannie offered.

"Cock! And as soon as I began coming, Twinnie, I started yelling, all kinds of stuff, like his name and then 'God' and then 'Fucking Jesus Christ!' I didn't know what I was saying, not really, but it didn't matter, it just felt good, like some of the pressure was coming out of my mouth while the rest of it was being released through my cunt. I dug my nails into his shoulders. He came then, too, but he just groaned, no words or anything. We cuddled. It was good there was a towel on the bed because I'd scratched him so hard with my nails he was bleeding."

"Wow."

"He didn't complain. I think he liked it. We said some sweet things to each other and then we did it again. It was way better than masturbation or dry-humping or anything. You've gotta do it."

"Yeah," muttered Jeannie. "I do. But with who?"

Patty shrugged. "Why not with Jason? He's really good."

Jeannie shrieked. "Aren't you in love with him?"

It was Patty's turn to shriek. "Of course not. I'm in love

136

with Pat. Or maybe Gene."

"Me too," said Jeannie. The girls doubled over with laughter, and then, at the sound of grumpy footsteps approaching, they dove under their covers, one in her nightie and the other naked, and feigned sleep when their dad stuck his head in their door and, unfooled by their angelic faces, grumbled, "Go to sleep."

Jason was the first time Jeannie and Patty shared a man, but it wasn't to be the last. Patty usually went first, weeding out the duds, and Jeannie always went last, dumping the boys with no tears and an ear deaf to their protests, but since they pretended only one of them was ever with any one boy, neither acquired the bad reputation they both deserved.

The next summer, arriving at the Twin Convention was a big event for the girls. They came without their parents for the first time, and they fully intended to fuck Pat and Gene, as soon as they decided who would be fucking whom. It was Jeannie who insisted they not share the twin blonds of their affection. They discussed it for most of the drive.

"These are our husbands-to-be," Jeannie admonished her sister, and when Patty protested that as such they *ought* to sample both boys each before making up their minds, Jeannie put her foot down. "Absolutely not," she said. "I will always be faithful to my husband."

They both loved Gene and Pat and were sure the twin boys loved them, too, and equally. But choices needed to be made, and soon, as the car was fast approaching Twin City.

Jeannie made the final decision. "It's best you go with Gene and I go with Pat," she said.

Patty was surprised. She'd been sure her sister would go for the quiet one, but Jeannie's reasoning was sound.

"Gene will steady you and Pat will challenge me," she said. "I think that's better for long-term relationships. Also, we're more likely to do stuff together, as we get older, if we share each others' interests."

Patty could see her point, but the biggest reason she agreed to the match was what Jeannie said next.

"This way," said Jeannie, "There will always be a Gene and a Pat and a Pat and a Jean." The symmetry was neat.

Twins greeted twins with customary enthusiasm. In fact, the boys glowed with a new intensity that the girls took for lust. They were disabused of this notion during the opening night barbeque.

The four of them sat at the end of one long table, under the same massive white tent that sheltered the throng of hungry duplicate diners every year. The food was great, as always. But something had definitely shifted.

"We've taken the Celibacy Vow," said Gene.

"Christ!" Patty dropped her fork on her plate.

Jeannie covered Patty's hand with hers. "Go on." She spoke with admirable calm.

The girls had always known that Pat and Gene were religious. It hadn't mattered, until now, that the boys were and the girls were not.

"It's simple. No sex until marriage." Pat shrugged.

"But ..." stammered Patty, "we had plans!"

"So do we," said Gene. "We want you to be our first. And our only."

"We hope you want the same," said Pat.

"Oh we do," said Jeannie, quickly, before her sister could betray them with her frankness. Her hand on Patty's tightened. "Now that we're almost eighteen, well, we were hoping it would happen soon."

"It will," said Pat. He knelt by Jeannie's wooden chair. He produced a blue velvet ring box from the pocket of his khaki shorts and opened it, displaying a solitaire diamond, small but not tiny, set in gold. "Jeannie? Will you marry me?"

Gene knelt at Patty's side. He too produced a blue velvet box within which nestled a ring, identical to the one Pat held in his hand. "Patty," said Gene, "will you marry me?"

"Yes!" the giddy girls replied in unison.

That night, in their room, Patty and Jeannie couldn't sleep, and who could blame them? They'd spent the evening making out like maniacs with their respective fiancés and hadn't said goodnight until the wee hours. They fell, exhausted, into their beds, but whenever one managed to doze off, she'd be awakened by the other, shouting, "I can't believe it!"

It hadn't actually occurred to them that the boys might decide between themselves who would marry whom. What luck! And look at the way the diamonds sparkled in the light! The bedside table lamp would be switched on and the sleepy twin would suddenly be wide awake, more than eager to thrust her left hand into the glow from the lamp and admire her sparkling ring, and her sister's sparkling ring, and join in her sister's joy with exclamations of her own.

The two sets of twins announced their engagements at the conclusion of their rendition of *My Heart Will Go On* at the annual Talent Contest. The crowd went wild. The applause was thundering. An encore was demanded, and since they hadn't prepared one, they sang the same song again, to more deafening applause. They won first prize.

It was a double wedding, of course, in the girls' hometown. They were young for marriage, but neither set of parents could argue the rightness of the union. The girls wore identical dresses, though Patty's was sashed with blue satin and Jeannie's with pink. After all, they didn't want to marry the wrong guys by mistake! The grooms wore matching black tuxedoes but Gene's boutonnière was blue and Pat's was pink. It was a winter wedding, February 14, in fact. Immediately following the reception, the happy couples boarded a plane for Barbados. Immediately upon disembarking, the happy couples disappeared into their bridal suites, and neither made an appearance the next day, or even the next.

On the third day they emerged, all fucked out and ready for some fun in the sun. The boys wasted no time hitting the surf. The girls stretched out in their deck chairs to chat.

"Do me," said Pat. She held out a bottle of suntan lotion and dropped the straps of her blue bikini.

"Didn't your husband?" Jeannie giggled as she slathered lotion on her sister's shoulders.

"Oh God. Gene's good. Really, really good." Patty sighed contentedly.

"So is Pat," said Jeannie. "What he lacks in experience,"

139

she whispered, "he makes up for in enthusiasm. Well worth waiting for."

"Well, mine claims I'm his first but if it's really true, he sure did a lot of research. When we couldn't fuck any more he ate me out until I begged him to stop."

"But you love oral! It's me who gets bored with it," said Jeannie.

"I couldn't stand another orgasm."

Jeannie rolled her eyes. "Did you do anal?'

"Yes, did you?"

"Yes."

The girls had decided that, since they weren't actually virginal brides, they would remain celibate for the duration of their engagements *and* save their bums for their husbands. In this way they successfully assuaged any guilt they had about their sexual histories.

"And?" Patty cocked her head at her sister.

Jeannie thrust the lotion in her sister's hands. "Do me," she said. She dropped the straps of her pink bikini.

"Tell me! Did you like it?"

"I found it humiliating and degrading," mumbled Jeannie.

"So you loved it."

"Yup." Jeannie giggled.

"I thought it was OK."

"Well, I think it's my favourite," announced Jeannie.

They hooted in unison.

"This is heaven. I wish we could stay here for ever." Patty stretched and sighed contentedly.

"I know exactly what you mean," said Jeannie.

Once Fall came, all four of them would be attending SFU, living in student housing townhouses. That was all arranged. But until then, once the honeymoon was over, Jeannie would move into Pat's apartment, which was in Oregon, where he worked as a lifeguard. And Patty would move into Gene's apartment, which was in Texas, where he worked as a junior programmer. For the first time in their lives, the girls would be separated.

"Pass me your hat," said Patty, "I forgot mine."

As Jeannie passed her sister her straw hat, their fingertips touched.

Jeannie whispered, "Twinnie, I'm scared."

"Sssh," said Patty. "We have ten days left in paradise."

"We've never been apart."

"It's only for a few months."

"A few?" Jeannie's voice squeaked. "Six! Half a year!"

"Christ this sun is hot." Patty dragged a beach towel over her body, up to her chin. "I'm going to sleep."

"Fine. Be in denial. You'll miss me as much as I'll miss you when the time comes."

Jeannie flipped through a magazine for a few minutes, but the sight of her sister peacefully snoozing in the sun was so appealing she soon closed her eyes to join her. Just before she drifted off she pulled a towel over her body, too. The last thing either of them needed was the kind of tropical sunburn that would put an end to honeymoon sex.

Patty was awakened by soft lips pressed to hers. She responded enthusiastically. When a hand slipped under the towel to cup her breast she arched her back, pushing her hot nipple into his hand, cool and wet from the ocean. The kiss deepened. The towel fell.

"Hey!"

Patty opened her eyes to a surprised, red-faced boy in hot pink and black trunks backing away from her.

"Your hat," he sputtered. "The band is pink."

Patty glanced at her sister. Patty's husband Gene, in blue and black trunks, was backing away from Jeannie, who sat up, shocked, and met her sister's eyes.

"Get away from my wife!"

"You get away from my wife!"

The brothers pushed each other, hard, then started wrestling in the sand.

"It's my fault! I borrowed Jeannie's hat!" Patty's heart was pounding in her ears. The situation had to be diffused before tension could threaten the twins' idyllic vacation. That must be why her pulse pounded in her ears, and elsewhere, too. It couldn't be from Pat's kiss. Could it?

141

"Stop it, you guys!" Jeannie jumped to her feet. "It was an honest mistake. Anyway, we've all kissed before, remember?"

The men ceased wrestling to consider this. They cut a fine sight, their blond hair shining in the sun, their wet bodies, sculpted if not yet tanned, patched in places with glistening white sand.

"True," allowed Pat.

"But we weren't married then," said Gene.

"Yeah," said Pat.

The men resumed wrestling, this time laughing instead of hurling insults.

Patty threw Jeannie's pink-sashed straw hat to her. "I'll try not to forget mine again," she mumbled.

Jeannie couldn't take her eyes off the young men wrestling in the sun. "That would be best," she said. "I think."

The couples settled into a routine of sorts. After an early breakfast the girls would recline on deck chairs close to the surf, where they could tan, chat and watch their men cavort in the sea. In the afternoon they split off, sometimes to their respective suites for siesta and sex, or to take in the sights. They usually congregated with the rest of the hotel guests to watch the sunset, then returned to their rooms to rest and dress for the evening. Cocktails were followed by a buffet dinner, and then they'd dance under the stars or in a disco. After that came long, adventurous nights of passionate lovemaking.

"Gene is the best lover I've ever had," sighed Patty one morning.

"Me too," sighed Jeannie.

They both giggled.

"I mean, Pat is the best lover I've ever had," Jeannie amended.

Another morning, Patty said, "Gene is really hung. I suppose Pat is the same?"

"Should we be talking like this? They are our husbands, after all." Jeannie glanced out to sea. It was a windy day and Pat was teaching his brother to surf.

"They can't hear us. Anyway, they probably talk about us."

"You think?"

"No," said Patty. She laughed. "So, is he? Pat? Is he hung?"

"Like a horse," said Jeannie.

Their talk wasn't always so explicit. One morning, Jeannie initiated a conversation of another kind, by saying, "Do you think they're our best lovers because we're in love?"

"It's hard to say. Gene is a very skilled lover, and getting more skilled by the day. He takes lovemaking seriously. Speaking objectively, he's a great fuck."

"But are you? Objective? How can you..?" Jeannie dropped her voice to a whisper, as she always did when she talked about their past. "After all, we've each had the same lovers, for the most part, yet we both insist our husbands are the best."

"Our lovers never noticed when we swapped around. Maybe identical twins are identical in bed," said Patty.

"But we planned it that way. We swapped notes to make sure we didn't give ourselves away. Surely we aren't really the same, sexually?"

"I'm multi-orgasmic."

"Me too."

"Gene can get it up again, and again, and again, in the same day."

"So can Pat."

"He roars when he comes."

"Pat's noisy too."

They fell into a contemplative silence.

"We could always swap hats and find out," suggested Patty with a grin.

"You wouldn't! These are our husbands we're talking about!"

"Of course I wouldn't," said Patty.

"Of course not," said Jeannie. She stood. "I'm going for a swim. I'm hot." As she hot-footed toward the turquoise sea, the sound of her sister's knowing chortle followed her across the sand.

On the last full day of their holiday Pat and Patty went parasailing. Gene and Jeannie watched, hearts in their mouths, as their spouses sailed across the sky like big, colourful bats.

"If he dies, I'll kill him," said Jeannie. "And her."

"Ditto," grumbled Gene. "We can attend their funerals together."

Jeannie grinned. "Deal."

"He always has to show me up," grumbled Gene. "I go scuba diving, snorkelling and learn to surf so what happens? He has to go parasailing."

"So? You can parse code like nobody's business. It's just the way he is. The way they are." Jeannie put her hand on his shoulder. "It's fine."

"They're coming down," said Gene. His brother and his bride landed in the sea.

Jeannie didn't realize she was clutching his muscular arm until she saw her twin and her husband bobbing in the water, laughing and sputtering. Then she quickly let go.

Most of the rest of that day was taken up with last minute activities, but the two couples met at sunset for pina coladas and pictures. Jeannie was quiet, which wasn't unusual, but her sister was too.

The boys had often been apart, but they were respectful of the separation anxiety that afflicted their brides. The girls stood, shoulder to shoulder, as the orange fireball slid down the sky and drowned in the sea.

"More drinks?" Pat's solution to sadness was spirits. On this occasion, Gene didn't argue. Both girls nodded.

When their men had gone to get refreshments, wet blue eyes met wet blue eyes.

"I'm not sure I can do it, be away from you for so long," said Jeannie.

"Me too."

"We could make a pact –"

"We've already done that, Twinnie. We've done everything we can to keep what we have. You know that, Jeannie."

"Not everything," said Jeannie. Her eyes twinkled, made extra bright by unshed tears.

"Hmmm. Tonight's the night, is it?"

"Yes."

"No bra, white thong, white peep toes with kitten heels, pink chiffon strapless. I'll wear the same, no bra, white thong, white shoes and blue chiffon strapless. We swap dresses at dinner. Deal?"

"Deal."

And that, as they say, is exactly how the deal went down.

It'd been a while since Jeannie had played at being extraverted Patty, but she hadn't lost her chops. When Gene stripped her of the blue dress she'd exchanged with her twin for her pink one, she remembered to arch her back and pose for him, just as Patty might do. When he peeled off his white tee and dropped his blue shorts to his feet, she saw he was identical to his brother, right down to the fair, sparse down on his balls. Certainly, his cock was every bit as impressive and as rock solid as her husband's.

His lips on hers were soft, and his tongue, as it tasted her lips and then her mouth, was luscious and questing, so like Pat's, so familiar, but not Pat's, so different. She was excited, and secretly shamed by how extra wet her pussy was when his tongue slid along her slit, in agonizingly slow strokes, and then dipped inside. He moaned. She felt it more than heard it, a low, deep exhalation that warmed her inside and out.

"I love it when you lick my – um, my cunt," she said.

"Then I'll eat you until you can't come any more," he said.

Inwardly, she groaned at the idea. But as he laved and nibbled and sucked her to one orgasm after another, Jeannie groaned out loud, with gusto.

In the other bridal suite, Pat rolled Patty onto her belly. They were both naked and highly aroused from foreplay.

"I want your ass, Jeannie," he said. "I know how much you love it."

Patty shivered. Who'd have thought her fearful sister would've embraced this dirty act with such gusto? Still, she wasn't about to be found out and so, though anal wasn't *her* favourite, she giggled with delight and parted her legs wider, to welcome him.

She hoped he'd take his time but he lubed his cock and leant close, rubbing the head up and down her crack until it 'caught'

145

at her back entrance.

"You want it?" he asked.

"I want it."

"Tell me."

"I want it." Patty paused, then added, "A lot."

"What do you want? Tell me. You know I like to hear you talk dirty."

"I want your –um – prick in me, in my bum, in deep."

"Me too! I love to do your bum Jeannie." He leant in, pushing his way slowly inside her until she was full to the hilt with him.

"Do it," he said. "Do it like you know I like it."

Oops! Jeannie hadn't told her about this. He liked something that her sister did, something special, when he fucked her ass. Damn!

"If you aren't in the mood to do it that way, that's OK."

She was off the hook if she screwed up. Patty'd only had anal sex once with Gene and that had been pretty straightforward, so to speak. But she thought she could guess what her sister might do that was so special. After all, how can a girl do much of anything different when a man's weight is crushing her? What she did for Gene was the only way she could think of. She said, her voice husky, "Lift up, then."

He raised himself onto straight stiff arms and the tips of his toes.

"Are you ready?" she asked.

"Ready!"

Rotating her hips clockwise, she pushed up at him, skewering herself on his rigid flesh until the wet lips of her cunt kissed his dangling balls. She paused, then sank down again, rotating counterclockwise, until only the head of his cock was still trapped inside her.

"Oh fuck!" he groaned, "fucking fantastic."

She was surprised at the thrill that travelled her body at the sound of his breathless praise. Surprised and inspired. After she'd raised and lowered herself half a dozen times, undulating each time the obscenely split globes of her ass made contact with crotch, his lust seemed to take him over. He pushed her flat and pounded into her, fast and furious. The sex seemed to teeter on the very brink of craziness. Whether it was the taboo nature of the act itself or the depth of the sensations it created, she didn't know, but Patty was seized with a desperate need to come. She managed to slide her hand down between her body and the bed and rub her clit so that, a mere moment later, when Pat began to roar and jerk in ecstasy, Patty was ecstatic, too.

The next morning, the girls met in the pool's changing rooms and switched bikinis, so that Jeannie was once more in pink; Patty in blue.

They settled in their customary chairs by the ocean to wait for their men.

Jeannie said, "You were right about your husband." She pouted. "He is better in bed than mine, dammit! Not bigger, mind you, but, better. He ate me until I screamed for mercy.'

"Funny," said Patty, "because I was about to tell you the same thing. Your Pat is a dynamo, Twinnie. He fucked my ass like there was no tomorrow. It was so exciting! I have to apologise though."

"Why's that?"

"By the time he flipped me over and fucked my cunt – but I called it my pussy, don't worry – I was so out of my mind I raked my nails down his back. He's got marks."

"Oh well, they'll fade. Here they come!"

The girls watched their young husbands approach. Pat wore trunks and a white tee, and Gene was dressed similarly, though, as usual, his trunks had a blue streak on them, while Pat's had a flash of pink. As they neared their wives they stripped off their tees, rolled them into balls, and tossed them to the sand. Together, the boys dashed into the ocean for a final swim before departing the island.

"What the –" Jeannie's grin morphed into an open-mouthed expression of astonishment.

"Oh. My. God." Patty's face mirrored her sister's. For it wasn't Patrick's back that bore the mark of Patty's ardour – it was Gene's. Which could only mean one thing.

It seemed twins – at least these two pairs of twins – really do think alike.

Sculpted To Perfection
by Elizabeth Coldwell

"You're staring at my arse," he said.

I turned, startled. After all, it's not what you expect to hear from someone who is standing behind you. I looked from the tall, dark-haired man in the expensive-looking suit to the sculpture I had been admiring and back again.

"That's you?" I asked.

"Yeah." He laughed. "Well, part of me, anyway."

Cast in bronze, the sculpture was of a man's torso – this man's torso, as it appeared – and I had been drawn by the way the artist had captured the muscularity of his back and his exquisite, taut buttocks. It was one of half-a-dozen similar pieces which adorned the room, but it was by far my favourite.

"I never thought I'd end up posing for something like this," he said, "but apparently the sculptor saw me playing in a match and said he just had to immortalise my body, if you can believe it." A waitress was wandering past, clad in a black and red brocade corset, fishnet stockings and sequinned domino mask. My new friend helped himself to a couple of champagne flutes from her tray and passed one to me. "I'm Gary, by the way. Gary Collier." From the way he said it, he seemed to expect me to recognise the name, but apart from realising that he was a sportsman of some kind, I didn't have a clue who he was.

"Marianne," I told him.

He took a sip of his champagne. "You know, it's great to meet someone who doesn't ask me whether I think we're going to win the league this year, or ask me about that goal I scored against Everton." So he was a footballer. No wonder I didn't recognise him. Football was something which had kept my ex-

148

boyfriend occupied on all the Saturday mornings when he played for his best mate's five-a-side team, and all the Sunday afternoons, Monday nights and whenever else there was a match on television. In fact, it was quite a large part of the reason he was my ex-boyfriend – not that I wanted to think about him just now.

"So how do you know Bella, anyway?" Gary asked, referring to our hostess.

"To be honest, I don't," I told him. "I've got a couple of her CDs, but that's about it. My friend, Kelly, was one of the backing dancers on her last tour. I house-sat for her while she was in the States, and she got me an invitation to the party to say thank you." I looked round the room. "Kelly told me to expect something special, but I have to say I've never seen anything like this."

Everyone knew the launch parties Bella Capaldi threw for her albums were legendary in their extravagance. For the last one, *Three-Ring Circus*, she'd had a big top erected in the middle of Hyde Park and hired trapeze artists, fire-eaters and contortionists to entertain the hundreds of guests she had invited. Her latest album was titled *In The Boudoir*, and the surroundings Gary and I found ourselves in were suitably decadent. What was normally a rehearsal studio in west London had been completely transformed, with swathes of gold and purple fabric and thick velvet drapes separating large rooms into small, intimate spaces. Guests lounged on antique chaises longues while masked waitresses dressed in designer lingerie plied them with pink champagne and cocktail blinis topped with sour cream and caviar. As well as the sculptures, the walls were decorated with Eastern-influenced prints of lovers entwined in impossibly athletic positions. It must have cost a fortune to put together, but then Bella Capaldi's latest single had gone straight to the top of the download charts and tickets for her tour had sold out within 17 minutes of going on sale. Money was hardly an issue for her, or her record company.

There was no sign of Bella herself, but Kelly had told me that from past experience she didn't usually make an appearance until midnight, when she would entertain the guests with a couple of songs from the album she was promoting and then have lavish goody bags handed out to everyone. I was already starstuck as it was, having spotted a couple of soap stars and a well-known TV newsreader among the throng. And now I was standing talking to a handsome footballer and trying not to wonder whether the body beneath his suit was as beautifully put together as his sculpture appeared to suggest.

I heard shrieks of laughter and looked over to where a couple were settling down on one of the antique couches. They had a plate of exotic fruits and marshmallows dipped in melted chocolate, and as I watched, they began to feed each other succulent slices of kiwi and mango. That looked like fun, I thought, wondering whether I could persuade Gary to join me in a visit to the chocolate fountain. I could just imagine how it would feel to guide slivers of strawberry between his lips, and let him lick the dribbles of chocolate from my fingers.

However, he obviously had other ideas. As the giggling of the woman on the couch took on a lower and more intimate tone, he said, "Why don't we find somewhere a little quieter, so we can hear each other talk?" As he guided me away from the sculpture, I felt the gentle pressure of his hand in the small of my back. We'd barely known each other for five minutes and he was already finding excuses to touch me, which I took as a promising sign.

Knots of people were gossiping, accepting food and fresh drinks from the trays of passing waitresses or standing round a podium where a lithe, olive-skinned dancer in a bejewelled bikini was letting a python writhe sinuously around her shoulders. I wasn't sure quite how she fitted in with the boudoir theme, but I was still tempted to stand and watch her for a moment as the snake's tongue flickered out at the audience.

"Come on, let's go." I glanced back at Gary and saw that while I hadn't been paying attention, he had somehow managed to liberate a half-full bottle of champagne, which he clutched round the neck. Clever boy, I thought, and let him steer me through the room.

Pulling aside a burgundy-coloured curtain, we found ourselves in a small room which was dominated by a statue of a naked man holding a spear. "This looks perfect," Gary said, leading me over to the low couch which was the only piece of furniture in the room. The music and chatter were muffled here, and as I sat down, I took the opportunity to kick off my strappy sandals and make myself comfortable.

Gary looked over at the statue. "They never have much to write home about, do they?" he commented, and I realised he was referring to its small, neat cock and balls.

"That was how the Greeks liked them," I said, remembering something I had once been taught in a long-ago art lesson.

"They wouldn't have liked me very much, then," he replied, flashing me a wicked grin.

"So did we really come here to talk?" I asked. "Because I don't particularly want to hear about football, and I'm sure you don't particularly want to hear about all the house-sitting and dog-walking I do to make ends meet.'

Gary held his hands up in mock-surrender. "Busted!" he exclaimed. "Yeah, fair enough. You're right. What I really wanted to do was this–" And he leaned close and put his lips to mine.

My mouth opened without prompting and I returned the kiss, tasting a vague hint of champagne. As our bodies pressed together, I couldn't resist reaching down and tracing the contours of his cock through his trousers; it felt long and thick, already excited. Gary's hands were fumbling for the zip of my dress, which I had borrowed from Kelly for the evening; it was a tight, one-shouldered style, something I would never normally have considered wearing but which she had assured me was perfect for the event, and it was easy for Gary to push that one shoulder strap down and expose my bare tits.

"Lovely," he murmured, and started to suck my nipples. It felt so deliciously naughty to be pleasured in this way, to lie half-naked with a party going on just the other side of a velvet curtain. What would happen if someone were to push their way in here, looking for some privacy of their own? The thought of being watched seemed to rack my excitement up a notch, and I decided it was time to assert some control.

I pulled away from Gary's embrace and sprawled back on the couch. "Strip for me," I ordered him. He smiled, and shrugged out of his jacket. As the rest of his clothes followed, I took the opportunity to admire him, teasing my pussy gently through my knickers as I did. He was mouth-watering; muscular without being bulky, and he had a light golden tan. When he was down to his boxer shorts, he made me wait for a long moment before he took them off. Laughing at my pout of disappointment, he turned his back to me and slowly lowered them, giving me the view the sculptor had recreated so faithfully. Finally, he stepped out of his underwear and turned round again, revealing a cock that was already half-hard.

"Now you," he said, and knelt down between my legs to pull my knickers off. They were disgracefully wet by now, and he breathed my scent from them before dropping them into the pile of discarded clothing on the floor.

Still kneeling, he buried his head in my crotch, tongue tracing the folds of my pussy and flicking at my clit. The slight stubble on his cheeks brushed against my thighs, tickling them. I sighed, luxuriating in the glorious sensations of being thoroughly licked out. Suddenly, I heard laughter and raised voices, and my eyelids flew open. Had we been discovered? I looked round, but the conversation was fading away as the unknown guests walked past our little hidey-hole. And then I looked again, more closely, at something very bizarre on the other side of the room. The statue of the naked spear-carrier was directly opposite us, but it had changed noticeably since Gary and I had come in. The small, sleeping cock which Gary had pointed out so scornfully was small and sleeping no longer. It now stood proud, with a fat, glistening red head in contrast to what we had both assumed was white stone, but was clearly body paint.

"Gary," I whispered, "you need to see this."

Gary raised his head, my juices glazing his lips and chin. "What?"

I gestured with my finger and his gaze followed. He realised as quickly as I had that we'd had an audience all the time we had been in here; an audience which was clearly turned on by what we were doing.

"Okay, mate, get down off the plinth," Gary ordered. The statue did as it was told, looking at the two of us sheepishly.

"I'm sorry," he said. "I couldn't help it. They hired me to stand here and hold a spear all evening, so I couldn't exactly walk away when you started – you know … And I have to say this," he added, looking at me, "you've got such great tits anyone would get excited. I'm not in any trouble, am I?"

"What's your name?" I asked him.

"Matt," the statue said.

"No, Matt, you're not in any trouble," I replied, "but there is one thing I want you to do for me."

"Anything," he said, "just name it."

"Come over here and join us." Both Matt and Gary looked at me, startled, and then Gary started laughing as Matt practically snapped his spear in half in his haste to do as I asked.

My dress was still rucked up round my waist, and Gary pulled it fully off me. Then he laid me back on the couch, making me the centre of attention. I reached for the two nice, thick cocks in front of me, taking one in each hand and stroking them lazily. I hadn't planned on getting naked with one man tonight, let alone two – and certainly not one who was painted to look like he'd been carved from marble – but now I fully intended to make the most of this unexpected situation.

When both Gary and Matt were fully hard, I gave each of them a loving lick and a kiss on the end of their cock. Then I murmured, "Fuck me."

It was Gary who moved to oblige, spreading my legs further apart and raising my hips so he could enter me. Slowly, I felt him pushing his way in, stretching me wide. I had just begun to get used to his size when Matt decided to join in. My head was hanging over the end of the couch, and Matt fed the wet, briny tip of his cock between my open lips. It took a few moments for the two men to establish any kind of rhythm, but soon Gary was pumping hard into me, every thrust pushing me further on to Matt. With one hand I was holding on to Matt's shaft, guiding him where he needed to go, and with the other I was stroking my own nipples, lost in the sensation of being fucked at both ends for the first time in my life.

Nothing mattered now; not the party going on outside, nor the thought of being discovered. Everything came down to the soft sounds and movement in this room: hearts beating harder; breath coming faster; the slurping of my lips around the two cocks which were working away inside me; the primal, earthy smell of sweat and sex.

It was Matt who came first, pulling out of my mouth to shoot pearls of come over my breasts. Gary, with all the stamina of a professional athlete, was clearly going to last longer. Matt took the opportunity to play with my pussy as Gary continued to thrust into me. As I looked down through half-closed eyelids, I could almost imagine that the slender, grey fingers rubbing my clit were those of a statue, a Greek god come to life. It was such a surreal thought that it pushed me over the edge, and my body shuddered against the soft leather of the couch as Gary groaned and came, too.

The three of us collapsed together in a perspiring tangle of limbs, and when we finally broke the embrace it was to discover that we were all streaked with Matt's body paint; a strange souvenir of the strangest, but most exciting sex I suspected any of us had ever had.

As promised, Bella Capaldi rounded off a night of decadence by treated her guests to a stunning rendition of her new single at midnight. The later editions of the papers the following day were full of shots of her lying on a canopied bed, naked apart from a number of strategically placed diamonds. Unfortunately, I didn't witness her performance for myself, as I was still having a little party of my own with Gary and Matt; a party I wouldn't have missed for the world …

Coming Home
by Josephine Jay

The penthouse had floor-to-ceiling glass doors that opened up onto a private terrace, offering panoramic views across London and the Thames that were enough to take the breath away of even the most hardened individual. But that was just the beginning. Everything about the apartment oozed luxury: huge square sofas in dark brown hues were covered with expensive fake fur throws. Off-white walls revealed themselves to be lined with fabric on closer inspection, and a magnificent designer chandelier hung over a glass dining table. The floors were dark polished wood with hand-woven silk rugs: no expense had been spared. Even the refreshments were chosen with glamour in mind.

Sat on the low table in front of the sofas was an ice bucket holding a bottle of fine vintage champagne; two cut glass champagne flutes; a dish full of succulent deep red strawberries and another overflowing with Belgian truffles – the finest that money could buy. They were a mixture of dark, milk and white chocolate, some clothed in shiny foil wrappers of red and gold that glinted in the soft evening light and that begged to be eaten.

Satisfied that everything was in place Ruby bit into one of the strawberries. Its sweet red juice ran down her chin. She wiped it away with her finger then slowly savoured the juice on her tongue. Walking into the bedroom, complete with floor-to-ceiling windows, she admired the seven foot-wide bed opulently dressed with its sensuous fabrics in oranges and golds. It sat like a throne on a raised plinth to give the best possible view of the twinkling lights that made up the magical night time city skyline.

Ruby threw her bags on the bed and kicked off her shoes; the carpet felt rich and soft and made her scrunch up her bare feet so she could feel it softly tickling between her toes. She surveyed the room knowing she'd achieved near perfection for the setting. And now for the rest …

She carefully removed her purchases from their bags and laid them out with precision on the bed, smiling with pleasure at their beauty. Ruby could no longer contain herself and with her calm sophistication now totally abandoned she squealed with delight and hugged herself with excitement. Time to prepare herself.

She walked into the designer bathroom – complete with more expansive windows made from cleverly-tinted glass to hide her modesty while still allowing her the best view. In the centre of the marble room sat a large shiny copper bath with taps on a stand to one side so as not to interrupt the fairytale view. There were glass shelves with every conceivable wonderful-smelling lotion and potion beautifully displayed for both men and women. Piles of folded thick white towels and two heavy towelling bath robes sat waiting to engulf her clean wet body once she'd bathed.

Ruby turned on the taps and poured some citrus-scented oil into the steaming hot water, watching the soft foam appear as she swirled her hand around. She had a while until Dan arrived and so dimmed the lights right down, undressed and slid into the water, resting her head on the cushion in the tub. She felt her body relax and slowly started to work the moisturising bubbles into her skin. The very thought of seeing Dan after a three month absence was enough to make her body tingle and as she washed her breasts she felt her nipples harden beneath her fingers. She couldn't resist slowly running her hand down her body and slipping it between her legs, rubbing gently, the sensation making her arch her back in anticipation of what was to come later. But she soon removed her hand. She'd had three long months of satisfying herself and tonight it was most definitely Dan's turn.

By the time Ruby had wrapped herself in the soft white robe

156

she was so aroused that she needed to distract herself. She expertly opened the champagne, poured herself a glass and took her drink on to the terrace. The cool night air made her shiver as she sipped her champagne. It was chilled to perfection and the bubbles tingled and exploded against her tongue. With her senses already heightened, even that was almost too much to bear. Anyway, now it was time to dress. She knew exactly how to please Dan, and after three very long enforced months' separation there was an awful lot of pleasing to be caught up on. His work had taken him away and they'd talked, texted, e-mailed and kept in touch as best they could, but it hadn't always been easy and they'd had days on end sometimes with no contact.

But tonight was not about conversation, not about cyber sex, text sex or phone sex. It was about something very real, something very tangible. Dan had laughingly described the last three months as very long foreplay, but for tonight at least he was hers and she intended his home-coming to be one he would be unlikely to forget.

Ruby found her iPod in the bottom of her bag and took it over to the docking station. She selected the playlist that she'd made from their shared love of music. It had taken her hours, each track lovingly chosen, and now she smiled as one of her favourite mellow tunes filled the air.

She made her way into the bedroom and applied her make-up with perfection, enhancing her large blue eyes with a soft smoky pencil, before picking up the underwear from the bed. The waspie and its matching bra were a mixture of dark rich chocolate brown satin, velvet and fine black lace and felt exquisite to the touch, silky and sensual. She held them up to her face and luxuriated in the sensation of the fabrics against her cheek, knowing full well they were going to feel just as sensational against her own skin and to Dan's touch.

She put them on, smiling as the bra pushed her up and out in all the right places to give her an impressive cleavage. The waspie gently pulled in her waist so overall she looked curvaceous and sumptuously all woman. The expense of having them made for her was totally justified as they fitted like a second skin. She pulled on the delicate matching knickers and the final touch were sheer black stockings which she carefully and very slowly rolled up her long legs.

She admired her reflection in the mirror as she fastened the stockings with the soft wide velvety suspenders. Finally, Ruby slipped on a long chocolate brown silk robe, put on her high strappy black patent shoes and sprayed herself with his favourite perfume. She went over to check her make-up in the mirror, reapplying her lipstick, and then brushed her thick blonde hair until it shone in the soft light. Her pale skin was accentuated by the rich tones of her clothes and she felt and looked a million dollars.

Dan's weakness was his really sweet tooth. He had a passion for chocolate, especially dark chocolate, and as she looked at herself in the mirror she knew she'd achieved the desired effect. She looked positively good enough too eat.

There was a knock at the door and Ruby felt her stomach flip in anticipation, she'd been waiting for so damned long for this moment that she actually felt incredibly nervous about seeing him again. She opened the door and there he stood, tanned, with a smile on his face and that irresistible devilish twinkle in his eye. He started say something, but Ruby moved into his arms and kissed him instead. The kiss was soft and warm and their tongues gently played as she breathed in the familiar smell of him. His hands ran down over the silkiness of her gown until he was holding her buttocks as he pulled her towards him and she could feel his cock hardening against her body.

Ruby could feel herself going weak at the knees so she broke away from him, took his hand and led him into the sitting room. Dan's senses were overloaded, he couldn't take his eyes off Ruby, let alone his hands, but at the same time he was trying to take in the magnificence of their surroundings.

He turned to Ruby and gently slipped the robe from her shoulders.

"Wow," he said. "You look like …

"A box of Belgium's finest?" she laughed.

"Oh, and so much more."

He pulled her back into his arms; the luxuriousness on his fingertips of the feel of her clothes and the soft white skin exposed at the tops of her stockings were driving him wild. He was definitely a man who appreciated exquisite underwear.

Ruby slowly undid the buttons on his shirt, exposing his deep golden brown tan in stark contrast to her pale porcelain skin. She ran her hands over his chest and started to kiss him, removing his shirt as she did so, but impatience got the better of him and he removed the rest of his clothes quickly, leaving them where they fell, and led her into the bedroom. The sheets were cool and made of the heaviest cotton satin, which felt equally delicious against the skin, and he took Ruby in his arms and kissed her slowly and thoroughly. He slipped his hand inside her lacy knickers which were already soaking wet with her juices.

"I think perhaps these can go," he said, gently removing her panties. His hand ran between her legs and dipped into her slick wet pussy. She let out a low groan as his strong fingers played her like a fiddle then turned round so she was facing down the bed, and had easy access to his erection. It was standing up proudly, awaiting her full attention, while his fingers were still deep inside her and his thumb rubbed the nub of her clit.

She started to give little wet licks up his shaft, gently blowing so he could feel her hot breath while she cupped his balls in her hand. It was his turn to moan with pleasure now and she dropped her head down to suck his balls, gently humming as she did, knowing that the gentle vibration was enough to drive him to distraction. His cock rubbed up against her neck and the very smell and taste of him made Ruby want him to fuck her senseless. She lifted up her head and then gently took him into her mouth. Her warm lips wrapped around his hardness as she slowly took him deep into her throat and then rhythmically sucked his dick.

Dan pulled her legs across his chest so she was straddling him and then buried his face deep between her legs. This was what she'd been waiting for, for her the ultimate pleasure. He delighted in the feeling of her stockings silkily rubbing on his ears and he pulled her lips apart and started to work his magic with his tongue. He worked it as far as could inside her and as he removed it gently flicked his tongue over her clit. He nibbled it, sucked it and rubbed it with his nose until Ruby could barely contain herself, great waves of pleasure washing over her. She was still doing her very best to suck his cock and give it her full attention, but as her orgasm drew ever nearer she struggled to concentrate. Then he started: he slowly licked across the length of her wet slit and then ran his tongue firmly up over her clit and just kept repeating the process. He knew this would make her come quickly and she totally succumbed to him. She lifted her head and arched her back, pushing herself deeper onto his face, and heard his cock cruelly slap down onto his thigh.

"I'm so sorry," she breathlessly groaned

Dan laughed as he continued his long, slow, lascivious licks, as he knew what she was about to say.

"It's the only time in my life that I can't multi-task," and with that she felt her orgasm build from the very tips of her toes and convulse through her in waves of sheer unadulterated pleasure. She knew if she stayed in that position Dan would and could carry on for as long as she wanted; he was the most unselfish lover she'd ever known, put on this earth to please her. But tonight she had plans and so she rather reluctantly lifted herself off him and turned around to kiss him. She delighted in tasting her own juices on his mouth, but he flipped her onto her side so they were spooning, their bodies fitting perfectly together like pieces of a jigsaw. It was as if they couldn't tell where one finished and the other began.

"My God," he exclaimed as he slid his shaft deep inside her. "You're still so wet."

"You always make me wetter than wet," Ruby sighed.

His hand delved inside her bra and released a very hard taut nipple which he spun between his fingers. Then, with her breast exposed, he brought his hand up and clamped it over her mouth, bringing back her head onto his chest. Ruby loved it when he took control. She never felt threatened, it was total trust. She could feel the strength of his body behind her and it made her deeply aroused and took her breath away. She slid her hand down between her legs and felt his cock pumping inside her. It felt so good to have him inside her again and she was unable to resist stroking herself while she was there. She knew she was close to coming again, could feel all his muscles tensing and the fabric of her waspie caressing his skin. He released his hand from her mouth.

"Do you want me to talk to you?" she asked.

"Mmm," Dan replied. "You know I love it when you talk."

"Some things don't change then," she laughed. "You've been away three months and already she's back in our bed."

Their favourite bed talk always involved another woman and Dan loved nothing better than hearing Ruby telling him what she was doing to both of them. She didn't have a name, but Ruby had ground rules even for their imaginary friend and there was definitely no kissing on the mouth allowed and Dan was not allowed to imaginarily fuck her either. The other woman was definitely all about oral pleasure, for both of them. If Ruby felt she was intruding just a little too much then she'd flick her leg in the air.

"What the fuck are you doing?" Dan would ask.

"I'm kicking her off the bed," Ruby would reply indignantly and then they'd laugh. Their sex life involved a lot of laughter – a lot of chat and a lot of laughter.

Ruby looked up and she was standing in the doorway, right on cue, holding the bottle of champagne in one hand and the dish of strawberries in the other. Dan's face was still buried in Ruby's neck and so he wasn't aware of her presence. The thought that she'd been watching them made Ruby even hornier and she gasped nervously and beckoned for her to come over nearer the bed. The girl stood in front of them silhouetted against the twinkling city lights. She was wearing a fine golden lace bra and suspenders and black stockings, her dark hair cascading over her shoulders. She looked shimmery, like the foil wrapper on one of the truffles.

"Well," said Dan impatiently. "You're awfully quiet," and then he lifted his head and saw her. She felt a deep chuckle

161

rumble from within him and then a moan as he thrust himself even further into Ruby with anticipation and excitement.

"Oh God," he groaned, putting his hand up to his forehead to check he was OK. "I'm hallucinating."

The girl knelt beside the bed, took one of the strawberries, bit it in half then dipped it in the champagne. She rubbed the red juices over Ruby's exposed nipple and then leaned over and gently started to suck.

"No, she's definitely very real," replied a very breathless Ruby, barely able to speak. "Now who's gone awfully quiet?"

"You are simply ..." he started to say as he kissed her neck.

"I know," she replied smugly. "Just remember the rules and, oh yes, welcome home my darling."

A Night at the Opera
by Sarah Berry

Felicity had been so happy. She'd won the UK's *Warbler of the Year* prize of £1,500, a double spread in *Opera Weekly* and the title role in a production of *Mistress Bluebottle* directed by the great Ludwig van Ponci at Milan's *L'Impala* opera house. She was talented, beautiful and could speedily trill her way through the highest and lowest registers of a very large vocal range with little effort.

That day was the first run through in the piano room. She'd been ever so excited to sing for Ludwig and she felt she'd performed with her usual aplomb. But after the first act, it wasn't praise that Ludwig was showering upon her, but abuse.

"Theese Eenglish gels know nathing of the love. She ees preety song-bird ey? Puta her in a cage not on the stage. Send her away. She have no passion!"

With that, he spun around on a designer shoe and made for the door.

"Oh please don't go!" shouted Felicity desperately. "I do have passion. I mean I'm sure I have some somewhere. Thing is … I've just never … you know … had a boyfriend."

"Whata never? *Scopilo!*" screamed Ludwig, stopping in his tracks. He slowly turned around and started looking at Felicity like she was a science experiment.

"Well, you know, I've been too damn busy for all that," she faltered. "My mother thought it was more important I sing than get laid. I'm ever so sorry. All I've had is a quick fumble with a spotty lead clarinettist when I was a bit squiffy. You'd think he'd be good with his hands. But he was awful. And he blew his load before he was anywhere near me."

"I'll sort her out," jumped in her excitable co-star, the up-and-coming Brit sensation Boswell Bounder.

Now, in her more whimsical moments, Felicity had had fantasies of being swept off her feet by some hunky drummer. The percussion boys were always the hottest – all rock and roll with muscle and good rhythm. She could imagine them banging her like they did the bass drum. But she couldn't imagine Boswell sweeping her off anything. He was an amazing singer – that was true. But he was so skinny and flamboyant. He wore impeccably tailored velvet jackets and had a head of long blond locks that wouldn't look out of place in a hair commercial. In fact, she was pretty sure he was gay.

But now Boswell was walking around her. Looking her up and down with his arms folded. "Yes, I'll work on her passion," he said chirpily. "I think she's got potential. And I do *so* love a challenge." And with that he winked at her. That was the first time an opera boy had ever done such a thing in front of Felicity – they were usually so stuffy – and she found herself smiling. She didn't have a clue how Boswell could save her, but his enthusiasm was infectious. Maybe he could help?

"Veery well. You have a night to try. Fix her or she ees gone." And with that, Ludwig flounced out of the room.

Boswell took Felicity's hand in his and fixed her with determined stare, "Darling, meet me on stage at the opera at 11.30 p.m. sharp tonight. We'll get you singing, I promise." And he too flounced out of room.

The rest of Felicity's day was spent in pensive anticipation. She would have dearly loved to smoke, drink or at least have caffeine, but she really didn't do that sort of thing. And anyway she couldn't risk hurting her precious voice.

Instead, she wondered aimlessly around the streets of Milan, listening to the great Maria Malice on her iPod – the first singer to step into *Mistress Bluebottle*'s shoes. She wasn't used to having her performance criticised, but as her heart filled with sorrow when Maria realised that her child wasn't to know his father, she had to agree that she needed work. Somehow, she needed to pretend to be in love with Boswell.

That night, Felicity stepped onto the *L'Impala* stage for the first time. The set was beginning to take shape now. A marvellous melange of blue and silver velvet surrounded a glistening chandelier, an ornate dressing table and a rather splendid four poster bed upon which Mistress Bluebottle was to lose her virginity.

She had always dreamt of performing on that stage. She looked across the empty auditorium imagining the thousands of faces looking up at her, delighting in her. Maria had famously had a standing ovation lasting 30 minutes. She'd be lucky to get a solitary clap at this rate. The clipped footsteps behind her made her jump and she spun around expecting to see the foppish Boswell. Instead her eyes met a tall, handsome cavalier from the 1790s.

You might expect that a powdered wig, tights, breeches and a beaded satin coat would emasculate a man. But somehow the outfit had turned the refined, lean Boswell into a roguish lothario and he was now bending down to kiss her hand. Even this simple act served to make her blush.

"Why Ms Bluebottle, we must get you properly dressed for the occasion," he said and led her over to the dressing table. "Now my darling, until you feel the part you won't be the part. So strip."

"What?" asked Felicity, aghast.

"Darling, we need to attire you. And that's how the play starts is it not? You're being dressed by your maid, ready for your debutante ball. When you're all excited to meet boys and flirt? That is actually a very sexy scene."

"But there's no skin on show. It's not like I get my boobs out," laughed Felicity nervously. "You're not going to suggest I do are you? My mother will be in the audience and …"

"No no, don't worry. This is just an exercise."

Felicity guessed it was useless to protest. And she wasn't sure that she wanted to. After all, this was totally an artistic endeavour. There was nothing at all perverted about it, right?

She pulled open the sash of her simple wrap dress. She couldn't look down, she was too shy. She kept her eyes fixed on Boswell's big brown merry eyes. After a few seconds he allowed his gaze to travel over her body. Taking in her small breasts – she'd never needed to wear a bra – and simple white knickers. Felicity bit her lip, wondering if he would see the stain of moisture forming on her gusset. The pleased look in his eyes wiped away any thoughts that he was gay.

"Excellent. Now knickers off. We need to put these on you." And he handed her some bloomers. Feeling emboldened, she removed her knickers. She thrilled at the thought that her bushy mound was on show and kept it on show for as long as she could allow, while still being businesslike. She slowly eased on the frilly bloomers, thinking it was a shame he didn't take her there and then.

He pulled up the chair and ordered her to sit down. She rather liked being under his control, not knowing what he was going to do next. He bent down at her feet and took her small, French manicured toes in his hand and gave them a light kiss. Then, from his pocket he produced a pair of thick white stockings.

"Point your toes, my dear," he commanded. Slowly, carefully, he rolled up them up her legs. Felicity closed her eyes, feeling the tightness of the cladding move steadily up her legs, wishing the garment could reach all the way to the delicate folds of her sex. As he tied around the ribboned garters, it occurred to her that this delicious boy was having as much fun dressing her as he hopefully would have undressing her later.

"I feel like a doll", she giggled, as he strung up her corset, a little tighter than would normally be done for a singer.

"Isn't it wonderful?" he breathed. "I wish I'd been around in the eighteenth century. The men and women were bound into these remarkable, constricting costumes. The pomp, the ceremony, and then the unwrapping. You need to think about this when you sing in the first act, OK?"

She knew that she would. As she slipped her feet into the delicate heels, she truly realised for the first time what it meant to walk in someone else's shoes. Clearly there was a lot more to this opera lark than just singing.

Soon her bony hips were given life via a petticoat of cascading frills. Then he helped her into a beautiful sapphire blue velvet dress. She struggled a little to get her arms into the bell sleeves of the heavy, voluminous garment, and came up for air giggling but he stopped her with a kiss. She hadn't taken a breath and was startled. He smiled again and turned her round so he could do her up.

Looking down, Felicity was rather surprised to see her tits pushed up and looking at her. Her waist was sucked in and her hips were full. She was an object of desire and she melted as Boswell nibbled on her neck. One wig and some faux jewels later, Boswell led her to the centre of the stage.

"Now my dear, sing."

Fear encroached on Felicity once more as she felt dwarfed by the overwhelming set. She'd never been nervous before – she'd always been a controlled virtuoso singer. But here they wanted more. And in front of Boswell she hoped was about it give it.

A little more breathily than she liked, Felicity sang as Mistress Bluebottle and how she was excited about meeting her potential suitor that night. Boswell stopped her mid acciaccatura with a kiss. And this time she had breath aplenty. He sought to open her lips and gently pushed his tongue inside her mouth. She responded and leaned into him. According to the rather large bulge, Felicity was comforted to see that her trainer was enjoying her training.

"Carry on," he smiled, and she sang of the moment she met her Boswell. How she wanted him to take her and marry her and be father of her children. As she sang, Boswell kissed her neck, causing some of her pitching to be a little off. He then came in front of her and bent to his knees. She sang on, confused but aroused. "Will he love me? Will he be mine?"

Up went her skirt and soon Boswell disappeared underneath her petticoat. If someone came into the theatre now they wouldn't know he was there, she mused to herself. As she lamented her need for love, she felt her bloomers being eased down and two sets of fingers push into her bottom cheeks. As he probed her arsehole, his tongue was on her clitoris, lapping in time to her melody.

"I think I love him," she cooed, as he plunged his tongue

inside her. Now Felicity was no longer worried about the pitching. She sang out her orgasm, filling up every inch of the auditorium with the sounds of her pleasure.

Boswell crawled out from underneath her petticoats looking slightly pinker than before but still manly. As he breathed out his cravat billowed, like the crest of a lion. A bead of sweat decorated his brow – the heat from his wig no doubt adding to the fervour.

He took her head in his hands and kissed her again. Felicity could taste herself on his breath and wanted to taste him. She was being carried away on a wave of hedonistic, artistic bliss and it felt only natural to fall to her knees and unbutton his silk breeches. Any other chap would look a sissy in tights, but not Boswell. His legs were magnificently contoured and his sizable cock was stretching, desperate to be released. She eased down the waistband and he sprang free.

"Sing for me," she smiled up at him as she cupped his balls. Boswell hadn't expected his little prodigy to take to her lesson so well. As she sucked he sang about how beautiful Mistress Bluebottle was. And of how he would indeed take her. An accomplished flautist as well as a singer, Felicity suddenly realised why she'd spent all those hours perfecting her double tonguing as she played out a symphony around her lover's helmet.

After Felicity had swallowed his seed – it was necessary so as not mark the costume – and after Boswell had composed himself, he pulled Felicity towards the bed.

"Very good my dear. Now in the opera, don't we next come upon Ms Bluebottle when her lover has taken her virginity?"

"Why so we do sir," she smiled. "And I would say that I need to practise."

Felicity climbed on the bed and allowed Boswell to unwrap her. As each layer of her costume came off, Felicity wanted to scream. She needed him inside her. But she also knew the longer he took the more ecstasy she would feel. Finally he was peeling down her bloomers.

She spread her legs so he could see inside her as he hurriedly removed his jacket, his waistcoat and loosened his cravat. He looked dishevelled and she arched her back in anticipation. Then he was inside her. She moaned with tuneful ecstasy as he moved in and out of her sodden slit. As he bit her neck she filled the auditorium with a soulful scream. Her whole body was singing lust, love, life …

When she came to from her orgasm, Boswell was gone. And for the next week, she only saw him in rehearsals. While she was sad, she knew this ardour was reflected in her singing with him. She was more desperate and wanton than ever as art and life met. Was it just a trick to get her singing or did he really want her?

Either way, Ludwig was ecstatic with her performance. And Felicity wept with joy when her opening night yielded a 31.2 minute standing ovation. But the icing on a wondrously decadent cake was the bouquet of roses that she found in her dressing room afterwards, with a note asking her to meet on stage at 11.30 p.m. sharp that night.

Alice's Indulgence
by Adam Sawyer

Alice was fed up. The week before Valentine's Day was hardly good timing to split up with her boyfriend. Although she wasn't a fan of red hearts and soppy cards, she'd booked a hotel in London for the weekend as a surprise and the thought of cancelling that made things seem worse.

But Alice decided a self-indulgent splurge was just what she needed to cheer herself up, so she went ahead with the booking. "What the hell," she said to herself on the train up to London. "I deserve to spoil myself."

Once she'd checked in to the hotel in London's Shoreditch she went shopping for the afternoon, splurging on a new outfit, designer heels and something skimpy from Agent Provocateur. Alice instantly felt better and decided that a night alone in her room with a movie and a bottle of wine would be the perfect end to the day. She hadn't planned on buying the vibrator. But when she saw it, all boxed up and looking respectable on the shelf in the pharmacy, she thought to herself, "Hmm, this could be fun".

As she walked back to the hotel, her mind was buzzing with what she had in her carrier bag; it felt very naughty. Back in her room, Alice kicked off her boots and jeans and opened a vodka from the mini bar. She tried on the new clothes in front of the mirror and then took them off to try the new lingerie: a matching balconette bra and g-string in black silk. Stylish but very sexy; the silk felt great against her body. As she stood there looking at her reflection Alice noted how good she felt and her nipples hardened as she imagined a guy in the room with her.

Now it was time for the other gift to herself. Her heartbeat quickened as she took the vibrator out of the box. It was pink, rigid and thick.

"Oh God," she let out in a murmur as she held it in her fist, twisting the dial at its base as it started buzzing. She felt herself getting aroused in anticipation so she now lay back on the bed, running the buzzing vibrator gently over her breasts and tummy before placing it between her legs. She let its pink head graze her silk underwear and then placed its vibrating shaft against her clitoris. A huge surge went through her like a switch had been clicked; it took her breath away. As her right hand held the pink tool, her left hand swept over the cups of her bra, gently stroking her nipples.

"Oh fuck," she said out loud. Alice now pulled down her g-string and placed the pink head of the vibrator at the entrance to her pussy. Closing her eyes, she revelled in the connection as it gently entered her warm and now wet pussy. She bit her lower lip in response to the friction she felt between her walls and the realistic vein-like texture of the vibrator. Wow, it felt so good as she took its full length up her. With her head propped up on a cushion, Alice now brought the heel of her right foot up towards her pussy and gently nudged the vibrator back and forth – fucking herself – while her fingers found her clitoris and she started to stroke herself. Alice gulped heavily as she looked down and took in the horny sight of her fingers and the pink rubber cock between her legs. It was too much; it instantly overwhelmed her. As the pace of her fingers quickened, her heel nudged back and forth and Alice started to tremble. It was like she was surfing a huge wave. She let out an unexpected cry as her flesh pimpled, her eyes glazed over and a powerful climax gripped her. Her mouth quivered as she was rewarded with a mind-blowing sensation from the combination of her fingers and the pink tool. She threw her head back as the orgasm shuddered through her, leaving her breathless and satisfied.

After a relaxing bath, Alice thought she should put on the new outfit and grab a drink in the hotel bar – she was in the mood for champagne. She took the lift down to the lobby bar

171

where she ordered a Bellini. Not liking the idea of sitting by herself at a table, she decided to stay sitting up at the bar. She didn't need a boyfriend she thought to herself, especially after the great time she'd just had upstairs.

It was in the mirror opposite that she first noticed him. A guy with dark hair, shirt unbuttoned at the top, denim jacket and iPhone, sipping a pint of Guinness. Not the sort of bloke she'd normally go for, he looked a trendy creative type. But the champagne and her climax had given her a new-found confidence; so she turned and said, "Hi".

He looked up from his iPhone, and hi'd back. His name was Iain; he was from Glasgow and in town on a business trip. They started chatting and found a common interest in art; when Alice said she'd been keen on checking out an exhibition at the British Museum, Iain said he was going the next day and would she like to join him. Well it was hardly a date, but Iain looked like a really nice guy and it would be a cool way to spend a Sunday morning. But unlike a lot of guys that Alice met, she was confused as to what his motives were. Did he fancy her or just fancy some art? She certainly fancied him; his designer stubble and Scottish accent became more and more attractive as they chatted, but she wasn't sure how to play things.

Not wanting to appear too keen, and with the promise of a rendezvous the next morning, Alice decided to quit while she was ahead and go back upstairs to find that movie to watch. Iain had given her his business card with his mobile number and shook hands as Alice got up to say goodbye and moved through the lobby. As she glanced back she could see the way Iain was looking at her, not in a predatory way but certainly admiring her. Alice wondered whether she should have left. Could she have had a nice evening flirting at the bar with him?

She tutted at herself as she walked into the lift, but then asked herself if she was really ready to meet another guy. As she posed that question and caught her reflection in the mirror, she decided something.

"Fuck it," she said out loud, grabbing her mobile from her bag. As the lift ascended to her floor, she sent a text message, typing so quickly that she didn't think much about what she was saying: "Sorry had to dash Iain, fancy another drink, room 322? A x" She then punched in his number from the card, shaking slightly, surprised by her own confidence.

Alice felt very naughty as she closed the door to her room but also frustrated; there was no reply to her text. Would Iain come or not? She decided to think confident and dimmed the lights of the room and found a station playing chillout dance tunes on the TV.

"This is so out of character for me," she thought as she sat on the edge of the bed. But there was no time for reflection, because there was a knock on the door.

And there he was, looking gorgeous.

"Thanks for coming," she giggled as he walked in, wondering what to do next.

"Shall we get that first kiss out of the way now then?" he said, laughing, and they bent forward, their lips meeting in a soft kiss. They then moved to sit on the edge of the bed as, breathing more heavily, their tongues explored each other, his hands stroking her back and face.

"Wow!" Iain said, drawing back. "That was nice. Now where's that drink you promised?"

She took a can of cold lager out of the mini bar and passed it to him.

He looked into her eyes. "So what's next on the menu Alice?" he asked. "What do you fancy now?"

Alice smiled and replied with the same directness, looking right in to his eyes. "I'll tell you what I want," she started. "I want you to …" she paused for breath, "to … lick … me … here," and then her hands went down across her navel and she spread the palm of her hand over the taut top of her skirt.

While her own words had surprised her, she knew that's what she wanted more than anything – she wanted him to go down on her. She didn't want to kiss him again or touch him yet; she just wanted his tongue on her pussy – it was that simple.

Taking off his denim jacket, Iain knelt down by the bed at Alice's feet. He carefully pulled her silk skirt up over her knees so she could gather it up at her waist and he then pulled down her black g-string. He looked at her – her flesh naked, a neatly trimmed pubic triangle greeting him, the tops of her patterned hold-ups framing the view, her 'fuck-me' heels still on. And he exhaled in anticipation.

Iain knelt until his face was inches away from her pussy. Alice's breathing had quickened and her fists tensed in anticipation of what she desired. Slowly and tenderly, he pushed out his tongue and went to greet her pussy. Flicking his tongue over her clitoris she flinched in response, sucking the air through her teeth. Giving one or two firm flicks he then placed the palm of his left hand over her pubic mound, gently stretching her skin taut to expose her clit. As his tongue engaged with her pussy once more, Alice bucked against his mouth where he lapped hungrily at her juices. Just as an hour and a half earlier she'd been lying there with a vibrator, here she was again on the brink of another climax with a guy she'd just met going down on her. And he was good at it.

As she fucked against his lips, her juices changed to something sweeter as she felt a climax build. As he shifted the rhythm to more frenetic licking and nibbling, her bucking increased. Alice let out a moan and quick gasps, her body twitching as Iain realized that this woman he'd just met was about to do something very intimate: she was about to come in his mouth. "Ah fuck," she exclaimed, "F- f- fuck!" and then she was there. On the edge of a mind-blowing orgasm as he carried on licking, keeping his tongue rigid, flicking over her clit as she released a flood of juices drenching his stubble and face with her sweet aroma. And then with a final release and gasp she was finished. She collapsed on the bed, her face and neck flushed, her breathing erratic.

"That was just amazing," she said finally.

As Iain stood up Alice went to kiss him on the lips and then unbuttoned his shirt and unbuckled his belt. She sat back down, her face level with his cock as she let his jeans drop to the floor. As he stood there in his white briefs Alice noted a complete shift in the dynamic as she now took control, emancipated by the confidence of her post-climactic glow. She now pulled off her strappy shoes, rolled down her hold-ups and took off her bra and top. The hotel room looked so seductive in the low light; dark walls and tan bedding, the gentle rhythm of music echoing the sexy mood of the two new lovers.

"Lie down," she said. Iain said nothing as he lay back on the bed and Alice climbed over him on all fours, sweeping her hair behind her ears, her bare breasts touching him. She started by his feet, gently kissing closed-lip kisses on his legs, up to his thighs, her lips tracing a trail up his body. He shivered in response as she paused by his cock. Still encased in the white briefs, his tool was throbbing and where his helmet urgently nudged the fabric of his pants, it was translucent with the glisten of pre-come. Alice lent and licked up the shaft of his cock, through the fabric, stopping just below the ridge of the helmet. Then she licked up from his navel all the way to his neck where she gently kissed him, her lips once more tasting her own juices on his mouth. She moaned back in recognition of something so sexy, but kind of dirty too.

Finally Alice slipped his briefs down, taking care over his cock, and gasped at the throbbing erection. It stood proudly upright, finally liberated from the constraints of his underwear. She bent her face and kissed his helmet, her lips withdrawing with the glisten of his pre-come. Then she gripped the thick base of his cock with her right hand and skilfully took its full length in her mouth. Holding him like that accentuated his erection and he felt huge in her mouth. She closed her eyes and dipped her head to take him deeper in her mouth, sucking tightly on his shaft, her tongue flicking over his helmet. Alice repeated this process and Iain gently held the back of her head in his hands. Encouraged by his tenderness, Alice built up a quicker rhythm, bobbing her head up and down as she continued to suck him. He let out a moan. "If you carry on like that, I'm going to come," he blurted out.

Alice took that as her signal to stop and sat back, wiping her mouth. "Not yet – I want you to fuck me," she said.

She lay on her back, her legs raised to reveal the lips of her pussy. In response Iain knelt at her bum and she exhaled as he entered her smoothly and deeply, her muscles clenching as they felt the intensity of the penetration. Still kneeling he gripped the sides of her thighs and started pumping into her with such force that her body moved with each thrust. In each movement he withdrew before taking her deeply once more, stopping to kiss her tummy or lick her nipples and neck. Although they were strangers fucking, their connection had a tender intimacy to it, like two long-term lovers with a real chemistry; not two people who'd never done this before.

Iain was building up such a frenetic rhythm that sweat was showing on his brow and chest but as Alice looked up she found it really sexy how his body glistened in the low light.

"I want you to come for me," she whispered, and with those words Iain's frown of concentration became more intense as he bit his lip and she registered a deeper arousal in them both. He didn't need to say anything; she could see it in his face and feel it in his cock. She felt his cock tense and his eyes glaze as he let out a deep moan and now, clutching her sides more than ever, she felt a surge as he came into her. Clutching her bum cheeks tightly, his finger stroked the entrance to her anus as she now tensed before finally releasing the wave of her own climax that overtook her senses. He stayed focused as he came again, shooting into her with each thrust, as they gripped each other tightly, climaxing at the same time.

They lay back panting, their bodies now unlocked, revelling in the warmth and perspiration of frenzied love-making.

Alice had never done anything like this before. It felt really naughty but empowering to be so self-centred, so focused on her needs. As she lay there reflecting on the evening so far, she thought perhaps it would be a good idea to split up with a boyfriend more often.

Sweet Like Chocolate
by Mark Farley

"I need to run some errands, love. Can you come and watch the shop?"

I rolled my eyes with the phone receiver between my ear and shoulder. My mother had been increasingly using her 'daughter-living-at-home-for-free' card ever since I'd moved back in with her and my father. I'd been made redundant from my office and discovered that my husband was fucking the account manager of his biggest client once a month at the Travelodge in Kings Cross, all in the same week, so I had retreated back to the family home on the outskirts of Brighton to regroup and figure out what the hell I was going to do with the rest of my life. Because at the time, it pretty much equated to watching *Sex and the City* DVDs, draining bottles of Tesco Soave and moping in my childhood room with the only release from boredom being masturbating to girl-on-girl porn on my laptop. Not that William had ever shared my desire for such Sapphic voyeurism. Odd, considering that it's supposed to be a man's ultimate fantasy.

"Do I have to, Mum?" I sobbed pathetically down the phone.

"Why, Claire?" she demanded in that dominant maternal tone. "Is there something more pressing going on in your life?"

We both knew that there wasn't, of course. We both knew that she'd pretty much rescued me when I'd walked out of my marital home one Sunday night, tears streaming down my face, with a half-packed carry on, vowing never to go back.

My mother would tell you that she was a 'confectioner' but

when people enquire of me about her business and what my life is currently filled with, I tell them that she owns a cake shop. Because that's what it is, essentially. Granted, the online part of her venture branches out into sandwiches, rolls, sugar-based Turkish Delight-type goodies and creamy vol-au-vents in a hundred different flavours (including Champagne and Somerset Cerise, whatever that is) which are all designed for catering to the growing local office party market, not to mention the odd celebrity wedding. But the part of her vast, sweet empire that I come across and that she is currently guilting me into aiding with is basically a cake shop. A till, an old English bell above the door that rattles a Victorian shrill when someone enters, a few tables and lots and lots of cake. There are three- and four-tier gateaux sitting proudly in the window, wide and flat one-tier sponges complete with your favourite photo of the intended recipient transferred onto sugar paper to slice into, and a whole host of indulgent cupcakes that are ideal for that office girl on the go looking for a momentary lunchtime spot of escapism.

I soon found myself standing outside the Co-op on Portslade High Street sighing to myself and waiting for a bus to take me into town and towards the North Laines. I puffed on the last of my pack of ten as I arrived at the shop. My mother seemed flustered. Before I even got the chance to take off my jacket, I got: "Heavens, I have to go … God, you took so long … Why on earth do you wear your hair like that?… What have you done to find a job today?… Have you sent off those CVs?… I'm so late … I can't believe the delivery didn't show … I must dash … You may have to close up again …"

The door slammed. A waft of some sort of cheap Arabic spritz slowly dispersed, leaving the familiar aroma of stale vanilla and cocoa in the air. I looked around, sighed again and peeled off my jacket, tossing my handbag under the counter. I glanced at my watch and looked forward to a long afternoon. It was deathly quiet. I served about three people and took two phone orders in three hours. The watch on my wrist slowly crept around nearer to 5 p.m. I read and re-read that week's *Grazia* more times that I can remember (thus knowing far too much about 24-hour anti-ageing creams) and studied the ingredients on the side of the box of Ritz cheese crackers to the point where I could probably recite them word for word.

Then the bell went. I shook myself awake. A couple entered. They held hands and giggled coquettishly at one another, gym-fresh with holdalls and racquet bags thrown casually over their shoulders. Her hair, wet from the communal showers, was held up by an HB pencil, and cotton training-wear hung tight and casually in all of the right places. I huffed to myself at the inconvenience of their timing and looked back down at the latest rumours of the Brangelina split, thinking that the idea I had had of closing a half hour earlier than I should and hitting the themed pub next door had just flown out the window, with the rest of my wasted day. I submitted myself to the situation and decided to fantasise instead about the man in front of me, hoping that it would make the day pass faster.

Dark, shaven head, goatee. The mutterings between them about the display of treats in the glass cabinet revealed their Italian origin. He was thick-set, tanned and probably quite toned underneath the Nike shell suit I was taking off his broad shoulders in my head. She held him close, wistful and proud. Probably used to watching other women staring slack-jawed at him like some kind of temptation we specialise in on the premises. I caught her eye for a second and realised that not only was I doing just that but I was also sucking quite unattractively on the end of a biro. I disengaged it with my teeth and it clattered on the counter. I looked down, blushing as I heard them laugh in the corner by the door to the prep kitchen.

Her demeanour suddenly changed and she straightened up like a peacock. She began to beam with confidence and a subtle bravado as she hung tighter to her prize, rubbing the back of his muscled neck with her hand. Petite with small, ripe plums for breasts, she hadn't bothered putting her bra back on, it seemed. Her perky nipples indented into the lettering on the chest of her training vest and cinnamon curls flowed around them from her fringe. Dark eyes and full lips complimented her full figure and my mind soon wandered to what they might look like naked. Perhaps, I thought, their skin would melt into one another's and their limbs would entwine together like neighbouring sweet pea bushes. I imagined their nether regions regimentally tended to like the most passionate gardeners would attend their crop. I pictured each of them plucked and shaved themselves, pruned within an inch of their lives. Bald, stripped and smooth like the halved, fresh peaches currently lined up for glazing in front of me. At least my wandering imagination wanted them to be.

My mother swears that the key to all sales is visualising your customer's every need. To put yourself in their shoes and imagine what it is that they truly wish for upon visiting your establishment, which is then when you must tailor your interaction towards making a sale. It always sounds a little cut-throat to me. Like Arkwright in *Open All Hours*. This crossed my mind as I slipped my bare feet back into my flip-flops and schlepped across the floor towards them with the lunch plate I hadn't bothered taking out, hours before. The sale-making interaction could wait this time, I thought.

They were still happily chatting away to themselves as I passed them. She had her face buried in his neck as he punched away on the keypad of his Motorola RZR. As she saw me coming towards them, her hand appeared from the front of his pants, rather suspiciously. I don't think she'd meant me to see, especially as her head was turned away, but I did start to wonder what their game was as I placed my crockery into the large industrial washer. I mean, they weren't exactly our sort of clientele at all and didn't seem to know precisely what they required. Hey, maybe they were killing time or they just got off on doing it in cake shops, who knows?

Maybe they would do it here. In this cake shop. Maybe that was their plan all along. They could, I thought. And they would let me watch and then utilize my body and appreciate my own furry lips, wet with moisture – the fantastical images of a scenario yet unfulfilled in my own life. That scenario was quite simple. It was the one that I had in my hand and had brewing there, ever since my private life had changed so abruptly. I desired a couple like this. To want me, to take me, to have me.

I wanted to have my first ever threesome and it couldn't have come soon enough. I took a quick second to put a hand up the front of my medium length skirt, pulled my panties to one side and pinch my clitoris hard between my thumb and my forefinger.

As I left the kitchen and entered the front of the premises again, I was dying to know if they were still feeling frisky so I glanced their way. Nothing. To be honest, I was hoping to see even more. Like her wandering hands again but this time I had her in my imagination, peeling down his trousers and sucking him off for my viewing pleasure as I took my place nonchalantly behind the counter. I certainly wouldn't have minded. It was then that she spoke for the first time, "You have some lovely cakes ..."

"Thanks," I replied. "My mother makes them."

"Wish my mother made me cakes ..."

"Well, it's her place so ..." I looked down, embarrassed. She purred to herself, looking around at absolutely everything on offer, before continuing the conversation.

"I have no idea how you can work here and not get fat ..."

I laughed. "It's very tempting ..."

We both nodded. Her partner looked up from his mobile and snapped it shut, looking over the brim of a pair of mirrored shades and chewing gum, registering the comment and looking me up and down for the first time. He turned to his girlfriend and raised his eyebrows. She looked back my way and said, "But with a body like yours, it would be a shame to ruin it anyway ..."

I blushed.

"Really," she continued. "You have an amazing body."

"Thanks," I said, getting redder by the minute. Like the strawberry shortcake, pulsing with baked, dried fruit in large oven trays and cooling at room temperature, sliced and ready for sale. I would be lying if I said that I wasn't enjoying the sudden attention.

"I agree ..." he said next to her. The first thing he had uttered since he had arrived. He was a man of very few words, clearly.

Meanwhile though, time was ticking and the end of my day was fast approaching. My guests were still idly chatting about what cupcake to purchase, when I rose to flip the sign in the door to read CLOSED and turn the key in the lock to prevent others from entering, the guy commented cockily that he was now my 'prisoner', while I groaned audibly.

His girl politely announced, "Oh, I'm sorry. We'll go. Didn't realise you were closing …"

"No. It's OK. I'm in no rush," I said. "You two carry on. Besides, I'm enjoying the view."

My heart lurched in my mouth as I said it and I cringed inside before looking their way again, hoping I hadn't offended. The couple smiled naughtily at one another and continued their whispering.

"Feel free to try some cake too," I said. "On me …"

I sat back down and watched her break open the soft sponge of a chocolate cupcake with both hands, handing half of it to her lover. He took a large bite, as did she. They munched away, gorging on its creamy sweetness. I saw her hand hover once again over his crotch and she laughed playfully. She rubbed the growing length between his legs with her already sticky hand, dirtying his pants, and happily continued as she looked over to me, comfortably sitting watching. She took her finger and sunk it into the thick butter icing of another one of the cakes on show and placed it seductively into her partner's mouth. He looked towards me as he sucked it off and made her purr contentedly. He reciprocated and I began to wonder how far this was going to go, as my insides started to moisten. She took another few fingers full and playfully slapped it onto his neck, making us all chuckle.

"I hope you intend licking that off …" he complained jokingly.

"Oh yes …" she replied, taking her tongue across his skin, up towards his ear, collecting every last bit. I felt a twinge down between my legs and the urge to join in came across me.

"Oh no," she announced, probably worrying at the extent that she was going through our cake display. "We've run out of icing … and we were just getting started … Oh well …"

She shrugged and continued pawing at her man's neck.

"I can help you there." I said, jumping to my feet and heading to the kitchen.

"Brilliant!" he said, clapping his hands together as I returned with a plastic container, filled with butter icing, chocolate, intended for the next morning's batch. He fooled with the bottom of her shirt.

"Take off your top, honey …" She looked at him and then me, incredulous.

"Honestly, you can't take him to seduce pretty cake shop girls anywhere, can you?"

She slapped his arm hard and continued. "I mean, anyone could walk past …"

That was true. I laughed, put down the container in front of them and released the blinds, obscuring us from the tourists who ambled by and gawked through the window.

"There you go. No excuse," he bellowed. I shrugged at her in agreement and leant against a nearby work surface. She pondered thoughtfully.

"You know where this would taste good, don't you?"

"Where's that?" he replied to her.

"On your cock …" she cried. "Come on, where is it?"

Now it was his turn to look shocked, although I was sure they were both doing it to tease each other. He glanced my way and put his hands on his hips and watched me signal him to drop his pants. With that sort of encouragement, how could he say no?

I stepped a little closer and watched her crouch on her feet in front of his exposed thighs. They were massively hairy, but as I suspected, all around his cock and balls was completely waxed. This was just as well as she soon coated the whole area and his thick erection with the sticky brown mess. She wanted to place a row of chopped banana up the length of his shaft too, but he just threw them back at her. It soon descended into all-out anarchy of course and, soon enough, I had to politely call for a truce as bits of fruit were getting stuck quite amusingly to the walls. She had now stripped down to just white cotton panties. I stood there, still fully clothed, but with a hand in my knickers, wondering how dirty she was expecting to get. More to the point, how much I was about to play a part in their filthy, chocolatey antics. She spread a little on her bare, tanned chest with her fingers caressing her small titties.

"Mmmm," she moaned with delight, before taking his coated length in her mouth and as far into it as she could manage. When her lips touched his abdomen and she began to gag slightly, he took a messy handful of her hair. She pulled away, catching it in her mouth, and let it spill out onto her chin and cover her face as she continued gorging on her lover's cock. He smeared it into her nose and cheek and she soon had to come up for air.

"Hungry?" she offered.

"Always …" I said, dropping my skirt to the floor. I peeled off the soaked knickers I'd been fiddling inside while they were putting on their show. My angora jumper followed before I joined her. She moved aside for me so that we could both come at him from different sides. Our mouths and tongues instinctively met as his sunkissed, Umbrian tool disappeared and then re-appeared from each of our mouths. She took cream from her cheek and reached across to my ample bosom, slowly coating my tits to match hers. Soon, both of our faces were coated in butter cream and the thick substance soon developed into a warm, darker brown ooze as it mixed with our saliva and we passed it between one another in deep, engorged kisses.

I climbed up to meet her man's chest, nuzzled on his neck and bit his lip as his girlfriend found her way down below and sucked hard on my vagina. He grabbed the back of her head and pushed it harder into me, making her snort and pant harder on my clit.

"She loves that, baby. Do it more. Make her come."

That she did. All over her sticky brown face, making it creamier still. She got to her feet and we kissed, touching our sliding bodies together. He leaned in for a kiss. To taste me, I didn't doubt. His bald head bent over to eat from my chest as she soon took the prompt and went to my other side. I put an arm around each of them, feeling very dominant all of a sudden. As I was being indulged for the very first time like

184

this, I considered it not too bad an idea to help out in the shop more often.

He took a handful of sauce in his hand, slapped it between my soaked pussy lips and rubbed it in quite hard, sending a lovely wave through me. He thrust globs of it inside me with his fingers, getting into all the deep folds, as his girlfriend held my wrists behind me and bit hard onto my nipples.

He looked into my eyes as he coated his hard penis with yet more sauce and waited for her to goad him into sticking it inside me. He lifted my hips onto the surface behind me and they both pulled my legs wide apart for him to take me, to use me like some coarse, human mixing bowl. I knew right then that it was going to feel great.

"Oh, I have a great idea.." she piped up, taking a handful of the squares of hardened cooking chocolate.

"Do you have a microwave?" she asked me as her boyfriend was teasing the tip of his cock at my entrance below.

"Yeah …" I said, laughing at my state. How I got from reading the side of a cracker box to this is anyone's guess. I was naked and covered in chocolate sauce with two strangers and I still didn't know their names.

"It's in the kitchen," I said.

He slowly eased his cock into me and past the gooey mess as I listened to the distinctive beeps and closing of the microwave door in the distance. Her man casually and slowly fucked me as she returned with a plastic measuring jug.

"Playing nicely you two?"

"Your boyfriend is fucking me …" I cooed.

"Yes, he is," she purred, stroking the small of his back as it moved towards me.

"He's driving his cock into my chocolate flavoured pussy."

"He is indeed, my sweet little whore. Now, do you like your nipples tweaked?"

"Oh yes."

"How about that?"

"Oh yes, harder …"

"Very well. But I have something nice and warm for them too. Would you like that?"

185

"Oh yes, while this bastard shags me."

"Don't worry, he won't stop until I tell him. Now are you ready?"

"Yes. Please, give it to me."

As I gave her the nod and as my sex dripped onto the slate floor a mixture of our bodily fluids and rich, chocolate icing, my new friend, her face covered also, poured piping hot sauce onto my breast and nipples, making me call out with a delicious shriek of agony. Our pleasures and ecstasy combined.

"Thanks ever so much, Claire. I really appreciate it. I had to go to three different cash and carries for glace cherries. Can you believe it? I mean, honestly …"

"That's OK, Mum. It was fairly quiet."

"Oh OK. How come you're back so late?"

For a split second, my mind went back over the few hours before with Silvio and Anna and in particular how we had finished together in a heaped, spent pile on the dusty floor.

"Oh, I got a cleaning bug and got carried away," I said with a hidden smile, thinking about the extent of the mess we had created.

"Thanks again. Oh, you are a good girl."

Yes, I thought. Yes I am. At least that was what Anna whispered into my ear sweetly, as she brought me off with her hand on my crotch, filled deeply with her man's cock. After a quick exchange of email addresses and the promise to get to know each other soon, we hugged intimately and parted ways. Yes, yes I am.

"No problem, Mum. Any time."

Henry
by Mistress Grace

Want to share the excitement that comes from exploring and opening up to possibility with your partner? Want to learn more about the fetish world but don't know where to start? Try me. I'm a sexually confident woman; tall, striking, open, you may call me Mistress. Over five years I have evolved from a Stepford wife, having very little sexual intimacy, to a lifestyle dominatrix. I share tales of my exploits in order to spread the word that experimenting and pushing boundaries makes sex great and love stronger.

Strawberries and cream instantly bring to mind Wimbledon, summer and Henry ... Henry spends a lot of time abroad for his work so our trysts are few and far between. As a result I am always happy to move things round to make time for him while he is here. This time he mailed me to say he was flying in from Canada. Would I meet him in central London? There was only one answer to that.

Preparing for a date always takes effort but the rewards for taking the time are enormous. Unless I want a sub to shave me I always de-fluff from head to toe and then layer the perfume range I use with body cream, talc and finally the perfume. Scent is so important; dab behind the backs of your knees as well as your wrists and neck.

My underwear always matches and is expensive. It makes me feel incredibly sexy to pull on silk knickers, to have fully fashioned nylons shape my legs – mmm! If I am using public transport I will either tone down my dress or wear a big coat!

Settling on a black wraparound with a plunging neckline I

slip on my five inch stilettos, brush my lips with cock-sucker red lipstick and look for my 'kit' bag.

I keep a travel bag containing toys and tools under my bed ready for sessions away from home. I have a few dildos of different sizes, a strap-on, nipple clamps, cuffs, collars, crops, paddles and of course piles of condoms and lube; dirty sex that isn't safe is just dirty. All of these items form the basis of my 'kit': depending on the event I could have saran wrap, feathers, silk scarves, butt plugs, blindfolds et al.

Henry loves having his arse played with but is not turned on by pain in any way so I threw out the clamps and paddles, replaced them with some nice lace underwear in his size and I was ready to leave.

The journey to the West End had me wriggling in my seat. The tube was rocking from side to side, producing a lovely level of friction in my knickers. My nipples were hardening and none of this was being helped by the stares of my fellow passengers. It's the lipstick, so bright and red, it always makes me smile.

My heels clicked as I walked across the marble foyer of the hotel, my dress swishing round my thighs. I saw the concierge look up from his post. I smiled at him, still walking towards the lifts.

I checked myself out in the lift mirror – gorgeous – then took a deep breath and stepped into the corridor. The clicking disappeared into the pile of the carpet and everything was silent. Hotels have that peculiar effect of compartmentalising everything, so experiences become more intense but disjointed.

I knocked on the door, turning my body sideways to avoid the face front approach. I always do that, it profiles my large chest and allows me a few moments to collect my thoughts and make them move to me. The door opened and there he stood, all twinkly-eyed and smiling. He looks like such a sensible grown-up until his eyes twinkle. At that point the lothario is clearly visible.

Instantly I felt my heart beat a little faster as I offered first my cheek, then lips, for kissing. His kisses started strongly and just get deeper. He began to fuck my mouth with his tongue before he even moved to let me in the room.

We paused, laughing, and I passed my kit bag to Henry as I walked into a lovely room. On the side, instead of the usual flowers, were punnets of strawberries, a pint of cream and two glasses of champagne. Heaven.

I pulled out the silk knickers and indicated I wanted Henry to undress and put the knickers on. His cock looked so lush straining against the pretty fabric. He stroked himself as I began to divest myself of clothes. In short order I was naked aside from my heels and lipstick. I lay down on the enormous bed, sliding my hand over the Egyptian cotton sheets.

I opened my legs wide to show Henry just how pleased I was to see him, and how ready I was for him to please me. Running my hands down to my groin I felt my clit swell and knew how ready I was to play.

Reaching for a strawberry, Henry looked me straight in the pussy as he knelt at the foot of the bed.

"You like strawberries, don't you?"

I nodded.

"Want this strawberry?"

He took my smile as acquiescence and so very slowly pushed the strawberry between my labia.

"Hold it there for me."

I nodded again and closed my eyes. It felt a little odd; naughty, but nice. The next sensation took my breath away as I felt the cream being poured over my breasts. I gasped, damn it was cold and heck, how much did he have, and what about the sheets? The thoughts stopped abruptly as the stream reached my cunt. Then he was between my legs eating the strawberry out of my pussy. I laughed with the sheer joy of it as he made his way up to my mouth, passing mulched strawberry, cream and pussy juice into my mouth to swallow. Yum!

We ate the strawberries as he massaged the cream into my body: the mess we left on the sheets was outrageous. Squished strawbs leaving bloody pulp trails around islands of fat cream. Rivulets of champagne joined the picture before soaking into the counterpane, followed by cum which seemed to fly everywhere.

It was great fun, decadent and frivolous. I fingered his arse, manipulating his prostate as I rubbed my breasts across his body; we watched each other masturbate, coming together.

Time for a shower and dinner. The maitre d' made me smile when we left the restaurant by wishing us a good sleep. We did, eventually, only to start all over again in the early hours. Henry loves adding kink to our sessions, it makes them special for both of us. Can't wait to try my violet wand on him next time.

Cocktease
by Rachel Kramer Bussel

"No, I'm not gonna do it," Brad said, sounding more like a petulant child than the self-made chef he was.

"Not for everyone in the world, just for me. Right here. That's what I want: to see you touch yourself. I want to watch, baby. You know I love looking at your cock, right?" I was starting to whine, but I couldn't help it. Seeing him do his own private circle jerk had become the reigning fantasy, playing on rotation in my mind non-stop.

I was poised in front of him, on my knees, within easy sucking distance, like I'd been plenty of times in the last six months. Truth is, I wanted to suck him, too, but even more than that, I wanted to update the homepage in my mind, to see what he looked like when he wasn't with me, but was getting off.

But for the life of me, I couldn't get Brad to comply. He even started, his hand moving up and down, playing hide and seek with his gorgeous cock, but then he burst out laughing and looked away.

"Baby, I wish I could do it for you, but I just can't. I feel awkward with you watching."

I couldn't understand it; I'd seen his dick hundreds of times. So I decided to take matters into my own hands – and out of his.

"Fine, then, if you can't do me this one itsy little favour ... I have another idea."

I fished out a pair of black and gold fishnets of mine that I know he loves, bending over to reach them so my ass would be right within his reach. He started to fondle my bottom, but just as he got into it, I shifted around so I was behind him, and

191

started to tie his hands behind his back with my stockings.

"What are you doing, Brenda?"

"Oh, nothing. I'm just going to show you how excruciating it can be to not get what you want. Kind of like what you did to me."

If he wasn't going to jerk himself off, I was going to avail myself of the pleasure. But I know from previous handjobs and blowjobs that at a certain point, he's enjoying himself almost too much, and wants to jump in and get involved. His hands start playing with my nipples, or he starts 'helping' me, and this time, I wanted things done my way. He shifted against the bonds, and even though he made some protests about his state of immobilisation, I heard his breathing change and noticed that his dick was even stiffer.

I moved so I was once again in front of him. "There, isn't that better?" I asked as I leaned down and gave his dick the gentlest of kisses.

"Oh yeah, lick it, Brenda," he said.

"Maybe," I said, smiling impishly, before getting up and walking into the bathroom. I knew he could see me, and I made a show of rummaging through my makeup cases before finding a box holding various shadows, blushes, and lip glosses. I dipped a brush into some pink gloss and swiped it over my lips until they gleamed. I was wearing my favourite pale blue lingerie, a wispy nightie that hovers just at the line of my nipples, sometimes allowing for a peek, sometimes not, and a pair of mesh panties the same colour. I also knew they were Brad's favourites.

I liked that suddenly, he couldn't move, all because of a little ingenuity and one of our favourite items of clothing. I'd have liked it more if he would've just shown me how he masturbated, but that wasn't to be, at least, not yet. I pulled back, only letting my lips lightly graze the engorged flesh of his cockhead.

"You're driving me crazy," he said.

"That's the idea," I said as I squeezed his cock in my fist, relishing the power I suddenly had over him. Much as I had wanted one thing from him earlier, now I wanted something else. I lightly licked, resisting the heat radiating from him; funnily enough, I was restraining myself almost as much as I was restraining him, just in a different form.

I stepped away and blew lightly on his dick, laughing. "You wanted a blowjob, right?"

"Come on, you know what I want," he growled, twisting his wrists against the bonds that held them together. I knew that, strong as he was, if he really, truly wanted to escape, he could, but some part of my macho man was enjoying being tied up, at my mercy. He knew I wasn't the truly sadistic type who'd hurt him just to hurt him. A pinch of his nipple, a light slap against his cock, a squeeze of his balls, maybe, but nothing major. No, what I wanted was even more valuable. I stood and very slowly moved to get the lube. I wanted a handjob, and I'd be damned if I wasn't going to get it.

I was naked, which suddenly seemed like a shame, like I should be sashaying around in some skimpy, sheer nightie that would cling to my ass and make it all the more alluring. Oh well. Instead, I made sure to stick my butt out and flaunt my backside for all I was worth as I leaned over, extending my ass and exposing my pussy lips, while pretending to rummage for the bottle I could easily find. My hand passed over the suede of a beloved flogger, the smoothness of a patent leather paddle, the chill of nipple clamps and the clamminess of a silicone dildo, beloved toys all. But the most beloved of all, I'd have to say, is the lube. We have several bottles, so we never run out. He likes to pour it between my breasts and then fuck my cleavage, while I press my tits together to form a tight tunnel.

He'll use it to finger my asshole while I'm on top of him during sex. He'll let it slip and slide against my pussy until I'm aching, the frustration extending into what feels like for ever. Turnabout's fair play, so that's exactly what I planned to do to him. I took it out, then poured a little down my chest, letting the cool liquid slide over my breasts, drip down the curve of my belly. I rubbed it into my skin the way I often rub his come against me, and when I looked up, Brad's eyes were locked on mine.

How's your cock?" I asked, though I could see perfectly

well that it was tall, erect, proud, and horny.

"Good," he said, mock-casually, though I knew the tension ran through his blood. "Get over here, though, I need you, I need you to fuck me." I heard the strain in his voice, heard that the need was real, and felt a shiver chill me from my toes to my ears. I love to see him reduced to that need, to play just hard enough to get that I make him hard, make him think about what it's like to fuck me, make him miss me even when I'm in the same room.

"Be patient, my sweet," I said as I approached, leaning down to tenderly kiss his forehead. If his hands had been free, he'd surely have grabbed me, mashed my mouth to his, insisted that we kiss and fuck and come immediately. But he couldn't, and I knew it was driving him crazy.

We both stared down at his dick, and the sight made my inner ache even stronger. Oh, I wanted him, but that primal, feral need warred with the excitement of my power over him. Which would win? I knew I wasn't likely to get him to submit to bondage again soon; he liked it, sure, but the waiting was too much for a man who practically defined immediate gratification.

I took the bottle of lube, flipped the plastic opening, and upended it. Slowly, the clear, thin liquid drizzled down, landing directly on the upright head of his cock. It slowly made its way down his length, and then I poured more, into my palm, before wrapping it around him and gliding it up and down.

"Since you won't show me what you do to yourself, maybe you can tell me," I said, my voice gone deep and husky as I switched my gaze from his member to his mouth. His lips were parted, his breathing heavy and dull, as I squeezed tighter, then used one hand to massage his balls. I moved much slower than normal, because I had all the time in the world. Still holding onto his cock, I peeked behind me to confirm that my favourite fishnets were still holding his wrists in place. They looked both out of place and perfect there, the holes bunched together, strands of gold glistening from the pile of black.

I shifted so I was half-kneeling, one foot on the ground, one on the bed, my pussy hovering over him. I rubbed myself gently against the head of his cock, not letting it enter but simply grazing it, then moved back and returned to my task. I placed both hands, fist on top of fist, on his shaft, the head disappearing between my fingers before peeking out again.

"Oh God," he groaned, and I pressed harder, started moving faster. He pushed his hips upward, trying to control my motions, but he couldn't. I was 100 per cent in charge, and I loved it. The tease, I saw now, was everything; bondage was just a means to an end. His face, when I glanced up at it, was contorted, brow wrinkled as he processed my torment, counted out in each agonising stroke.

"You want to come, don't you? You want to come all over my tits, or my face, or in my mouth? You want to shower me with all your hot come, drown me in it." I wasn't asking, I was telling, because I know exactly how he likes to come. He almost always pulls out and makes sure I'm the recipient of his cream. Brad just moaned as I kept on stroking. I knew it wouldn't be long. I had to act fast. I took one hand off him and reached between my legs, flicking my clit, which was extremely hard by then. It almost hurt, but soon I got a familiar rhythm going, doing double duty as I pumped his dick and played with my clit.

I knew his eyes were on the hand between my legs, but mine were fixed on him. I wanted to watch him come, wanted my very own money shot. I stroked faster, squeezed harder, remembering how I once thought it possible to squeeze too tight, only to be assured that for him, there was no such thing. I played with the pre-come that had seeped from the tip, longing to lean down and suck just the swollen, blood-filled head, but I didn't. I just stroked, up and down, up and down, a twist here, a ball fondling there, working myself up to a tremendous climax.

"You're going to come when I do, or I won't let you come at all," I told him. Then both hands moved at a feverish pace that would rival my favourite vibrator. I was inserting and flicking myself, so wet I could smell my arousal, while pumping him hard, feeling the motion in my arm muscles. "Yeah …" he gasped, and then slowly my orgasm burst forth, going from an ache, a tingling, to something so much more as I shuddered against my hand. Just then I felt the eruption; my eyes had already drooped closed in ecstasy when I came. Feeling his climax, I looked down and saw the milky thick cream cover my hand.

Only when I'd stopped trembling did I lean down and lick his semen off my fingers and his skin. And only then did I kiss him, offering Brad a taste of himself. And only then did I untie him, letting the used stockings fall to the floor. And only then did I ask, "So, was I close?"

He laughed, and pulled me towards him. "Very close, my love. But you're not quite there yet. I'll have to give you some pointers tomorrow." I kissed him, full and deep and horny yet again, excited for the sexual secrets that awaited me.

Indulgence Calling …
by Angel O'Neill

She sighed as she closed the door softly behind her and walked into the room. It was exactly as she'd wanted. The suite was large enough for a small family to move into, and the bed! Roughly the size of two normal king sized beds side by side, the four-poster, with its dark wooden posts and heavy red velvet drapes, suited her purposes perfectly. She checked the food service trolley, ensuring everything she'd ordered was there – champagne, lobster, strawberries. Yeah, it might be clichéd but what the hell. It was what she wanted.

Checking the time she realised with a thrill it was almost zero hour. Shedding her coat she sat down slowly on the vast chaise longue and poured herself a glass of bubbles. Not too big, she didn't want to kill the buzz. But enough to relax. She lay back, and waited.

She didn't have to wait long. In a few minutes, the buzzer went and, feeling butterflies in her stomach, she went to answer the door. There they were, exactly as she'd imagined. Really, this was all going very well so far. She opened the door wider, allowing them access. One tall blue-eyed blond with long legs, a muscular model with dark brown hair and brooding dark eyes, and finally, soft glossy black skin and a body to die for. They were all perfect. She smiled a hello, and they all walked into the suite together.

She'd made her requests clear when booking this, so she kind of knew what was coming up – but she wasn't prepared for the sheer thrill of making it happen. The blond – Sven – disappeared into the bathroom and she could hear the bath running, while Milo, the black guy, cracked lobster and poured more champagne. Meanwhile Rory, proper Heathcliff eyes locked with hers, making her slightly shivery, was slowly taking off her clothes. His gentle fingers undoing the buttons, sliding her skirt over her bottom, softly pulling her knickers down, before wrapping the silk robe around her. Just lightly twisting her nipples as he did so. She jumped, gasping at the intimacy of it.

They led her into the bathroom and tied up her hair like a child before encouraging her to step into the rolltop Victorian bath stood in the middle of the room. As she lay back in the deliciously hot bubbles a silk blindfold was tied around her eyes. Left only with her hearing and physical sensations, she could hear them moving around the room, knew they were on both sides of her ... then hands, cool in the heat, plunged under the water's surface, stroking her skin. One set of hands at her feet, working the soles gently, massaging. One set further up, circling her stomach, moving slowly upwards, sliding round her breasts, brushing lightly across the nipples and making her stomach clench with excitement. While the third set of hands gently stroking her legs, working up her thighs, making her throb between the legs, shivery with anticipation.

She felt her legs being gently but firmly pulled apart, one hand sliding more intimately up her inner thighs, until finally touching her cunt, sweeping movements stroking the surface, pressing more insistently as her lips parted, rubbing now rather than stroking, finding her swollen clit rising to the pressure. She felt her body responding, twisting towards the sensation, her breath coming faster, and as fingers pinched her nipples, more fingers came gently around her neck, holding her still as she started to climax. As the waves hit her, she could hear nothing but her own gasps and the water splashing, could feel only the hands on her body. Slowly, she subsided, her breathing regulating as the hands, not withdrawing but slowing down, gave her some time.

The blindfold remained in place but she was instructed to stand, helped to step out of the bath. She felt warm towels around her, her body being dried carefully, thoroughly. Her hair released from its tie. Scooped up in a pair of strong arms she was carried rather than led into the next room, before being laid on the bed. Silence then except for movements around the room … then the smell of fresh strawberry close to her face before the gentle touch of it nudging her lips, gently forcing them open. The taste was heaven as she bit into it. And as she tasted the strawberry in her mouth, so too did she feel the coldness of another separating the lips of her cunt again, gently probing, rubbing her slit. She felt her head lifted for a sip of champagne again before being allowed to fall back onto the pillow.

Suddenly the tempo changed. She was turned over, quickly, her legs pulled open, her arms too, and very firm hands held her fast as she felt ropes around her wrists and ankles. Not seriously trying to escape, but testing the tension, she pulled against the bonds, feeling how much room she had for movement. Not much. She was now laid face down, blindfolded, star-shaped, her legs wide open and cunt fully on display, with three total strangers preparing to go to work on her.

Her body was lifted slightly, a pillow pushed under her stomach, her bottom raised even higher now. She felt soft hands start to work gently at her back, oily hands massaging slowly and working downwards all the time. As this was going on, so too could she feel another hand slip under the front of her cunt, rubbing it gently, in rhythm with the hands on her back and her own movements as she started to thrust slowly, her hips rising and falling. She felt the bed dip either side of her head, and then something thrusting on the side of her face, and realised one of them was straddling her face, rubbing his cock on her as she lay there.

The fingers on her clit became more insistent, and the hands massaging her back moved down. Oil was then trickling down the slit between her anus and her cunt, and fingers started massaging there too. Her legs wide open, there were sensations everywhere, probing at her anus, the other fingers still on her clit and finally a third set of fingers in her cunt. She couldn't stop, she came hard, long, almost howling with the intensity of it. And as she did so, the unmistakeable feeling of a cock nudging at her lips.

As she slipped it into her mouth, the familiar salty taste on her tongue, the other fingers withdrew and were replaced by two things – one she knew to definitely be a cock by its texture, nudging insistently at her anus, and the other, a vibrator, which she soon realised was a rabbit as she felt the vibrating prongs touch her already swollen and sensitive clitoris. Moaning as she felt she could hardly bear such intense sensation so soon after coming, she felt the weight of the man fucking her in the arse at the same time, thrusting harder now, deep inside, and at the same time the cock in her mouth thrusting faster, definitely building in pressure. Despite her hypersensitivity, she felt another orgasm, almost forced from her, rising like a tide, and as her climax started to hit, so did the man fucking her. His groans were matched by hers, and then, a split second later, she felt the cock in her mouth throb, hands grabbing her hair as the other man thrust it deep into her throat, grunting with pleasure as she took it all.

There was a long pause then, nothing but panting and gasping. The vibrator was pulled gently out of her, she almost sobbed with relief, the almost painful pleasure had become too much. And as she rested, the binds were removed from her legs and arms, and she was gently turned over.

She knew it wasn't over yet though. The third man, his smell and heat close to her face, climbed on top, nudging her legs open with his knees, kissing her softly on her neck, stroking her body. The gentle touch was exquisite after the pounding she'd just taken and she opened her legs, feeling his cock slide between the lips of her cunt. Wrapping her legs around his body, she could feel the tension in his muscles, knew he wouldn't take long. He rode her harder, his cock really deep as she could hear his breathing hard in her ear, close to her head, hear his mounting pleasure. He came, groaning loudly, pushing hard, thrusting as deeply into her as he could.

The third man rolled off her and they all lay there in peaceful silence for a while, enjoying the pleasurable buzz that follows sex, waiting for a burst of energy. Then she felt the blindfold removed and blinking, looked around at the soppy grinning faces, her own face pretty soppy and grinning too, feeling the thrill of not knowing which one had done what to her.

"That was perfect," she said, "you guys are brilliant!"

They all looked pretty pleased with that, and Milo scooped her up again. They took her back to the bath and gently cleaned her up, softly washing away the evidence of excess and indulgence. Following the bath, they all dressed, and shared the trolley of delicacies before the boys departed, leaving her replete, well fed, well watered, and extremely well fucked. Pondering, she reached into her handbag, flicked through the leaflet again, re-reading what had caught her eye in the first place. And she decided, without a doubt, that the 'Ultimate Indulgence' package had been worth every single penny.

Fantasy
by Sarah-Louise Young

I could hear them breathing. As I crouched down I held my breath. A sudden thud then a female voice, laughing gently.

I'd been sitting on a bench in St James' Park, quietly reading to myself, when I saw them: a young couple, driven by a sense of urgency, rushed, on borrowed time. I glanced up from my book and caught sight of them, twenty metres away, scurrying along the path, their bodies leaning close, a secret between them. From the benches which line the path leading around the park, the only thing that can be seen of the island in the centre of the lake are trees, leafy, tall, their branches tipping the water's edge in the bright August sun. I looked around. I seemed to be the only person who saw them, the only one moved by this sudden rush of activity.

I put my book away in my shoulder bag and picked up my camera. I smiled a goodbye to the old gentleman who had been feeding the ducks beside me and chatting away. I hadn't minded. I was between appointments and happy to have some free time. But now I wanted to slip away, unobserved. I nodded to the man and left him, still talking and chuckling to himself. I walked briskly round the pathway and stepped over the low gate, about a foot and a half high, which marked the out-of-bounds entrance to the island. Trying to appear as relaxed as I could, I followed the smaller track where I'd seen the couple go. Within a moment I was at the edge of the island. Another second and I would have drawn attention to myself, so I stepped inside the thickness of the garden and continued nervously forwards.

After a while the space opened out slightly and I crouched behind a bush so as not to be seen. Far off I could hear the noise of children, families, people out and about, but here, all I could hear was my heart, racing as I listened for movement. I edged further still, all the while keeping low to the ground, my camera clasped close to my chest. The grass underneath scraped softly against the inside of my thighs and I waited, panting, out of breath in the heat. And then I heard her laugh. I looked up through the foliage and, framed by green, could just make out the middle of their bodies. He pushed his full weight against her delicate waist and pinned her to the trunk of a tree. The urgency was intoxicating. His fingers struggled with the bottom of her white shirt, tugging it forcefully from her slender neat hips. As he pulled at the garment I saw the soft beauty of her skin, before she ripped at the blouse with her own fingers, frantically struggling to reveal her bare stomach and breasts. She tore with her nails into his shirt and back and ground her hips into his crotch, losing herself. Their tongues and limbs all seemed tangled, mouths eating, devouring each other. She let out a deep sigh and then a gasp. But then their bodies stiffened as he cupped her mouth in his hand. I froze too. Had they heard me, my own breath joining theirs as their passion grew? I did my best to remain invisible, squatting in the leaves, one hand clenched over own lips. There was a heavy silence.

Then she pushed his hand away, giggled and grabbed him in her arms. I took this moment as my cue, and slowly, silently edged my way backwards, half crawling half falling, my knees brushing the slightly damp soil beneath. Then out into the open, back down the path, the noise and daylight flooding my senses. As I reached the little gate I felt a rush of relief – I had been lucky no one had seen me, least of all the man and woman currently devouring each other inside. Once on the other side, I turned again to face the island, so innocent from the main path. I noticed properly the warning sign, nailed to the barrier: 'Private. No Admission' it read. As I looked up something caught my attention from the small gatekeeper's cottage on the left. A pair of beady eyes looked out at me from a tiny darkened window. Someone was watching me, disapproving.

The gate keeper would have had a fit if he had known what carnal delights were being enjoyed inside his island. I smiled to myself to think that I has distracted him and maybe bought a bit more time for the illicit pair.

For the rest of the day I thought about them, wondered who they were, how long they'd been together. Were they married or having an affair, a moment of forbidden passion stolen in the middle of a duck-inhabited island in the late afternoon in St James' Park? I hadn't wanted to disturb them, but being close enough for them to hear me if I moved was so exciting. If only they knew what pleasure it gave me to see them enjoying each other, the spark they had lit in my belly, the smile of wickedness they brought to my lips that day.

I'd spent a beautiful summer with Marcus. The mysterious beginning of our affair had been so intriguing, so dramatic, so all consuming, I'd wondered where else there was left for it to go. Knowing it was allowed, that Anthony has chosen him for me, even fantasized about us being together, made me feeling deliciously decadent. Whilst I wasn't against the idea of falling in love, it seemed as though Marcus had been put in my life purely to enjoy and be enjoyed. I was determined to know him but not to lose that spark of passion and desire. He always kept our adventures a surprise so I could never quite know what to expect.

I worked for most of the summer in my sweltering studio. Some nights I'd stay awake alone in my dark room, slinking about the house in just my briefs, feeling the cool night air on my body and thinking of our previous encounter or the evening to come. At the end of an agreed day, Marcus would arrive, dressed to perfection with an expectant look in his eyes. We grew closer as lovers and indulged in each other, but always kept each other guessing as to what would happen next.

When he called to say he had an offer to work abroad, that he'd be gone for at least six months, initially my heart sank: an end to our games, an end to our fun. But a moment later I felt almost excited – the close of one wonderful chapter but the possibilities of a whole new novel to come. Our affair had been perfect, passionate, powerful and now that it was going to end I felt like celebrating its success. No malice or confusion or broken hearts, just sexy, fabulous memories and a tempting open door if ever I felt the urge to travel. We met one last time, and toasted ourselves, chilled Vespers raised to our futures. He made slow tender love to me and left, his scent draped over my bed and my hair and my skin.

In the four months Marcus and I had been together I had not spoken to Anthony once. While he'd orchestrated his replacement with unquestionable flair and commitment, it was one thing to know your girl is being royally fucked by a hand-picked friend, but another completely to be flooded with the intimate details. I wanted to reassure him, thank him. Let him know that our chapter, Anthony and Fantasy, would never be a closed book.

Anthony wasn't due back for another two months and I found myself sitting on the end of my bed wondering, 'What now?' I drew a clean circle around my relationship with Marcus, perfect in its completion. I had been so busy with work and Marcus so attentive that I hadn't really kept my eyes open for another suitable match. Besides, I felt this natural break was what I needed, to take stock, remind myself of my own company. I spent blissful evenings in, bathing, moisturising, preparing myself for what might come. Sometimes I would spread myself across the bed and let my gentle fingers playfully wander over my body, caress my soft supple skin and delve finally between my legs and circle the delicate moist opening of my cunt. Sometimes I thought of my evenings with Marcus and sometimes I let a stranger's face, someone I'd seen out that day, enter my thoughts. I felt open and free and totally absorbed in my own desire. As I brought myself to orgasm I would rock myself back and forth, letting the silky juices rush through my fingers as I rubbed myself against the satiny sheets. I sighed and smiled, happy with myself and my complete satisfaction with having been born with a clit.

It was at this time, towards the end of August, that I received a letter from my old photography college. I'd stayed

205

in touch since leaving and had recently gone back as a guest speaker. I was something of a celebrity there, which surprised me. The letter was from a young man in his twenties called Daniel. He'd come in late, half way though my last talk back in May. I remembered him because he came up to me afterwards and apologised. He was sweet and enthusiastic. I'd looked at a couple of his pictures and offered some advice. Then, I remembered, he'd produced a copy of some journal I'd written a column in, headed with the usual moody black and white photo of me posing, rather uncertain with my camera in hand. The young man had said how much more attractive I was in real life and I blushed at the corny line, flattered nonetheless that it came from such an attractive attentive man.

It was part of the training that all students find a work placement in their second year and although I'd received the odd request before, I'd never really given them much thought. The odd seminar was easy but being trailed for a week might be difficult in my busy schedule. However, my impressions of Daniel and my few weeks spent alone, made me curious. I also needed help moving some heavy equipment and it was this last excuse that led me to pick up the phone and dial Daniel's number.

He sounded surprised to hear from me, his voice bright and open. I said I could do with a bit of man power and in return he was welcome to spend a week picking my brains. As I put the phone down I started wondering what it would be like. Although my studio was my professional domain it was still my home. No one ever saw further than the main room or the hallway. I kept the door to the adjoining hallway firmly closed.

Although the question mark of sexual possibility had been raised the moment I agreed to help, it gave me an equal thrill to consider *not* seducing Daniel. After all, I was supposed to be his tutor. As the older woman, experienced and confident, it would not be vain to imagine that his intentions might not be wholly fixed on work experience. That he was hoping for some kind of education I could be sure of. I didn't feel the need for an affair, but how sweet might it be to fill his head with images, unattainable desire then leave him frantic and excited and ready to go out and burst himself fucking an appropriately younger girl. Sex with Marcus had been so fulfilling, his manliness so essential, the idea of a younger, clumsier lover seemed unattractive. For a moment I thought of calling him back, changing my mind, but then I though about how pleased he had sounded, how disappointed he'd be if I let him down.

He arrived on the Monday, early. By the nervous look of him I'd guessed he'd been pacing about the lobby for at least ten minutes. He looked as if he'd camped out all night. He was clean but his tousled hair stood up at odd angles and his sharp jaw wore an even layer of stubble.

'Fantasy', he breathed, as if relieved to say my name.

'Come in, come in," I urged. As he entered the studio I noticed how tall he was. Over his broad shoulders he'd slung an old army bag.

"Sorry I'm early.'

"Don't be," I said, "First professional test and you passed."

I showed him where to put his bag. Under his other arm he held his portfolio and in his hand he clutched a white paper bag.

"Croissants," he offered. I smiled.

"I'm going to like you."

The morning passed quickly as people came and went. Daniel took their coats, helped me shift lights and was generally very helpful. I felt a bit guilty giving him such menial chores but he seemed happy, watching me closely as I gave instructions, his eyes serious and intent. We were both tired by the end of the day but I still had some photos to develop.

"I could always help," he said. I looked at my watch. It was past six – over time already.

"Look, I've got a friend's exhibition opening tonight. I can work later. Do you want to come?"

I knew it would a good opportunity for him, though strictly speaking it was out of hours. He looked at me, delighted. "I'd love to."

The opening started fashionably late at nine and I needed to shower and change. As Daniel left I called out to him, "Wear something smart."

When I arrived at the gallery it took me a moment to recognise him. During the day he'd been in tatty jeans and a T-shirt. I normally kept to a smart black shirt and trousers myself but now had on a low-backed silk Chanel in dazzling silver. I looked out though the sea of faces and there, standing at the bar, was Daniel, clean-shaven, resting on one elbow, dressed in a smart black suit with a cream shirt, open at the neck. He'd done something with his hair and stood serenely, unfazed by all the big names and talk about him. He looked up, caught me staring at him as I approached and straightened himself. He raised a suggestive eyebrow and made a low, appreciative hum. Cheeky, I thought, but intriguing. He ordered me champagne and we watched the art world gather around the room.

"I'm not a big fan of these things," I admitted, "but the artist's a friend of mine."

Daniel just stood there looking elegant and relaxed as if big gallery openings were second nature to him. I had to abandon him for most of the night as I chatted to friends and associates. Occasionally I'd glance over. He didn't need any introductions though and more than once a female friend touched me on the arm to inquire about my dashing new protégé. After one day he was certainly making a very good impression. I left at midnight, aware of the busy day ahead. Daniel put me into a taxi and I felt strangely young, as if I were his guest and he were in charge.

The next day, five minutes early, came the knock at my door. He was back to his ruffled self but his eyes betrayed a new confidence, a sparkle from the night before. I didn't have a client until eleven so our first job of the day was developing some pictures. Daniel was keen to see my approach and I admit I was quite keen to see him in my lair. The dark room was small, constructed out of the sloping underside of the stairs from the flat above and an old cupboard knocked through. I'd built it myself, never really imagining it would ever house more than one person.

As he stood close behind me I could feel his breath against my neck, warm and soft. I worked my way through a series of pictures and gradually he began follow my lead, helping to pin up the finished prints. I was trying to concentrate on the tones and shades but his strong physical presence was like an arm around my waist pulling me into him.

"That's St James' Park, isn't it?" Daniel asked.

"Mmm," I said, innocently.

The story progressed. A cluster of trees, a wooden bench, an old man feeding the birds. A little closer still and there it was. Duck Island: my lovers' retreat. To anyone who didn't know, it wasn't a particularly interesting set of prints, but when I thought back to that afternoon where I'd crouched, unobserved, witnessing two lovers tear at each other's clothes and moan deeply, I felt suddenly overwhelmed. I turned to Daniel a few inches away and reached out to touch his arm. At that moment there was a knock on the door and Daniel looked up from his work.

"I'll go," he said cheerfully and strode off out of the dark room and into the light. I stood there, breathing heavily, staring at the photos hanging up to dry and allowed a wicked thought to enter my head.

For the rest of the day we worked closely. I let Daniel check the lens, offer suggestions and even take a few shots. He was good – invaluable with a difficult older woman in her sixties, a fading glamour star who needed constant praise and reassurance. By six we were done and as he collected his things I took my chance. Casually, as if the thought had only just entered my head, I said, "Those prints today – I'm not quite happy. I've got a few things I need to do in the morning, but how about we meet at 3 p.m. tomorrow at the entrance to Green Park? I'll bring some lunch – it'll be good to get out of the studio."

He paused for a moment taking in the change of plan.

"Great, see you then," and he was gone. I fell back onto the sofa content.

I dressed deliberately the following morning, taking care of my light make-up and painting my toe-nails a pearly pink. I slipped a pale blue flared skirt over my smooth toned legs and put on a close-fitting white halterneck that clung to my skin and revealed the faint outline of my dark nipples. I stepped into a pair of low heeled sandals and pinned back my hazel hair with a clip. Simple, classic, carefree – that was the desired effect. The one item of clothing I dispensed with at the last minute was my thong. If I was going to do this at all I wanted to do it properly. I packed my shoulder bag and as I left the studio I caught sight of my reflection in the elevator glass. I looked young, mischievous and determined. A rush of air touched my naked bottom and my face flushed with anticipation.

As I stepped up out from the tube I checked my watch. I was ten minutes early. I leaned against the wall at the entrance to the park. The traffic along Piccadilly raced by and the late summer sun shone down on my face. I tried to remain calm but a familiar wave of danger and desire I hadn't felt since Marcus left was returning to the pit of my stomach. I felt elated. How would I approach him, I wondered? How would he react? Just then I felt a strong hand on my shoulder. Daniel.

"You look lovely," he said.

"Thank you," I said, a little taken aback.

I led on and as we walked down through the park I felt at once released from the tension in my stomach. Being outside in the sun, office workers stealing a crafty picnic lunch to our right, families with children playing, I wanted to enjoy this afternoon, the build up, the unknown elements of my planned liaison. Out here it seemed impossible to re-capture the intensity of the dark room. I had no idea how it would work. I didn't say much but let Daniel chat on about his studies, his lecturers and the clients we'd met the previous day. He was so young and vibrant, his positivity was infectious. As I walked on, the softness of my naked thighs brushed together and my little skirt rippled in the gentle breeze. My pink parted pussy started to moisten as the air lifted the edges of my skirt. I felt like the keeper of a wonderful secret.

We reached the end of the park and crossed the road, marvelling at the hordes of eager sightseers' never ending fascination with Buckingham Palace. We followed the new path down into St James' Park. Daniel started to point out some of the spots from my pictures and I laughed inside at my mistreatment of college time! We continued on through the park, the sun opening out onto us like a blessing from above. As the path curved to the left once more we came upon the little cottage and the route to Duck Island. I stopped and Daniel turned to face me.

"Hope you're feeling brave," I whispered. "In here." I tipped my head in the direction of the island, my eyes wide like a naughty child.

He nodded at the sign and I looked towards the little house where I'd been observed that afternoon.

"While the cat's away …" I purred and took his hand gently in mine. With one last look over my shoulder I stepped up and straddled the little fence. He paused, his hand still in mine, standing on the other side.

"You're crazy," he said in amused defeat and stepped over to join me. We ran quietly up the path and into the bushes, an energy of forbidden pleasure passing between us. He squeezed my hand and I wondered if he knew what I had planned. I hadn't been able to venture very far inside the island before for fear of being seen. It was only about thirty metres wide and much of it was too thick with wildlife to access. Some slightly annoyed ducks quacked and took off as we moved deeper still into the heart of the secret garden. We found ourselves in a clearing and then I let go of his hand.

"I hope you're hungry," I said, turning away from him.

"Ravenous," he replied.

I heard him drop to the floor and, kneeling, start rummaging in his rucksack. Still with my back to him I slowly lowered my bag to the floor but, instead of crouching down to empty out the picnic things, I bent right over from my waist, my legs straight, so that my bottom was all at once revealed and in line with his face. My short skirt lifted to unveil the perfect peach of my nicely-toned bottom and the glistening opening of my now soaking cunt. I waited for a second, hardly daring to turn. I was about to stand up again when, confronted with this unusual presentation of floorless Fantasy, Daniel raised his large hand and placed it firmly on my buttocks. The touch I had been waiting for sent a shock through my entire body and I gulped. As his two strong palms clamped down on my waiting arse cheeks he moved his face closer to my mound, his breath cool on my skin, his weight holding me in place.

"You naughty, naughty lady," he said, his voice full of pleasure.

He loosened his grip a touch and started working his hands around the pert curve of my expectant, inviting bottom, then brought his face closer still so that his nose and mouth nuzzled in between my cleft. At last, in one firm stroke, he licked my waiting, wet pussy from top to bottom with his firm rough tongue. I wanted to thrust my groin onto his mouth and grind my juices all over his beautiful face. He licked again and this time pushed his tongue right inside my opening and sucked on my dripping juices. Still with his hands on my rear, my skirt pushed up over my muscular thighs, he gradually stood up so that his whole body touched the length of mine. Standing, he turned me round to face him, working my thighs with his touch. Face to face I finally felt the full youthful swell of his cock, forcing its way through his trousers and pressing angrily against me. Our eyes locked, and Daniel kissed me for the first time with hungry, all-consuming kisses. I responded with equal drive. We were a tangle of lips and tongues, my arms searching roughly through his hair and down his back around the full girth of my new lover. His smell and the light sweat on his neck all seemed to me like the sweetest perfume and I longed to lick his whole body, to taste him in my mouth. Then he pushed me backwards and I stumbled, clutching onto his arms for balance until I felt the rough trunk of a large tree behind me.

Daniel pushed up my top and began sucking at my beautiful breasts, alternating tongue and hand, squeezing them together and tweaking their taught upward-pointing nipples. I ran my own hands over and around them, the shock of excitement making me frantic. Then he sank to his knees and parted my legs. He took a moment to take me in as if worshipping at an

212

altar and looked up to me with a flushed face, hot but ecstatic. I loved how wild and lawless this felt, how completely different from the hotels and parties of my time with Marcus. Then he plunged his face and tongue into and around my cunt, flicking his tongue over the tip of my clit, then gradually concentrating his stroking on my flushed peak. As he circled I looked up and saw the clear sky, smelled the undergrowth and the scent of our sex all merge together. One final tug at my glorious clit and I came, wildly all over his face, spasming and grabbing hold of him to steady me.

As he stood, his look triumphant, I saw that he had already got his cock out in his hand and was pumping it hard. This young man who I'd thought I would have to teach seemed to know exactly what he was doing. I was enjoying his control. Daniel put his hands once more on my hips and turned me so that I faced the tree. I lay my palms flat and pushed out my rear, my pink open lips defiant to the world. At once I felt his hard prick push into me and I clenched my stomach muscles and tensed my legs. As he thrust into me I took the force of him onto my hands and lowered myself so that we pounded harder and closer together. He grunted and sighed and I could feel a deep swell growing in me as he was about to come. His hands grabbed at my breasts swaying beneath me and as I straightened my back he shot through me, his whole body giving way to his climax.

Still inside me, his breathing heavy, he held me close and drew me to him, kissing my neck and my shoulders. He started to straighten my clothes and stroke my skin as if not wanting to leave me ruffled and unkempt. As he pulled out his soaked member I turned to face him and kissed him firmly.

"I think we found our location," I laughed gently.

He looked at me with strange admiration and kissed me back.

I looked at our bags strewn across the floor and our flushed, rumpled hair. We looked thoroughly reckless and I started to wonder if anyone could have heard us, not least the beady eyed man in the cottage. I picked up my camera and took a couple of quick shots of our nest, our love makers' lair.

213

I decided to abandon the picnic and take Daniel back to my home, beyond the studio into my bed and my arms and feast on him there. Creeping off the island and out of the park we must have looked like two guilty criminals. We fell into a taxi and raced back to the safety of my flat to spend the rest of the day in bed.

During our last two days in the studio we worked very closely and discovered that the dark room was definitely big enough for two.

A few days after Daniel left I developed the photos from our afternoon. I picked my favourite, the clearing, the tree and our bags laid out. Almost out of shot was Daniel's profile, his lips parted, still slightly out of breath, his shirt off his shoulder and his hair tousled just the way I had come to like it. I made a print and wrote on the back of it:

"For Daniel at the start of a very promising career. If you ever need any professional advice just call."

Then I slipped the photo into an envelope and posted it to the college, wondering just how Daniel would manage to sum up his week of 'work experience' to his tutors. I walked around my flat, reclaiming my space, and smiled at the millions of possibilities that lay ahead.

Take Me to Carnevale
by Maxim Jakubowski

They had arranged to meet in a small cafe on the left hand side of Campo Santa Maria Formosa, right opposite the church and the hospital. It was February. It was Venice. A thin morning mist still shrouded the city, floating in from the lagoon like a shimmering curtain of silk, half obscuring the old stones, the canals and the normal sounds of the floating city.

The connection had been made over the internet. He hadn't even brought his laptop with him on this Venice trip, but the apartment they were staying in, which he had agreed to house-sit for friends travelling in India, had a computer in almost every room and a wi-fi connection and it had been, for both of them, almost too much of a temptation. Like allowing their fate to be decided by the vagaries of electronic availability.

Emma had been sitting on one of the sofas, half reading and half daydreaming, while he listened to music on his iPod. Right then the soundtrack by Nick Cave for *The Assassination of Jesse James*, he would remember later.

"I don't know," Emma had said, and he had known exactly the precise words she had uttered, just from reading her lips behind the threnody in his ears. It was something she often mumbled when things were not quite right.

He'd switched off the music and turned towards her.

"What is it?"

The green of her eyes emerged from a sea of sadness.

"You know …" she replied.

He knew. Oh yes, he knew. They were just going nowhere, and no earnest conversation could put them back on track. Even in Venice.

They had reached the city a week or so earlier, arriving at Marco Polo airport. To save money, they had not gone to the extravagance of taking a water taxi but, instead, the bus which took them across the Ponte Della Liberta to Piazzale Roma where they had caught a vaporetto down the Grand Canal to the Rialto Bridge stop and, following the map they had been emailed by his friends, had somehow made their way on foot to the apartment, dodging the customary labyrinth of small bridges and lesser canals.

By now they had seen a multitude of churches, several handfuls of Titian and Canaletto paintings, eaten enough exquisite food to jade the best of palates and suffered an indigestion of baroque and classical architecture and the silences between them were growing longer.

From their bedroom window, they could see St Mark's Place and the Doge's Palace and the Campanile across a bend in the Canal. But the weather was cold and humid and the old building's heating was stuttering at its best and they'd had to wear sweatshirts most of the time both inside and outside.

Maybe he should have chosen the Caribbean where they could have lazed naked on a beach and the warmth might have seeped into their mood. But Emma had never been to Venice and he had promised her he would take her anywhere she wanted, and she was aware that Roberto and Marta had offered them the apartment here should they ever wish to visit. Geoff had been to Venice several times before, and to be frank had never been too much of a fan. In summer, the canals smelt and he disliked being just an anonymous part of the tourist crowds. In truth, he was not a great traveller. Emma, on the other hand, was twenty years younger and always sported an enthusiasm for new places and experiences that he no longer could pretend he had. And he secretly knew he'd never possessed the joy or curiosity even when he had been younger himself.

Although it remained mostly unsaid they both knew to a different degree that their relationship was doomed. The age difference, the opposing temperaments, the cultural differences, the weight of his own past, her own ambitions in life. But love still bound them. His, full of despair that she might well happen to be the last great love of his life; hers, full of wonder that Geoff had somehow become the first great love in her life but with her mind, her imagination nagging her daily about the roads not taken and all the future roads that were still to be reached.

In an effort to combat the due date on their affair, they had come to Venice. In her mind, she had wanted to confront beauty. In his, it was just a melancholy vision of past literary memories of Thomas Mann, Byron, Dickens or Nic Roeg which resonated in the greyness of his soul, the delusion that a trip to a new place could repair the stitches that were coming apart in their affair.

"Carnival begins tomorrow," he had pointed out to her.

"Really?" she had exclaimed, her eyes widening in anticipation.

"Yes."

"Will you buy me a mask?" Emma had asked.

"Of course."

"And I will get one for you," she suggested. "Something darkly romantic, that would just suit you."

"Why not?"

"And we acquire them separately, and they remain secret until the first evening we go out and wear them. A surprise!"

"A lovely idea," Geoff had readily agreed, the fleeting thought of Emma quite naked except for a delicate white Carnival mask shielding her face, and her green eyes peering through the disguise already warming his heart and suggestible loins. His finger lingered on her knee, and he shuddered. The electricty between them still worked.

"Can we go online and read all about the Carnival?" she asked.

"Of course," he said. They made their way to the guest bedroom where the nearest connected computer stood on a rickety trestle table their host often used to mix his paints on. Above it, by coincidence, hung slightly crooked on the wall by the window, was a gaudy painting of a woman in chains wearing only a black mask which obscured her eyes. Roberto's latest BDSM variation.

217

They surfed freely for the next couple of hours, learning all about Carnevale and its origins, the stories of Casanova, the types of masks and their significance. One link led to another and yet another until an aimless stroke of the keyboard took them to the website where out of sheer prurient curiosity they arranged for the meeting in the bar on Campo Santa Maria Formosa the next day.

At first, Geoff had been somewhat hesitant, but Emma's enthusiasm had swayed him.

"It will be an adventure," she said.

"I suppose so," he answered.

"Don't be so old," she added.

Geoff smiled wryly. She always knew how to silence him.

"Yes, it's all because of Attila the Hun."

They were sipping espressos at the back of the small cafe. The man was in his fifties and had silver hair and was explaining how the earliest inhabitants of Venice had been exiled all the way to the lagoon by the invasion of their native lands by foreign hordes.

"Fascinating," Emma commented.

"And the bridge that connects us to the Italian mainland was only built by Mussolini under a century ago. Before that we were isolated and you could only reach the city by water."

Geoff ordered another round from the hovering waitress. Mostly San Pellegrino mineral water; neither he nor Emma could cope with too much coffee at this time of day.

"It's a party," the man who called himself Jacopo said. "But we try and organise matters so that we adhere to all the old traditions of the Venice Carnevale, not the diluted versions that have sadly evolved over the years since Carnevale's heyday."

"We understand," Geoff said. Emma looked him in the eyes, and nodded.

"It is strictly by invitation, of course," he continued. "Normally, we try and restrict attendance to pure Venetians, but as you know, there are fewer of us now. The younger generations are all leaving the city. So sad."

He looked at Emma. Her dark hair shone glossily; she had

washed it just before they had left the apartment to walk here. When wet, her curls ironed out naturally and her hair extended then to the small of her back. Geoff observed her, too. She looked luminous. Already excited by the prospect of the party they were being informally interviewed for. As if a fire was rising inside her, bringing light to her features, heat to her hidden senses. Geoff recognised that gleam in her eyes. It was invariably present when she had been fucked. He kept on watching, transfixed as Jacopo's words swept soundlessly over him. The man with the silver hair also kept on observing Emma, as if weighing her in his steady gaze.

Geoff returned to reality, reluctantly abandoning his vision of Emma's fascinated attention to the man's words.

"Naturally, you remain masters of your destiny. A polite 'no' will always be an acceptable response to overtures, although it is hoped that all guests will participate freely and openly in the proceedings." Again, Emma nodded, her chin bobbing up and down.

Geoff sighed discreetly. It was true that they had often discussed the remote prospect of others joining in their games, their lovemaking. But they had never reached the stage where they had actively done anything about it.

Something inside him – something rotten or diseased? – had always imagined what it would be like to see Emma mounted by another, harboured the curiosity to witness how another man would touch her, make her moan. Because he found her so beautiful, part of him felt she should be shared with the whole world, so that all and sundry could truly understand why his love for her was so strong and overpowering. But it was a long road from thoughts to the realities of the flesh.

She had even asked, "Would you be jealous if it happened?" and he had been obliged to dig deep into his thoughts and had finally answered quite truthfully, "I'm not sure, maybe not if I could watch. I wouldn't want you to fuck another man behind my back, that's for sure."

"Wonderful," Jacopo said as he rose from the cafe table. "You are a lovely couple. I think you will enjoy our parties a lot."

They jointly agreed to attend the opening of Carnevale the next day. He had slipped over a piece of paper with the address.

"Every party takes place in a different locale," the man with the silver hair had said. "They can only be reached by the canals, so you will have to make arrangements accordingly."

They all shook hands and he departed.

Left alone, Geoff and Emma looked at each other. He tried to smile, but couldn't raise the right rictus. He knew already that they would go. Emma had always been a woman of her word and once a decision had been taken, only hell and high water could ever change her mind.

"Well," she said.

"Hmmm …"

Emma was dressing.

"Don't wear panties," Geoff suggested.

"Really?"

"Yes. I think it would fit in with the spirit of the occasion."

Emma chuckled softly. "If you say so. Anyway, the dress is quite heavy, so I shouldn't feel the cold …" She gave him a twirl. He applauded theatrically. "Flattery will get you everywhere …" she said.

They had been shopping in Mestre. In Venice, the prices were much too unaffordable. She had found him a sleek black silk suit made in Thailand which Geoff wore with a black shirt and a scarlet bow tie.

"My prince of darkness!" Emma laughed. As if he now reminded her of a vampire.

In contrast, the dress they had acquired for tonight's event for her was white and made from thick linen, falling to her ankles with ornate elegance from her bare shoulders downwards, thin, almost invisible straps holding the dress up above her small, delicate breasts, unveiling just a discreet if appetising hint of gentle cleavage. Underneath she wore just dark hold up stockings reaching to mid thigh, their black veil as sharp as her luxuriant pubic hair. A perfect conjugation of nights, when she cheekily raised the dress to her midriff, exposing herself to him. God, she was stunning! Her lipstick was fiery red and she had surrounded her eyes with a grey circle of kohl.

They had found masks at Mondonovo, on Rio Terra Canal, near the Campo Santa Margherita, where masks could still be found that were replicas of the old historical, traditional models, and were different from the traditional fare on offer to gullible tourists in search of local colour. For Geoff, in his black outfit, they had chosen a larva, also called a *volto*. It was white, made of fine wax and should have typically been worn with a tricorn and cloak, which he had of course absolutely no intention of doing. After all, this was the 21st century! The shape of the mask would allow him to breathe and drink easily, and so there was no need to take it off, thus preserving anonymity.

Emma, on the other hand, had been coaxed by the old wrinkled lady at the store to select a *moretta* instead of the more traditional *bauta*. It was an oval mask of black velvet that was usually worn by women visiting convents. Invented in France it had rapidly become popular in ancient Venice as it brought out the beauty of feminine features. The mask was finished off with a veil, and was normally secured in place by a small bit in the wearer's mouth. As this was not appropriate to participate in a modern party, Emma's model had been modified so it was held by a clip at its apex that was attached to her mountain of curls.

"Bella," the old woman had said when Emma had tried the mask on.

"Bellissima," Geoff said in turn, with a painful stab of fear coursing through his stomach, as Emma stood, fully attired in dress and mask, and the jungle of her curls peering impudently above the formal mask.

"Grazie mille," she laughed.

There was so much more he wanted to say to her. Like, "Do you really want to go?" or "What will you do if another man proposes to you?" or "Do you still love me?" but the gondola they had booked had just arrived. They walked down to the waterside entrance of the building. The night air was cold and

221

the sky full of scattered stars whose reflection glistened over the waters of the small canal like a million phosphorescent fish. Geoff read the address out to the gondolier in his French-accented Italian.

"It's party time," Emma said.

The half-abandoned palazzo dominated the Grand Canal halfway between the Ponte del Rialto and the Ponte dell'accademia, with the Campo San Polo visible from the ornate balconies on the land side of the building.

The tall man who wore the white mask with the elongated beak, similar to the head attire medics had worn in the years of the Plague, when pepper had been lodged into the furthest reaches of the bird of prey-like beak to shield its wearers from the illness, had been hovering near them most of the evening. They had briefly been introduced by Jacopo, earlier on in the festivities. Occasionally he would approach them with new glasses of Champagne and would whisper in Emma's ears, or casually allow his leather-gloved hands to brush against her bare shoulders. His English was nigh perfect, albeit with West Coast American inflections. Geoff couldn't remember his name. Real or otherwise. They had been introduced as Byron and Ariadne. As neither Emma's or his Italian was fluent enough, they had been isolated in the margins of the party and its flowing conversations. They had both drunk too much by now. Which meant he was retreating, as he did, into longer and longer silences, whereas her demeanour was becoming looser, more joyful by the minute. How many times now had she wondered at the sheer elegance of the evening and its incomparable setting, the candles illuminating the cavernous, marble-floored rooms, the gold dishes laden with fruit, the never-ending flow of booze? She was intoxicated by both the alcohol and the sense of occasion. Was this the adventure she always claimed she was seeking when he would raise any questions about the future?

A hand took hold of his. Geoff turned round. A woman in a red velvet dress and a white powdered wig pulled him a metre or two towards her. He looked up at her. She had endless legs enhanced by thin six-inch heels. Behind her mask, he could see her eyes were the colour of coal.

"You are English, no?"

"Indeed," he answered. Her scent was sweet, cloying almost.

"So you like our Carnevale?"

"Absolutely," he responded, ever polite.

Her purple lipsticked lips moved into the shape of a kiss.

"Is it your first time in Venice?" she asked.

"Not quite," he answered. "But the first time I've been here at Carnival time, though."

"Ah …" She moved nearer to him. He realised they were now alone in the large room; the woman with purple lips, Emma, the tall guy and him. Somehow all the nearby partygoers had drifted out silently into the other neighbouring rooms, leaving faint echoes of conversations and the tinkling of crystal glasses sort of suspended in the tobacco smoke-infested air. He took a step back.

"Oh … Shy?"

"No," he muttered.

"So?" She extended her left arm and her fingers swept across his dry lips.

"Your woman isn't as shy, I see," she remarked.

Geoff's heart dropped all the way down to his stomach as he glanced round. Emma was now being embraced by the tall stranger, who held her tight against the far wall of the room, his hand burrowing under her dress, his face muzzled into hers. Her eyes were closed.

"Come," the woman with the white powdered wig said, taking him by the hand and leading him to a low couch at the opposite end of the room.

He followed, as if in a trance. Time slowed down to a crawl. Her cunt tasted of exotic spices. Pungent, strong, savage. His tongue lapped her generous juices with quiet and studied abandon. She spread her legs wider apart and pressed his head down firmer against her. Geoff gasped momentarily for breath.

"Lick me harder," she ordered him.

Once she had tired of his worshipping the thick folds of her

223

labia and the invisible radiating heat pulsing through her opening all the way from her innards, she pulled him onto the worn-out couch and slipped his trousers downwards and began sucking him off. Somehow, even though she was talented and imaginative, he failed to get totally hard, and she gave up within a few minutes.

"No worry," she said. "It happens."

Red-faced, he looked her in the eyes, attempting to find out how old she might be behind that mask. Her skin was spotless and taut and her unending legs were those of an athlete at the peak of her form. He gulped and recalled instantly the taste of her and its striking flavours. She had been on her knees and rose to her feet. He just stood there, his black silk trousers bunched around his ankles.

"Undress," she said. It was more of an order than a suggestion. He meekly obeyed. He wanted to turn around and see where Emma was. And the tall man. Their own noises had been muted, distant, but nevertheless insidiously present all the while he had been involved with the purple-lipsticked woman. She sensed this.

"Do so as you are. Don't turn," she said, unclenching the black leather belt that circled her thin waist. "Look down to the floor as you undress."

He noticed the smudged purple stains of lipstick on the mushroom tip of his cock, like dried wine against the ridged flesh of his masculinity. He pulled the trousers down over his laced shoes. Then kicked the shoes off and quickly slipped off his socks. Surely there was no more ridiculous sight than a naked man wearing just black socks? He then pulled himself up and began unbuttoning his shirt. As he did so, he saw the woman reach for her matching red handbag, which had been lying on the couch and pull a devious contraption, all leather straps and ivory trunk from it. His stomach froze. There was a faint cry from the other end of the room. He was now naked. The woman pulled her ruched dress upwards and belted the strap-on to her waist. The artificial cock jutted ahead of her like the prow of a boat. Hard, inflexible.

"Maybe this will give you a hard-on?" she suggested.

"Legend has it that English men are much appreciative ..." He knew he could say no, and just leave the room with no further words of protest. But the words wouldn't pass his lips. And then he knew he could not leave Emma here alone anyway. She indicated the couch and how he should bend over its sides and she positioned herself behind him. Now, through the corner of his eyes, he could finally see Emma and the other man. She had also been stripped naked, and wore only the hold up black stockings. The pallor of her body was unbearable to watch. As was the shocking contrast between her skin and the dark as night material of the remaining stockings.

The other man's cock was thick and dark pink and was ploughing her roughly and systematically, pulling out of her almost all the way with every stroke and then digging back into her up to the hilt with every return thrust. Machine-like, metronomic, like a deadly instrument of war. He felt the pain explode through his own body as the woman's artificial member breached him with one swift movement. He swallowed, almost bit his tongue. As he did so, he realised why Emma was so silent. A red handkerchief had been stuffed into her mouth, as her face rhythmically banged against the wall with every repeated movement in and out of her. He couldn't help noticing the handkerchief was the exact same shade of red as the lipstick she had decided to adorn herself with to attend the party. Also, her hands were tied behind her back with brown fur-lined metal cuffs. She must have agreed to this. There was another huge stab of unbearable pain as the strap-on began stretching him and he felt himself being filled like he had never been filled before. For a brief moment, he feared he was going to defecate, as the pit of his stomach went totally numb, but the pressure against his inner walls soon reasserted itself and the pain slowly began to recede. Not that being fucked in this manner, gave him any pleasure. He felt as if was becoming detached from his own body as it was being defiled. And his eyes kept on hypnotically watching the abominable movements of the other man's massive member inside Emma, the way the tight skin around her opening creased inwards and then outwards again as she was being implacably drilled, and the eyelet of her anus winked open and shut with every movement below it There was sweat dripping from her forehead. Her calves tightened, her ass cheeks shook, her hair was undone, her curls spilling in every conceivable direction as if moved by an invisible wind rising from the nearby lagoon and flying over the Giudecca to shroud the city on its way to the marshes and Trieste. From the tremors mechanically coursing through her body, Geoff knew Emma had come. The stranger had succeeded in raising her senses, playing her like Geoff had rarely been capable of doing. But the man did not cease. He would continue fucking her until she begged for him to stop. Would she ever?

Back at the apartment, they at first could not bear to look each other in the eyes. They went to bed in total silence, still coated by the dry sweat of their exertions, of their shame. They slept late into the morning.

After breakfast, they took a vaporetto to the Lido and later to the Isola di San Servolo. A trip they had agreed to undertake a few days before they had stumbled across the website which had lured them to the party. Over dinner in the San Polo district, they began communicating again.

"Talk about an adventure!"

"I suppose you could call it that …"

"Regrets?"

"No."

"Sure?"

"Absolutely not."

"Were you jealous?"

"A little, I suppose."

"You?"

"No. It's … how can I put it … life …"

"Certainly one way of putting it …"

They tried to go for coffee at Caffe Florian, but it was closed on Tuesdays in winter. They made their way back to the apartment. There was no power. They tiptoed their way through darkness to the bedroom.

"It doesn't change anything, does it?" he asked.

"I don't know," she replied, spooning against him.

It was at that precise moment Geoff knew he was about to lose her. That it was too late to plead, beg, affirm his love, however impure it now was.

He didn't sleep that night. He stayed awake in the darkness, listening to the vague sounds of the canal delle Due Torri lapping against the building's rotting stone facade and the imperceptible melody of her breath, as her chest moved peacefully up and down against him under the duvet. He smelled her, listened to her as if trying to fix these memories in his brain once and for all. What he would one day be left with. He finally succumbed to sleep around seven in the morning. When he awoke, she had left the apartment.

The morning went by. He tried to read, but couldn't concentrate on the text, whether a week-old newspaper or an anonymous serial killer thriller. Emma returned at the beginning of the afternoon. She was wearing that black skirt he had once bought her in Barcelona and which held so many memories. The one with the giant sunflower patch sewn into its flank. And a T-shirt he had once loaned her in the early days of the affair when their lovemaking had proven a tad rough and messy and he had left compromising semen stains across the blouse she had been wearing that day. The T-shirt that advertised 'Strangers in Paradise' across the Aubrey Beardsley-like face of a woman. He was sipping a glass of grapefruit juice at the kitchen table. He welcomed her.

"Had a good walk?"

"No."

"Oh …" A shadow passed across the room, shielding her eyes from his examination.

"I saw him again," Emma said.

The pain inside returned. "Have you fucked him again?"

"No."

"I see."

"There is another party tonight. A different palazzo this time, near the Campo San Silvestro. He's invited me. Wants to introduce me to some of his friends …"

"Do you want to go?"

227

"Yes."

"Without me?"

"Yes."

"Why? I still love you, you know."

"I know. But love is not enough. I need adventures, you see. On my own. I don't want to be owned …"

"I've never tried to own you, you know that. You're too much of a gypsy to be kept in a cage."

Emma smiled. "You can come, if you wish, I reckon. As long as you'd promise not to interfere and allow whatever happens to happen …"

"I don't think so," Geoff said. "Don't much care to repeat yesterday's foursome. Just didn't feel right to me somehow."

"I understand."

She walked to the bedroom they had been using; she was holding a large Mondadori canvas tote bag.

"What have you got there? Been shopping?" he asked.

She looked away. "No …" she hesitated, then came clean. "It's the outfit he wishes me to wear tonight."

"Can I …"

Emma interrupted him. "I'd rather you didn't see it, Geoff."

That evening, he left the apartment to wander the narrow streets and have several coffees in a row to allow her to dress in privacy. By the time he returned, she had already left for the Carnevale or had maybe been picked up. She did not return that night or the following day. His days and nights were haunted by obscene visions of her with other men, and the abominable images of alien cocks of all shapes, sizes and shades invading her. Her mouth, her cunt, her arse, her hands. Orgasmic flush invading the delicate pallor of her skin. The indelible marks of hands, ropes, whips and paddles across the familiar geography of her body. And the sound of her voice just saying 'Yes', 'Yes' and 'Yes' again, like Bloom's Molly. And the grateful acceptance of her smile, of her eyes.

Finally, she reappeared halfway through Carnevale. She looked radiant. More beautiful than ever.

"You haven't shaved," she remarked. "It's so grey."

"Couldn't bother," he said. "So, you're back."

"Not really," Emma said. "I've just returned to pick up my stuff, my clothes and all that."

"I'm sorry," Geoff said.

"It's the way things are," Emma remarked. "After Carnevale ends, Master has promised me that the adventure will continue. He wants to take me to Mardi-Gras in New Orleans and also the Carnival in Rio one day …"

"How exciting," he said bitterly in response.

"Don't be like that, please, Geoff," she protested.

"You should be happy for me. Respect what I am doing, surely."

"I find that difficult, Emma. I would have given you everything. Surely you realise that."

"I know, but it would never have been enough. You know that. I'm young. I have a life to live. My life." Her skin shone in the pale light coming through the window, the curls in her hair like the gift of Medusa. Geoff closed his eyes. Promising himself he would not open them until she had left with her belongings.

He never saw Emma again. He stayed in Venice until the end of Carnevale. At dinner one evening, he met another woman, a legal interpreter from Arizona. They had a few drinks together and he was pleased to see that he could still chat a woman up, be reasonably witty and seductive. But when he took her back to the apartment and undressed her after some willing fumbling and a cascade of mutual kisses, he wasn't capable of fucking her. Just couldn't get hard enough, despite her assiduous ministrations. Lack of inspiration or wrong person, he wasn't sure.

The next day as he sat at a cafe by the Rialto bridge, he caught a glimpse of a small water cab racing down the Grand Canal. A woman was standing at its prow. For a brief moment, he thought he recognised Emma. Same skirt and T-shirt, but the embarkation was moving too fast for him to be certain it was actually her. At any rate, she was alone on the small boat, standing erect behind the driver, facing the breeze.

Shortly after, his friends returned from India and he quickly made his way back to London. He left the two masks they had worn on that fateful evening behind. Not quite the sort of apparel you could wear for the Notting Hill Carnival. He would never go back to Venice.

All or Nothing
by Henrietta Maddox

Never could you meet a girl more free-spirited than Lilly. Through all her ups and downs, trials and tribulations, she never failed to find a reason to party. Since her mother's death, she had always known that life was too short to postpone any desire. And so, without hesitation, her adventures were always the wildest you could imagine. From slumming it at squat parties to fine dining at some of the top restaurants in the world, she had gone wherever the wind could take her furthest.

People were drawn to her happy-go-lucky attitude, jovial laugh and classic, versatile good looks. With fiery red short hair, lilac blue eyes and a slender figure, she looked stunning in anything she decided to wear.

On this particular summer's Sunday night, Lilly was feeling particularly mellow. So she decided to go to London to meet her neurotic friend Susie and sip cocktails at the opening of the Zip Zip Zippers JazzClub. After a few drinks, they found themselves being more entertained by the guy on the next door table showing off to all his debaucherous, glamorous-looking friends than by the band onstage.

"I'm not bi, I'm greedy," Tom bellowed in his usual flippant tone. Everyone at the table roared with laughter except for Tom's best friend and loyal sidekick, Mickey, who'd heard it all before. Never one to shy away from attention, Tom stood up with his glass of champagne and toasted, "To good things, my friends, and the goodness they bring." With an eye for anything unique, genuine and priceless, it was no surprise that Tom noticed Lilly and couldn't help being drawn to her.

From the other side of the table, Mickey had noticed her too and was finding it difficult not to stare. Their friends carried on with their trivial chatter while Tom snuck over to Lilly's table with every intention of seducing. Gregarious and charming, Tom was used to getting whatever he wanted. But Lilly did not make it easy for him. In fact, she thought he was an arrogant, stuck-up toff, out of touch with reality. This may have been a bit harsh, but it was true that he didn't seem to notice how she became a lot chattier when Mickey joined them.

To look at, Mickey and Tom were like chalk and cheese. Tom was tall and slender, with legs like Naomi Campbell and a lustrous mane of caramel brown hair. He looked like he had just walked out of a Dolce & Gabbana advert. Meanwhile, Mickey was muscular with green eyes and a head full of thick, black curly hair. He looked more like he belonged in *Gladiator* than in *Vogue* magazine. He was down to earth and a man of few words, and Lilly was attracted to his mystery while, even though she didn't want to admit it, she was entertained by Tom's humour and vibrant energy.

Before the threesome could so much as say, "Another Long Island Iced Tea please," it was closing time. Everyone had disappeared, including prudish Susie, who had stomped off after realising this was not the girlie night she had hoped for. So, with glazed eyes and a slight wonky walk, Lilly was happy to go back with her new boys to Tom's pad.

By the time they arrived, Lilly had sobered up enough to appreciate the lavish eyesore that was Tom's home. Looking around her in awe, she was impressed by the living room's palatial high ceilings and grand thick drapes that hung gracefully but dramatically in deep red tones. With Louis XV loveseats on either side of the French windows, the apartment reminded her of an old, classic-looking Parisian flat she had seen in a movie once. She felt a little intimidated by the sleek opulence of the place, but was too intrigued by her new friends to leave.

As the night wound down, they talked zealously of random things like only drunkards can. What they generally liked and disliked in people; the weirdest things that had ever happened to them and anything that would allow them to be the glorious story teller. Morning hinted through the curtains.

"Right, I'm off to bed guys," Tom said with a yawn and kissed them both goodnight. Although he was liberal in nearly everything he did, he was compulsive about sleeping alone.

"Is he always that ... um .... energetic?" asked Lilly. Amused, Mickey smiled and pulled her in one strong swoop onto his lap. I think you're the most beautiful girl I've ever seen, he thought but dared not say.

"Yeah – he's hilarious." He looked pensively into the coffee table trying to think of something interesting to say, but she beat him to it.

"It's a shame Tom went to bed. I was looking forward to a threesome."

He couldn't believe his ears. Looking at him sheepishly, she asked, "When are you going to show me your room?"

Mickey's bedroom was cosier and more understated than the living room, and Lilly felt more comfortable there. It was filled with mahogany Louis Phillipe-style furniture and Lilly felt a warmth that she had only been able to get from the red wine before. Mickey stood in the doorway in anticipation, watching her seductively walk to his sleigh bed, stripping off her clothes as she went.

"This bed's amazing," she giggled, sitting on it, facing him. His dick hardened as he watched the movement of her breasts as she bounced on the bed.

"Do you want to tie me up?" she asked.

Not only did he accept her proposition but he thought he'd add his own fun too. He smeared streaks of chocolate all over her thighs, then licked them off all the way to her toes. Pulling her lips apart, he nuzzled his mouth into her pussy and licked all the way up, flicking her clit with his tongue. Pouting, he sucked her erect womanhood, plucking at it inside his mouth. Groaning and wriggling her restrained arms in delight, she pulled her knees up and he pushed two fingers into her wet, juicy cunt.

Smooch kissing her stomach, he caressed her breasts, his thumbs circling her nipples until she begged him to release her. Liberating her from the silk ties, he lay back and let her take control. Taking some lube from the bedside table, she teased his hard cock, gently twisting the tip between her thumb and forefingers. Then she wrapped her hand around the base and brought her mouth down upon it. Like the iron grapevine sconce lights so perfectly intertwined above them, their bodies united. For him, having sex with Lilly was like the first day of spring, Christmas and New Year all rolled into one. Relishing her warmth, grip and velvety depths made him shudder all over.

Busy with their passion, they did not notice Tom entering the room, sitting in the armchair and taking pleasure in watching them. His long, toned legs stretched out, Tom stroked and pulled on his erection, watching their bodies move gracefully together in the moonlight.

Lilly pinned Micky down, straddling him and riding him rhythmically, her hands clasped with his. "Tell me when you think you're going to come, OK?"

He nodded, smiling. Pushing her pelvis back and forth, her firm breasts in front of him, a loud groan gestured that he was almost there. Mischievously, she grinned at him, closed her eyes and squeezed the muscles between her legs every time she moved her hips forward. Heating up, he closed his eyes and focused on the orgasmic sensations she was sending all over his body. Electric tingles shot down her legs until with ultimate satisfaction she burst onto the satin sheets. Simultaneously, Tom spilled his juices all over his hand and leaned back in the big armchair wearily.

As you would expect, Lilly was a little groggy, not to mention disoriented, when she woke up mid-afternoon in Mickey's bed. But as she looked around at her clothes scattered on the floor it all came flooding back to her. She thought to herself what a lovely night it had been, sneaking out of the bed quietly.

On seeing a naked Tom passed out in the chair, she gave a small startled shriek that woke both of the boys.

Her host stretched, grinning. "Good morning, m'lady. Looking lovely this morning, may I say?"

Lilly jumped back under the covers, speechless.

"Breakfast?"

While he cooked them up a feast, Mickey explained to Lilly that this had happened before. Voyeurism was one of Tom's many fetishes. Though he told her in an offhand manner, Mickey secretly wished that his buddy would respect his privacy, but, knowing how irrational and temperamental Tom could get, he had never brought it up.

Over breakfast, Lilly probed Tom about his sexual habits. Tom was very happy to openly answer her questions as his two favourite talking points were sex and himself. From holding depraved orgies in extravagant hotel rooms to dirty dogging sessions in dodgy parks, every story grabbed her full attention. She felt as if she had met a true kindred spirit.

Known for his spontaneity, Tom invited her to come and stay with them. "I know it seems crazy but you're at a loose end and we could do with a girl around the house. Makes things more fun, don't you think?" He noticed her hesitate. "Don't worry if it's money that's holding you back. It's of no object in this house."

"It really isn't," Mickey agreed, wishing Tom would back off and let him have her all to himself. Lilly thought for a moment. They were both gorgeous and fun. She was booked to go to an ashram in India but that wasn't for another two weeks. So why not?

"OK," she said. "Let's see how it goes."

Clapping his hands, Tom cheered and high-fived Mickey. "Right then, come with me. I have something to show you." Jumping up excitedly, he led her to his bedroom, which was filled with vibrant vintage retro furniture. Opening the double doors of his walk-in wardrobe with dramatic flair, he presented an abundance of erotic toys, props and costumes, filling her imagination with an overload of fun possibilities. Love balls, strap-ons, dildos, ticklers, butt plugs and even artificial vaginas filled shelf upon shelf. Corsets, leather cat suits and school uniforms were among the outfits hung on the rails.

Morning, noon and night, they gorged on each others' bodies, imaginations and fantasies. Two weeks later Lilly decided to postpone her trip. And time flew by until before they knew it, they had been playing their games for over a month. Usually Lilly would've had itchy feet staying anywhere for this long, but she was becoming accustomed to the lifestyle.

They relished their games, choosing what kind to play according to their mood for the day. If they were feeling mischievous, they would play schools for hours and be spanked with a thick wooden ruler by schoolmaster Tom. Sometimes Lilly would find herself doing too much of the cleaning, so would dress up in black leather and whip the boys into shape. Both of them loved being slaves for their dominatrix. But every day, Mickey's love for Lilly and loathing for Tom grew.

It was on a night when they had decided to take a break from all the games that the trouble started. Having a civilised dinner, they were discussing how they should start getting out of the house and perhaps going out to more parties. Mickey had drunk too much and was coming out with a plethora of snide remarks all aimed at Tom. Every eccentric quip was either shot down or met with sarcasm. And repeatedly Mickey would slur, "Not everything's about you, Tom. I know you think the world revolves around you but it doesn't."

Eventually the tensions started to upset Lilly and she told them that they were acting like children and went to bed. For most of the night she could hear their muffled shouting through the thick oak door between the living room and Mickey's bedroom. Their voices were so angry and loud that finally she took a sleeping pill to drift off. In the middle of the night, she heard a booming thud and awoke panicked. She tried to get up to see what it was but the pill had been too strong and so she helplessly dozed back off to sleep.

Late the following morning, she awoke to a cacophony of drills and hammers. Standing in the middle of the commotion, squinting in the glaring light of the living room, she was shocked to see all the beautiful furniture being taken away and the walls being sanded by a bunch of busy builders.

Tom and Mickey were nowhere to be seen.

"Lilly?" A slightly overweight, very sweaty builder came towards her.

"Yes."

He passed her an envelope. "I've got this for you."

Inside was a wad of cash and a card with a taxi number on it. On the back of the card, Tom had written: 'Too much of a good thing isn't good for anyone.'

At first her heart heaved with sadness – she felt rejected. But then she started to think about it. What did this all mean? That she'd just been some temporary tart to them? She wanted to destroy everything they owned, but clearly they had no sentimentality. Seething with fury and frustration, she walked away in the clothes she'd worn the night they met. She left everything else, including the whore payoff.

About the Authors

All the authors in this book donated their stories free of charge to help Burlesque Against Breast Cancer raise money for Macmillan.

Sarah Berry is joint editor of *Penthouse Forum* magazines and writes the Berry Outrageous column in *Scarlet*. She's also a reluctant burlesque dancer: after training at the London School of Striptease, she now dons a habit and whip to save the souls of her audiences.

Wersha Bharadwa is an award-nominated writer, journalist and social commentator. Her work has appeared in *The Guardian*, *The Observer*, *The Independent on Sunday*, *Glamour* magazine and *Cosmopolitan*. Wersha features regularly on TV and radio and is also an Ambassador for the Women of Achievement. She is currently writing her debut novel.

Daphne Bing is the pseudonym of a writer whose erotic fiction has until now only been available on the internet, although under other names she is a published author and occasional journalist. In her spare time she has run multi-million pound projects and dated inappropriate men.

Rachel Kramer Bussel (rachelkramerbussel.com) is an author, editor, blogger and reading series host based in New York City. She has edited more than 25 anthologies, including *Bottoms Up, Spanked, The Mile High Club, Do Not Disturb,* the IPPY Award-winning *Tasting Him: Oral Sex Stories* and *Tasting Her: Oral Sex Stories*, and is *Best Sex Writing* Series Editor. She is Senior Editor at *Penthouse Variations* and hosts the In The Flesh Reading Series. Her work has been published in more than 100 anthologies, including *Best American Erotica 2004* and *2006*, and she has written for *Cosmopolitan, Diva,* Fresh Yarn, The Huffington Post, *Newsday, San Francisco Chronicle, Time Out New York, Zink* and other publications.

Elizabeth Coldwell is an erotic author who has also commissioned some of the best erotica authors around as editor for magazines including *Penthouse Forum*.

Emily Dubberley founded cliterati.co.uk and was founding editor of *Scarlet* magazine. She script-writes for the *Lovers' Guide*, writes for magazines including *Look*, *More*, *Elle* and *Glamour*, and has been syndicated worldwide. She's written 18 books, and created Burlesque Against Breast Cancer with Sam Eddison, Fiona Fletcher and a team of incredible volunteers to whom she is eternally grateful.

Jeremy Edwards' greatest goal in life is to be sexy and witty at the same moment – ideally in lighting that flatters his profile. Drop in on him unannounced (and thereby catch him in his underwear) at http://jerotic.blogspot.com.

Justine Elyot's short fiction appears in numerous Black Lace anthologies, and her first single-author title, *On Demand*, will be published in December 2009. You can find out more about the author – and read a free serialised story – at http://smutoliloquy.blogspot.com.

Mark Farley spends far too much time obsessing about the book trade and celebrities. He has contributed to *Scarlet* magazine, *The Idler* and books from Xcite. He has a cat and a girlfriend and lives in London.

Alyson Fixter is a freelance journalist and writer and edited *Cliterature*, *Scarlet*'s free erotic fiction magazine, for two years.

Miranda Forbes is an editor for Xcite books, with an archive of erotic stories that has to be seen to be believed.

Laura Godman is editor of *Scarlet* magazine, having started as an intern and worked her way up. She previously edited the

Cliterature section of *Scarlet* magazine so has seen a wealth of erotic writing talent over the years.

Mistress Grace is a Dominatrix, writer and all-round debauched individual (in thoroughly nice ways).

Maxim Jakubowski has written or edited more than 100 books (novels, story collections and anthologies). He is best known for the *Mammoth Erotica* series. His last novel was *Confessions of a Romantic Pornographer* and the next one, if the gods of Eros permit, will be *I Was Waiting For You*. He lives in London.

Josephine Jay has worked for numerous magazines and spent many years researching erotic imagery and calling it work.

Karen Krizanovich is Britain's much-loved American commentator on films, modern culture, relationships, sex and other fun things. Born near Chicago and trained as a philosopher, Karen came to Britain in the late 80s where she first wrote under Auberon Waugh for *The Literary Review*. Appearances on *Sky News* and *Sex Talk* followed, as did a stint as *Sky* magazine's comedy agony aunt *Dear Karen*. Karen has also had her own radio and TV shows, namely *The Karen Krizanovich Show* on Liberty Radio and *The Movie Show with Karen Krizanovich* on Channel One.

Henrietta Maddox is the pseudonym for a freelance journalist who's been published by numerous magazines that might not approve of her naughtier side …

Kitty Meadows is an adventuress, orphan, (semi)-retired pirate and owner of the world's most extensive collection of handmade silk fans. She lives on a houseboat near the Spain/France border, perfecting her linguistic skills, is published by Xcite books, and can also be read in *EK* and *Scarlet*.

Madeline Moore is the author of three Black Lace novels: *Wild Card, Amanda's Young Men* and *Sarah's Education*. Her erotic stories have appeared in magazines and anthologies in North America and the United Kingdom. Madeline lives in sin with erotica author Felix Baron near Toronto, Ontario.
Visit her blog at moremadelinemoore.blogspot.com.

MonMouth is a part-time blogger and full-time pervert. His blog can be found at http://monmouth.blogspot.com. He welcomes email at mouth.mail@gmail.com.

Paris Orsini's stories have appeared on cliterati.co.uk and in *Scarlet* magazine's *Cliterature* section. Her pseudonym masks a woman of many talents …

Elizabeth K. Payne's stories have appeared in the Agent Provocateur anthology *Secrets: A Collection of Erotic Fiction*, winner of the 'Erotic Literature of the Year' category at the Erotic Awards in 2006. She also contributed to *Dark Desires: A Collection of Erotic Short Stories*, edited by Emily Dubberley, and to the best-selling anthology *Ultimate Burlesque*.

Marcelle Perks is a journalist and the author of *Incredible Orgasms, The User's Guide to the Rabbit* and *Secrets of Porn Star Sex*. Her fiction covers all the most important aspects of life: love, sex and death.

Suzanne Portnoy is the author of *The Butcher, the Baker, the Candlestick Maker* and *The Not So Invisible Woman*. **Simon Morgan** died of liver cancer on 9 September 2004.

Adam Sawyer is a freelance writer living in Essex. Through his writing Adam seeks to celebrate sex, to get people thinking freely about what turns them on and to stimulate that most important sex organ – the mind. He has written for *Scarlet* and other websites and publications. For more information see adamsawyer.blogspot.com.

Donna George Storey's erotic fiction has appeared in more than 80 journals and anthologies. Her first novel, *Amorous Woman*, a semi-autobiographical tale of an American's steamy love affair with Japan, was published by Orion/Neon. Read more of her work at donnageorgestorey.com.

Lauren Wissot is a gay boy born into female form. Currently working as a critic and columnist, Lauren is also an award-winning filmmaker bent on bringing an S&M flavor to the big screen. *Under My Master's Wings*, a sexual memoir about her time spent as the slave to a gay-for-pay stripper, is available from Nexus Books. For more information see laurenwissot.com.

Sarah-Louise Young is a writer, actress, singer and stand-up. She was a finalist in the Hackney Empire New Act Of The Year in 2006 and has performed in Stand-Up Women and The Very Best Of New Act Of The Year. For the past seven years she has performed in cabaret venues across London including the Jermyn Street Theatre, Old Vic Pit Bar and The Theatre Museum, combining songs and stand-up. As an actress she has performed in the National Theatre, the Royal Exchange Theatre and in the West End. Television credits include *Strictly Confidential*, *No Angels*, *The Jury*, *Casualty*, *Holby City* and *Doctors*. She also worked on *The Adam & Shelley Show*, directed by Tim Kirkby, with whom she worked on the feature film *The Blind Spot* and BAFTA-winning *Look Around You*.

Win a LoveHoney Ultimate Decadence Love Bundle!

By purchasing this book you're helping the Burlesque Against Breast Cancer organisation raise money for Macmillan Cancer Support. As a thank-you, Xcite Books and Burlesque Against Breast Cancer are offering you the chance to win an Ultimate Decadence Love Bundle from LoveHoney.co.uk. The prize is worth over £250 and consists of the following sensual treats:

• SaSi by JeJoue
• Durex Play Indulge Gift Pack
• LoveHoney Jessica Rabbit Platinum
• iBuzz Two
• LoveHoney Cosmos Glass Dildo
• LoveHoney Double Ding Ring
• LoveHoney Bang Bang Bullet
• Durex Love Condoms

For your chance to win, email competitions@burlesqueabc.com with your name and address, answering this question: What is the title of the first BABC fundraising book? For a clue, visit lovehoney.co.uk/babc. Normal terms and conditions apply.

NEW! XCITE DATING

Xcite Dating is an online dating and friend-finder service. With Xcite Dating you can meet new friends, find romance and seek out that special person who shares your fantasies.

Xcite dating is a safe and completely anonymous service. Sign-up today – life's too short not too!

www.xcitedating.com

More great books from Xcite...

Naughty Spanking One
Twenty bottom-tingling stories to make your buttocks blush!
9781906125837 £7.99

The True Confessions of a London Spank Daddy
Memoir by Peter Jones
9781906373320 £7.99

Girl Fun One
Lesbian anthology edited by Miranda Forbes
9781906373672 £7.99

Sex and Satisfaction Two
Erotic stories edited by Miranda Forbes
9781906373726 £7.99

Ultimate Curves
Erotic short stories edited by Miranda Forbes
9781906373788 £7.99

Naughty! The Xcite Guide to Sexy Fun
How To book exploring edgy, kinky sex
9781906373863 £9.99

For more information and great offers
please visit
www.xcitebooks.com